SNIFF THEM OUT, BROWNLOW!

Judy Upton

HOBART BOOKS

HOBART BOOKS

.

SNIFF THEM OUT, BROWNLOW!

ISBN 978-1-914322-13-6

First Published in 2022
by
Hobart Books, Oxfordshire, England

hobartbooks.com

Printed and bound in Great Britain.

Sniff Them Out, Brownlow!

By Judy Upton

About the author

Judy Upton is a playwright-turned-novelist from Shoreham-by-Sea on the south coast of England. She has written extensively for stage and screen and has won several awards, including The George Devine Award for stage play *Ashes and Sand*, Verity Bargate Award for *Bruises* and Croydon Warehouse International Playwriting Award 2016 for *Once Around the Sun*.

Plays include: *Ashes and Sand*, Royal Court; *Bruises,* Royal Court; *Sliding With Suzanne*, Royal Court; *Team Spirit*, National Theatre; *Sunspots,* The Red Room; and *Noctropia,* Hampstead Theatre. She has had seven plays on BBC Radio 4, including 2019 Drama of The Week, *The Bulbul Was Singing*.

As a screenwriter, Judy's feature films are Brighton-set *Ashes and Sand*, produced by Open Road Films and Matador Pictures; and *My Imprisoned Heart*, produced by Sci-Fi London. A TV drama *All in The Mind* was shown on BBC1, and her short films are *Exposed, Milk* and *Blame It on The Boogie*.

Judy's first novel *Out Of The Frying Pan* was published by Hobart Books in 2021 and is available from bookshops and online.

www.judyupton.co.uk

Chapter One

'Rouki Bennett's Cockers stolen.' That's not a headline you read every day. It was trending on Twitter too. In the process of making off with her two Spaniels, the thieves had also shot her personal dog walker. Thankfully he was not seriously injured, but he was in Worthing Hospital, having been peppered with shotgun pellets. Things had been worsening in the world of pet theft for some time, but this was the most significant case on our patch to date. Brownlow and I needed to get in on the action and fast.

Everyone's heard of Rouki Bennett. She started her career giving extremely obvious home decluttering tips on YouTube. 'Don't love it, don't use it, chuck it,' was one of her regular mantras. 'Skip it, skip it, skip it,' was another. After a few years of showing celebrities how to tidy their drawers and remove hair from their plugholes, her series had been cancelled and she'd had to reinvent herself by appearing on every reality show she could. Again, she struck gold, as people enjoyed her good-hearted but hopeless efforts at singing, skating, dancing and cooking. If you've not witnessed Rouki's recent misadventures while stuck in a forest with a bunch of fellow self-obsessed over-sharers, you must lead a busy life indeed. Pop into any newsagent and you'll find her improbably white teeth gleaming at you from the cover of just about every woman's magazine. Even her dogs have featured on reality TV. Her two Cavapoos were on a dog grooming special where for some reason they were pruned and accessorised to resemble tiny ponies, and the Cockers featured in a series about training animals where, much like their owner, they reliably came in last in every class and were saved from eviction by the public for longer than was really justified.

Brownlow and I have never been on reality TV or the front of a magazine. We're not, it has to be said, the greatest self-publicists in the world. In spite of that, we do have a respectably large social media following. Also, we are, I can safely say, extremely well known in the field of pet detection here in Sussex. In fact, I could go as far as claiming we'd be the first team you'd think of calling if your dog, cat, tree frog or whatever went missing. Rouki Bennett too is a woman of Sussex, at least since buying an ostentatious villa on the outskirts of Henfield, which she's renovating for her latest TV show.

Rouki's dogs had been stolen almost thirty-six hours before the news of the theft broke this morning. They'd been taken while being exercised by her dog walker on Broadmure Common, a couple of minutes' drive from her house. Although my sympathies were with Rouki and the unfortunate, and as yet unnamed pet exerciser, as well as the Cocker Spaniels themselves, I was, to be honest a little surprised that neither Rouki nor her people had been in contact. Brownlow and I are easy enough to find. You might've supposed someone as media savvy as Rouki would've checked out our socials and DM'ed us right away. Time is always of the essence when it comes to stolen pets, so I knew in these circumstances we had to be pro-active and seize the initiative ourselves.

Unfortunately, Rouki's popularity meant most of her twelve million followers were already replying to her tearful video about Lady Champignon and Mr Merrytrees' abduction. I should probably mention that whilst giving dogs twee names like these seems cute when they're a puppy, it'll sound embarrassing at the vets when they link it to your own surname to call you into the surgery. It's a bit like that game where you find your porn star name. My dog's vet name is 'Brownlow Gorrage'. Initially I thought it sounded like a firm of solicitors who'd represent you if you'd had an accident, but having got used to it, I now use it with an 'and' in the middle as our company name. It is I have to say, far preferable to 'Lady Champignon Bennett', a moniker more suitable for an MP caught in an expenses scandal. As for Mr Merrytrees Bennett, I rest my case.

I thought about leaving a message for Rouki, but it could've been days before she spotted it among the deluge of correspondence from both well-wishers and trolls. Fortunately, an online search quickly brought up the name of the talent management company who act on her behalf. They are called, for some reason, 'Kazowie'. Rouki Bennett's agent there was 'Sonia Rice' and conveniently there was a phone number listed for her.

I was about to call Sonia, when Brownlow pricked up his floppy ears, anticipating, as he unfailingly does, a ring of the doorbell. I checked through the spy hole and to my dismay saw our 'nemmy' – or arch nemesis, to be formal about it, lurking on the doorstep. PC Gemma Carmichael is a rural crime officer at Sussex Police and has been a particularly prickly thorn in our sides for the past three years. Brownlow and I seem to have somehow permanently rubbed her up the wrong way. No matter what the circumstances, I always say or do the wrong thing where she's concerned. I don't know exactly what she's got against Brownlow, but by the looks she gives him you'd think he'd drooled on her boot or peed up her neatly pressed trouser leg. To my knowledge he's never done either. If you meet Brownlow, I can guarantee you'll love him. It's impossible not to. That's why I can say, with reasonable confidence, that there's something seriously wrong with that constable.

'May I come in?' Carmichael snapped, striding in without waiting for an answer. I always find that so rude. Even Dracula doesn't cross a threshold without being asked. Brownlow though wagged his tail and grinned at our 'nemmy'. Annoyingly he can be a tad disloyal at times. I know it wouldn't be a good idea to growl at a cop, but he could at least give her the glare he reserves for cats with a bad attitude. Carmichael stood in the middle of our tiny lounge, wrinkling up her nose. I admit the place smells slightly of flatulent dog, but as a rural crime officer, you'd think she'd be used to the aroma of animal-emitted methane by now. I would've offered that she sit down, but I'd started reorganising my case files a month before and hadn't quite got around to finishing the job. Even though we hadn't been particularly busy, there'd still been a slew of emails to answer, photos to Instagram, tweets to tweet and a website to update. This meant that even my favourite armchair was piled high with paperwork, leaving no place for Carmichael to perch, should she have felt so inclined.

Our agency's only current case was that of a ginger house cat who tended to go missing on sunny days when a window was inadvertently left open. He'd return a few weeks later, by which time his owner would have all but given him up for dead. Brownlow had never, for some reason, obtained much of a scent to follow, but the cat lived in a ground floor flat, and my theory at the time was that he was a second homer. I imagined he might be climbing out of the window of owner number one and into the window of owner number two, who perhaps resided in the same block. The accidental cat bigamist might have been under the illusion that Gregory was a homeless stray, but when he or she next opened a window, the cat returned to home number one. It was only a theory, but it was one that could offer a rational explanation as to why Brownlow had failed to track this particular cat. That's a very unusual failure where Brownlow is concerned. Ordinarily, he always gets his cat. I had suggested the owner put a mesh over

4

his window, but he was unwilling to do so. At least the cat had so far always turned up, and Brownlow and I had been paid for not having to do very much. That week we'd also solved a missing budgie case, and although those rarely have a positive outcome, on this occasion my notice-board-checking round of vets, newsagents and supermarkets had yielded a 'budgerigar found' card in the Co-op. That meant one very satisfied owner, convinced I could work miracles and willing to give us a five-star review on all the usual tradespeople rating sites.

With PC Carmichael having nowhere to sit, her officious manner seemed even more overbearing than usual. She's not tall for a copper but she's still somehow able to give you the feeling she's looming over you. She doesn't take her cap off when she visits, like the police mostly do on the telly, but leaves it rammed down so far that you can't even make eye contact. On the few occasions I've seen her fiercely cropped and extra-hold gelled hair, I've noticed she's going prematurely grey. It can't be from stress, surely. I've always assumed from her demeanour she enjoys giving others cause for anxiety, rather than feeling any herself. A visit from Robocop would be a friendlier affair than one from our rural crime officer. 'No doubt you've heard about a certain high-profile incident,' rasped Carmichael, 'in which you might feel tempted to interfere?' Her voice always has a certain huskiness to it. It makes me feel like recommending Jakeman's or Strepsils.

'An incident? And what might that be?'

'Don't treat me like I'm an idiot, Ms Gorrage.'

'So what is this? Have you come to ask for my help with a case, Gem?' Her thin lips twitched with annoyance at my having the nerve to address her in this manner. Naturally, I only did it to rile her. I can't imagine anyone who's less of a 'gem' than PC Gemma Carmichael.

'No, Ms Gorrage,' she said, spitting out the words like a territorial cat, 'I have come bearing a message from my superiors, to inform you that should you in any way try to involve yourself in this matter, your interference will not be tolerated.'

'Offering my assistance to someone who's lost a pet is a crime now is it? Perhaps you can tell me exactly what law I'd be breaking?'

'Someone wilfully jeopardising a police investigation, can be charged with obstruction or wasting police time, or even perverting the course of justice.'

'I'd have thought the police would be glad of the assistance of a trained pet detection dog and his handler.'

'And I'm here to make sure you know that is certainly not the case.'

'So you're personally investigating the kidnap of Mr Merrytrees and Lady Champignon are you?' Carmichael bristled and blustered.

'No, I'm not involved in the dog theft case.' I hid a smile. I'd already guessed as much. As a lowly rural crime officer, she'd been overlooked once again. She'd be kept busy as usual, advising farmers how to security mark their combine harvesters or dispersing unhappy campers from illegal caravan sites within the South Downs National Park.

'Oh so you're just the messenger. Got it.' She must be around forty at least, our Gem, judging by the depth of her frown lines. It must be quite an achievement to have avoided any kind of promotion. Judging by her gym-honed biceps and hard-boiled attitude, she'd love to see a lot more action than she does, or frankly *any* action at all. 'Okay, message received...' I said to our own Dirty Harry, or to be more accurate, Dirty Harriet. '…though if Ms Bennett should wish to hire Brownlow and myself then…'

'She won't,' Carmichael snapped. 'You can be sure of that.'

'Are you going to tell her not to?' I wouldn't have put it past her.

'I won't need to. You've been warned off.'

'So who…' I said as she headed to the door, '…might you suspect of involvement in stealing Rouki's Cocker Spaniels and shooting her dog walker? If they were allowing you to investigate, I mean?'

'Organised…' Carmichael shut up abruptly.

'Organised crime you were about to say?' Rouki Bennett was a home makeover guru, but I doubted that Carmichael had been about to say, organised 'feng shui experts' or 'pre-loved furniture restorers'.

'I'm certainly not giving you any pointers.' Carmichael muttered.

'That's a shame. You don't see many Pointers about these days. Or Irish Setters come to that.' My humour was as usual lost on her, even before her radio interrupted our cosy chat. I earwigged on her message, hoping it was something about Rouki Bennett's dogs. It was however one of PC Carmichael's more usual calls. A cow had become stuck in a slurry pit. I bade her farewell, sure that at least my day was going to smell a whole lot better than hers.

Sonia, Rouki's manager, was abrupt to the point of being rude on the phone. If I'd been an influencer in need of representation, I'd have employed someone with a tad more personality and warmth. When Brownlow and I can afford a PA, our employee will be charm itself. When you're dealing with panicking pet owners you need to have a calm, capable manner about you. A person like Rouki's representative would lose me clients. She seemed to think I was someone she needed to get rid of as fast as she would a pigeon poop on her jacket. I don't like being treated as if I'm one of those tiresome folk who call up to tell you there's a problem with your loft insulation or that your 'window' has malfunctioned. Sonia informed me that Rouki had already that morning had numerous offers of help from pet-finding websites and private investigators. I pointed out that Brownlow and I were in a different league than the kind of general enquiry agent who deals with straying spouses and insurance scams. 'He's a fully trained pet locating dog, working with the odours of the missing animals. Plus, my knowledge of the world of pet theft is extensive.' She tried to cut me off, but you learn to be persistent in this line of business.

'Our results speak for themselves, Sonia: 94 dogs, 163 cats and 42 other animals from horses to tarantulas, reunited with their owners to date. In addition, we've been instrumental in bringing about a number of arrests and convictions for animal theft and other offences.' I sensed she still wasn't exactly impressed, but with a sigh, she did say I could send through my links and promotional materials to her 'info at' email address. She'd 'make Rouki aware of them'.

I'd been walking Brownlow in the park, while speaking to Sonia. I like walking while on the phone as it gives the impression we're busy, which is particularly useful when we're not. Fortunately, I was then able to find a bench without any joggers using it to aid their tiresome bending and flexing. Attaching our press and PR file to an email is a little fiddly and it's a task I'd rather tackle sitting down. The file contains newspaper reports of our biggest successes as well as feedback from a number of satisfied clients. I added details of our social media sites too for good measure. We hadn't even got back indoors when my mobile rang. I knew it would be Rouki Bennett.

'Sophie Brownlow?'

'Sophie Gorrage from Brownlow And Gorrage' I corrected her. I do realise that technically speaking it's not yet legal for a dog to be co-managing director, but Brownlow is, in my eyes at least, my equal partner in the firm. I recognised Rouki's voice from the TV and it was choked with emotion like the time her exploding soufflé had her ejected from 'Cookery Nook' or whatever it's called. It's the show where there are tears and tantrums every week as the heavily tattooed head chef says, 'You're toast' as she evicts the latest loser from the impossibly clean studio kitchen.

'I'll do anything to get my babies back,' Rouki quailed, 'anything. If there's anything at all you can do to help....' She suggested we meet at her place. I was secretly very glad of that, as the last thing I wanted was a former de-cluttering guru casting a critical eye over our place. For research purposes I'd already checked out a few old clips of her on YouTube. It had included one where she was showing people how to decorate the clay flowerpots she'd discovered scattered in their garden. Chez Brownlow et moi, flowerpots tend to be upended and covering doggy do on the patio, which I've not yet had a chance to clear up. I'm not sure there'd be much point in decorating those. Rouki told me she was currently filming an appeal for her dogs' return, for her YouTube channel, while the natural light was good. She suggested we met afterward, at around four. This worked for us as it gave us a chance to first pay a visit to Weatherall Fields.

Quinn James is the manager of an independent animal sanctuary that rescues and rehabilitates injured and orphaned wildlife, as well as rehoming unwanted pets. Quinn and I are old friends, but it had been a few weeks since I'd visited him at Weatherall Fields. The sanctuary is at the end of a winding country lane and previously I'd always driven straight up to its farmhouse and outbuildings and rang the bell. This time as we turned the final corner on approach, a very different sight greeted us. A tall gate with a barbed wire top and surrounding fences had somehow sprung up, blocking our way. Signs on the gate mentioned a state-of-the-art alarm system and CCTV. For a moment I found myself wondering if Quinn had secretly sold Weatherall to the military, the Prison Service, or even one of those sinister secret organisations that feature in every TV drama nowadays.

Spotting an entry phone, I left Brownlow sitting in the Clio while I used it. A posh, young female voice answered, and amid all the 'ums' and 'likes' I gained the impression she'd never heard of me and if I hadn't pre-arranged to leave or collect an animal, I wasn't getting in. Finally, though I managed to despatch her reluctantly to find Quinn. After a couple of minutes, the gates swung slowly open.

'Sorry about that,' said Quinn, taking a dog biscuit from his jacket pocket for Brownlow as he always did. 'Clemency's one of our gap year vet students.'

'Nuff said.' He grinned and poured me a mug of strong tea. 'But what's with Fort Knox? It would've been easier to get into Alcatraz. You've not had any recent break-ins surely?' Even as I asked, I knew that if this had been the case, he'd have called me. Quinn knows he can always rely on Brownlow and me to help him, free of charge, at any time.

'No, we've not been hit. But this year, it's been happening to more and more sanctuaries and boarding kennels, countrywide.' I nodded. It was a worrying trend. 'So for me, it was a case of shutting the kennel door before the dogs were stolen,' he explained. That made sense. 'It's mostly the pedigrees they're taking of course. And of those it's the breeds that are currently in highest demand, where they can get upwards of two thousand quid cash in a quick sale. It's still dogs more than cats, particularly the Instagram favourites like Cockers, Frenchies, Schnauzers and Dachshunds. Funnily enough though, we've just had a litter of Frenchies in.

Abandoned by the A23. Makes no sense, with people desperate for pups like that. I've seen them go for as much as 7k each. Now we've four on the premises. I mean I can't even advertise for homes with photos in the media, in case it causes us to be targeted. People have to prove their identities and be checked out before I can even let them see any of the dogs. It's slowing the whole adoption process down.' I noticed how tired Quinn was looking. When the sanctuary is overfull, he does tend to run himself ragged, what with the extra animals to care for, and the increased fund-raising needed to look after them.

Quinn James was an army sergeant until he was injured by a roadside bomb in Afghanistan. While recuperating, he came to help out at Weatherall, on the advice of his doctor. In those days, a sprightly octogenarian named Marjorie Weatherall, who was also, as it happened, a friend of mine, was running the place. When Marjorie died, she bequeathed the sanctuary and the attached farmhouse to Quinn on the understanding he continued to run it for the animals, according to her wishes. Since joining Weatherall Fields, Quinn has, in addition to keeping it solvent, established a separate charity of his own. This supports British service personnel who want to bring animals back from war zones, be that to adopt them themselves, or for the sanctuary to rehome. Brownlow was one of the first of the dogs and it's how Quinn and I first met and became friends.

At least 'a friendship' is how I think we'd both describe our relationship, though occasionally it does tip over into 'with benefits' territory, if you catch my drift. It's not something I usually talk about, but I'm certainly not trying to hide this fact. We are both single people after all, and both of us need our own space and like doing our own thing. The sanctuary takes up a huge amount of Quinn's time and finding lost pets with Brownlow keeps me pretty occupied, more often than not. It's usually only on those quiet days like over

Christmas, when the sanctuary is closed to the public, that you might find Quinn and me curled up together on either his sofa or mine, sharing a pizza while watching a film or boxset. In these few hours of leisure our viewing choices are understandably unlikely to include anything involving animals, though we do share a love of crime dramas.

Clemency walked through to the nursery carrying a wriggling badger cub and a bottle of milk with a teat on it. 'Now I've had to up security, it also makes it harder for people to bring us wild creatures they've found,' Quinn admitted. 'Barbed wire fences and entry phones aren't really what you expect to see when you turn up with a wood pigeon with a broken wing. I wonder what Marjorie would think if she saw all this.' I put my hand on his arm.

'She'd think you were doing exactly the right thing. As do I.'

Quinn, Brownlow and I strolled through the main kennel block. I always find it incredibly hard to look anywhere but at my own feet when surrounded by sad eyes and drooping or desperately wagging tails. 'The brutal truth', said Quinn, 'is I can now walk through here and put a price tag on every animal.' He demonstrated. 'Middle-aged mongrel – almost worthless, unspayed Yorkie girl – £3500, Labradoodle, neutered – £1500, Staffie – £3000, very elderly Jack Russell – worthless.' The Jack Russell jumped up at the front of his pen. 'You're not worthless to us of course, Rocco, and we'll find you a great home, don't you worry,' Quinn said as he fussed the dog through the side of the run. Indicating the building housing the cats he added, 'In there it's only the Bengals and anything with a bit of Serval or Leopard Cat in it that's currently worth silly money. They're far more in demand than the Burmese and Siamese now, well unless they've got a 'grumpy cat' flat face.' The human-like expressions of flat-faced animals might win you a few more 'likes' on your socials, but it so often means pets with eye and breathing problems. There was a reason that cats, dogs and rabbits started off with long muzzles. Nature rarely gets it wrong.

'So,' said Quinn, 'the Rouki Bennett case. That's the reason you're here isn't it?' He's always been able to read me like a book. It's incredibly irritating. 'Has she hired you two already?'

'I think she will. We're just on our way to see her, which is why we called in.'

'You'd like my advice about it?' He was surprised. 'I probably know even less about impressing home make-over experts than you do.'

'I'm not asking your advice on how to handle Rouki,' I clarified, 'I'd like to hear your thoughts on what happened. The dog walker getting shot and the fact this seems to bear the hallmarks of something that's been planned, rather than opportunistic dognap.'

'It might suggest involvement of a gang,' Quinn said.

'That's what Carmichael thinks too.' Quinn looked surprised.

'You've been chatting with her about it?'

'I'd hardly call it chatting. She snarls, I listen.' He laughed.

'But you're the one who keeps an updated file of known pet thieves,' he reminded me, 'if the police aren't yet picking your brains, they should be. Isn't there anyone currently on your radar who might be involved?'

'There've been no cases with thieves using firearms that I know of. Not in Sussex at any rate.'

'I think you need to look further afield, Soph. It doesn't sound like a local job.'

'Since Brexit it's been much harder to smuggle dogs in from Europe. The people involved in that will know the market is still white hot, and they'll have everything already in place to distribute and deliver the merchandise.'

'Crooked vets willing to offer false documentation and microchips, and householders pretending to be the genuine owners making a reluctant sale?'

'Absolutely. Whereas a few years back, dognapping was mostly confined to a few individuals trying to make a quick buck to fund their addictions, now it's becoming a much bigger and more serious game.'

'I suppose it was only a matter of time until it happened on our patch. When we were only up against a few chancers, junkies and gamblers, then it was a lot easier for me and Brownlow to solve the case.' He nodded.

'If things are, as you and I both suspect, becoming more complicated, not to mention dangerous, it would be good for Brownlow and me have someone else on the team.'

'Who'd you have in mind?' I pointed straight at him.

'I wish I could help. I would if I didn't have this place taking up all of my time.'

'Oh you mean to say Clementine, Satsuma, or whatever her name is, and her posh student friends aren't up to the task of scrubbing out kennels for a few hours? Clearly you're never gonna get to judge 'The Apprentice'.'

'So what is it exactly you'd like me to do?' Quinn said, resignedly.

'Provide some hired muscle.'

'Not me. Not anymore.'

'I just mean Rouki will need someone to walk her remaining dogs. While protecting them?'

'Canine bodyguard?' He looked at me quizzically.

'Why not? In a bullet-proof vest of course. You said the sanctuary needed money. You could charge around £500 a day…'

'How much?' Quinn gasped.

'That's the going rate. I've checked it out online.'

'And for that I'd do what? Wear a little cap and uniform? Call Rouki Mizz or Ma'am?'

'No seriously, Quinn. There are now firms advertising canine security personnel with bodyguard and self-defence skills. All vetted and mostly ex-military. I mean that's you to a 't'.' He was still looking sceptical, so I found the advertisement on my phone and showed it to him. 'Plus, it would help me and Brownlow to know someone else had eyes and ears on Rouki's two remaining dogs.'

'It would certainly be bad publicity for you if the thief came back and snatched them under your noses.'

'And bad for Rouki and bad for the dogs,' I reminded him sternly, in case he thought I was thinking only of the business's reputation. 'She sounded in bits on the phone.'

'No doubt. But you haven't bagged the job yet, Soph,' Quinn reminded me. 'One thing at a time eh?'

Chapter Two

As Brownlow and I drove away from Weatherall Fields, I reflected on how ironic it was that the sanctuary was currently underfunded and overcrowded, when owning a dog has never been more popular. Why would anyone pay a fortune for a dog when there are so many needing loving homes? I always feel a mixture of emotions visiting the sanctuary. Happy so many animals are safe and being cared for, but desperately sad to see so many pets with their confidence crushed by losing the owners they loved. I'd have more dogs if I could. Cats, rabbits and the odd chicken too. It's simply not possible though, whilst living in a small downstairs maisonette with a cleanliness freak above and a business cash flow that is erratic to say the least. For now, at least, Brownlow will remain an only dog.

You can't get greedy and charge the earth to find a lost dog or cat, even if a well-off person like Rouki Bennett owns him or her. People with money and people without can be equally distraught when an animal goes missing. It would be wrong to take advantage of that. I charge a very reasonable daily rate in addition to expenses and a modest finder's fee, payable only upon results. I inform the client of the likely costs upfront in our initial consultation, which is offered free and without obligation. If, as in the case of the man who'd lost his favourite guppy down his bath's plughole, there is no hope of a joyful reunion, I tell it like it is. There are no smoke and mirrors where Brownlow and I are concerned. What you hire is what you get.

Our ancient Renault Clio was making ominous noises as we headed towards Rouki Bennett's house, passing through Cowfold and Henfield on the way. (For those who don't know West Sussex very well, I hope you don't think I've made up some twee-sounding place names like Horsham, Fishbourne and Maresfield. If you've any lingering doubts as to whether these are real towns and villages, you can always check them out via your favourite search engine. Another local town, Storrington is actually named after the Storks that used to live in the area. They are now making a comeback here thanks to a rewilding project, but I've yet to spot one.) Our car spluttered and threatened to stall at the Henfield town centre roundabout, and I was relieved to see at least there weren't any warning lights winking from the dashboard. That could, I then worried, actually be because the warning indicators were broken too. My mechanic's called Gavin and just the fact we're on first name terms should alert you to the sorry state my car is in. If I tell you I can remember his phone number, and name at least two tunes he likes to whistle while examining an engine, I think you'll get the idea of how close to shuffling off her motor coil the poor old thing is. Also, one of those tunes Gavin whistles is 'The Final Countdown' by Europe, which says it all really. I do, in spite of the implied sexism, still refer to my car as 'she', but she doesn't have a name, unless you want to count 'Clio' as one. Even so, over the past few years she's come to feel like a part of our team, and parting with her when the time comes will certainly be a wrench, no pun intended.

We drove along through hedge-lined lanes, being overtaken by boy and girl racers, and even the occasional trailer-towing tractor. Brownlow had his head out of the window as usual, sniffing the air. Whereas I'm in seventh heaven if a favourite track comes on the radio, his drive-time wish list is made up of smells. A field freshly spread with manure or a roadside burger van will make his nose lift up in the air and his tail beat out a joyful rhythm on the back of my seat.

Rouki's house was one of those properties that gain a full-page spread in those glossy magazines you find in the GP's waiting room. It had a white-pillared porch, a terrace covered in grape vines, and a heated kidney-shaped outdoor pool. You could call it hard-core property porn, the sort we all might buy when our cunning side hustle makes us a million, or we wake to find a Banksy stencilled on our outside wall. Like Weatherall, it had a security entry system. Upon pressing the buzzer, I was rather surprised to hear Rouki herself answer.

'Hello?'

'It's Sophie Gorrage. Can I bring Brownlow in with me?'

'Who?' My heart sank. It was not a good sign if, having invited us over, she'd already forgotten who we were. I hoped it was just the slight background buzz of the entry phone stopping her hearing my introduction.

'The pet detecting dog.'

'Um o-kay.' The gate opened.

Rouki Bennett was sitting on a sofa that resembled an emerald scallop shell, if scallop shells came in dark green, which as far as I know, they don't. The walls were covered in pink striped wallpaper that, if you owned a pair of pyjamas like mine, you'd merge completely into. Not that I'd turned up in my pyjamas. I was wearing my long taupe raincoat which, this season, is back in fashion, according to 'My Weekly'. Shower-proof outerwear is of course a sensible choice for a pet detective. I had on a dark brown polo neck beneath, because it keeps out the chill, and dog hairs don't show up too obviously on its acrylic ribs. I was dressed for action, because as soon as Rouki signed our contract we'd start work immediately on the case. I didn't envisage getting an early night.

Brownlow had his harness on, with his wipe-clean hi-viz jacket that says 'Detection Dog At Work' on both sides. This is to discourage passers-by from petting him, which risks distracting him when he's following a scent. The polished floor of Rouki's lounge dazzled my eyes, and despite the sun streaming in through the tall windows, she'd still lit some chunky candles on the coffee table that were giving off a rather peculiar aroma. No doubt it was an expensive and exclusive perfume from Rouki's own range. In truth though it did whiff a bit, smelling to me of burnt milk and dandelions. What it smelt like to Brownlow I couldn't even hazard a guess. Unfortunately, he'd begun to sneeze the moment Rouki had let us in, hitting his big black nose against the hardwood floor with every involuntary spasm. For a sensitive nose like his, those candles meant a sensory overload. I resolved to discreetly move away the closest ones the moment Ms Bennett's back was turned.

Rouki's remaining dogs were two black Cavapoos who seemed unaffected by the expensive pong. They'd probably lived with her for long enough to be immune to the effects of an overpowering odour. The pair sat flanking her on the scallop, wearing little black and scarlet coats with their names on. They were Fennell Foxbrurgh and Morris B. I did wonder how Rouki chose the names of her pets. Brownlow, in case you're wondering, bears the name of a Sergeant Tom Brownlow, who rescued him from his former life.

With long gel nails, Rouki waved me to a chair that looked considerably less comfortable than her seashell. Rouki is one of those people who wave their hands about as they speak, and her nails, the same colour as the wallpaper, were quite mesmerising in their shininess. It made me wish I'd at least bothered to scrape the dirt out of my own. Up close her make up, particularly the foundation, appeared a little overdone, though I'm sure it looks flawless on YouTube. Her cream cable-knit sweater and artfully distressed jeans were inconceivably dog hair free, though in fairness her dogs were both far more expensively groomed and less genetically liable to shed than Brownlow. He did however know how to behave, lying down peaceably beside the engraved, frosted glass coffee table, while Rouki's dogs yapped and scolded at us both. They took no notice of her efforts to quieten them either. Clearly both were exhibiting the classic traits of small dog syndrome, but who could blame them for feeling insecure when their pack had been cruelly halved over night? It was enough to traumatise the calmest canine.

A personal assistant appeared and handed Rouki a mobile phone. She strode briskly into the hall on a sharp pair of heels to take the call in private. Meanwhile the assistant, who had a Scots accent, asked above the din of the tetchy Cavapoos if I would like a cup of tea.

'Shush!' I said firmly to the Cavas, rather than the PA, and silence fell. The PA looked impressed by that. I'm guessing she'd spent a lot of time being deafened by that racket while in Ms Bennett's employ. She wore grey dungarees and had a diagonal fringe that looked as if it had been cut with a desk guillotine. Introducing herself as Alex, she invited me to select a herbal infusion from a selection of teabags fanned out in a circle in a little basket. Wanting to appear decisive, I plumped randomly for liquorice and manuka honey, which according to Alex was a blend favoured by none other than Gwyneth Paltrow. Alex went to make the tea and brought my chosen infusion to me in a mug with the name of a TV channel on it. It was one of those 'More' or 'Plus One' ones that recycles old lifestyle shows. 'Rouki's beyond devastated. You cannot imagine.' I nodded. Actually I could both understand and empathise. I'd rather someone stole both my arms than Brownlow. If it were up to me, dog snatchers would all serve life with no parole. Still, never mind the owner, does anyone really comprehend how the poor stolen dogs feel? They can't possibly know why their adored human is no longer at their side. For all we know, they not only mourn, they blame themselves too. It's bad enough living with the knowledge that every time I go out without him, Brownlow has no idea if he will ever see me again. In the early days of our relationship he'd stress, wee and chew the furniture every time I went shopping. Nowadays he just utters a heavy sigh and walks dejectedly away up the hall, when he's left behind at home. Since it's no longer safe to leave a dog outside a shop and being home alone is a depressing experience for my faithful companion, I now buy nearly everything online. I miss the human interaction of shopping in the High Street, but not as much as my dog would miss me.

When Rouki finally returned, my tea was already cool enough to sip. It was clear from her manner there had been no news in the phone call, positive or otherwise, about her missing dogs. She sat back down opposite me, checked the time on the phone and yawned widely without covering her mouth. Her teeth (or more likely veneers) practically glowed in the light from the whiffy candles. 'So tell me,' she asked, 'exactly what a dog detective does?' I explained how Brownlow, if given the scent of a missing animal, can track it at even a minute amount, days, weeks and even months later. 'He can pick up a scent marker on nearly all surfaces, in all weathers and even where there has been maximum site disturbance. Faced with somewhere like a busy dog walking route, he will still be able to stick to the scent of the specific animal he has been tasked with tracking.' Rouki should've by rights have looked impressed at this, but perplexingly she didn't.

'Don't the police have their own sniffer dogs?' I tried hard not to take umbrage.

'Not ones specifically trained to find missing animals. A general search dog could go so far, but when the trail becomes faint, as like as not, he or she will lose the odour. You can think of it like this. A general search dog is a GCSE level tracker, Brownlow is a Cambridge professor.' It's a line I've trotted out a few times and it seemed to do the trick. She nodded and I hope she understood. 'May I ask,' I enquired, 'whether the police have offered the services of their tracker dogs?' Rouki grimaced, her brows straining against the Botox to attempt a frown.

'They've been asked, but it's not happened yet.' I nodded.

'And time in a case like this of course of the essence. Particularly, if the dogs being used are not specialists like Brownlow.' She eyed him somewhat dubiously, as he sneezed once more, his whole body spasming with the reflex. To her, no doubt, he looked like nothing special – simply a large, shaggy mongrel. 'I'm sorry, your candles are making him sneeze. It's due to having a top-grade nose, you see?'

'So some dogs have a better sense of smell than others?'

'Absolutely. Bloodhounds and others are specifically bred for it. But people also vary in their olfactory abilities,' I told her, warming to my subject. I always bought New Scientist if it featured anything about smell. 'Perfume houses only employ the best human noses to test their new scents.'

'I've my second fragrance coming out at Christmas,' said Rouki, almost as if she'd automatically switched to promotion mode, 'though I haven't decided what I'd like it to smell like yet. You tell them, you see, and they mix up some samples for you. The candles are from my first one 'Rouki – Strive'. The base notes are peach and pomegranate.' To me that sounded more like a yoghurt from Waitrose. No wonder poor Brownlow was sneezing. I was also concerned we were drifting away from the subject of Brownlow And Gorrage taking on her case.

I decided at that point to tell Rouki about my own personal skills, including my newly qualified proficiency as a drone pilot. Being able to use a camera to get an aerial view can be useful where lost or stolen pets are concerned. Last month I went on a course to learn how to operate them. I crashed the training version a good few times but I eventually got the hang of it. The woman training us had used a drone to film cheetahs in Africa for a wildlife programme, and she understood my needs of finding pets in the wild would benefit from the same skills. It was still hard to tell if Rouki was impressed or even interested. She kept cooing to the dogs and rubbing their ears, as well as looking over her shoulder as if she expected someone more interesting to enter the room. In the hall behind, Alex strode back and forth. She was constantly on the phone or scrolling its screen, occasionally coming in to discreetly whisper something in Rouki's ear. Despite all the activity, it seemed nothing was really happening where finding the stolen pets was concerned. If any of those calls or messages being relayed to the dogs' owner were from the police, then it sounded as if they had so far drawn a blank.

I couldn't resist hoping as I sat sipping my Paltrow approved tea that PC Carmichael was at that moment up to her neck in liquefied cattle poo. If Carmichael ever wanted to escape her career cul-de-sac, as her passive aggressive and sometimes genuinely aggressive attitude towards me suggested she might, she could do worse than ask me for a job. Brownlow and I could do with someone to run the office while we're out on an investigation. Despite her lack of interpersonal skills, I'd be the first to admit that Carmichael has, in the past, shown some good instincts where crimes involving animals are concerned. In one particular case involving a stolen Shetland pony, Brownlow and I were driving up to the remote barn where it was being hidden, when Carmichael emerged leading it by the bridle and two other missing horses besides. Of course, she gave me a horrible, smug look and gloated about it at length the next time we met. It was fair enough though, she had got there first, and three equines were saved from the horrors of a continental abattoir. Carmichael has received a commendation for nicking a thief of rare birds' eggs too, though that wasn't in competition with us, as we try not to tread on her toes where wildlife is concerned. City and town dwelling pets however are not part of her rural crime prevention officer remit. Rouki's house was on the outskirts of a small town, which some people might even call the countryside, but it was definitely not a farm, which I hoped meant Carmichael's superiors would be unlikely to change their minds and sanction her involvement in the dog theft case.

I asked Rouki if the police had been helpful thus far, and she said they'd sent a couple of detectives to see her. This was surprising. Normally a stolen pet or even two wouldn't receive this kind of VIP - Very Important Policing. In my experience you'd be lucky to get an email containing a crime number several days after the traumatic event. I guess having twelve million followers of your every breath has considerable advantages. 'Both my babies are microchipped, but I've heard they can remove them.' She winced as if she was the one having a chip cut out. 'I'm going to make sure my next dog walker has martial arts training.'

'A good idea. It's useful,' I told her. 'I wouldn't be without mine.' Even the Botox couldn't prevent her looking surprised at that disclosure. I couldn't help feeling a little indignant at that. Now I might not have a gym-honed, perfect body like Rouki and I must be well over a decade older than her, but I'm reasonably fit from the amount of walking I do. Certainly there shouldn't have been anything about my physical appearance to justify her shock at learning I'm able to defend myself. I went to both judo and taekwondo classes as a bullied school kid and, like riding a bike, those skills stay with you. I haven't so far been in many situations where I've needed to defend myself, but then we're still most usually called upon to find missing pets, rather than those that have been stolen in distinctly violent circumstances.

At this point Rouki said that it's a scandal pet theft isn't taken more seriously and informed me she was going to start a campaign about it. There'd be a documentary, fund-raising, some awareness sessions and even merchandise in aid of the cause. She'd already had a few ideas for t-shirt designs, which she showed me on her iPhone. They looked nice enough, but I was starting to worry that she still hadn't mentioned hiring us.

I took out our standard contract, moved aside the copy of Rouki's latest ghost-written home-beautifying tome and plonked it down on the coffee table between those reeking candles.

'This explains the scope of what we do, and sets out our daily rate and other charges, which I believe are very reasonable.' She didn't pick it up or read it.

'Oh, right.' she said, uninterested, 'You see I've just posted a reward actually. 300,000 pounds.' My heart sank lower than my ankles.

'Err, I'd have to strongly advise against that, Ms Bennett –'

'Well that's how I'm doing it.' She thrust her chin up the way I'd seen her do on TV when anyone dared suggesting saving a favourite knick-knack from the skip. 'And as I said. I have already done it. Just before you came in, actually.'

'Right.'

'This way, you see I can get as many people as possible looking for them, rather than putting all my eggs into one or two cakes.'

'Baskets.'

'Eh?'

'People tend to say 'putting all my eggs in one' –' I stopped realising it might not be terribly smart to contradict a possible client, even one who had just made my job, if hired, at least ten times harder.

'What I'm trying to say is I'm not so sure that setting a reward is such a good idea.'

'When you can reach millions of people, why would you not ask them all to help? Lives have been saved that way, you know? And a fortune raised for fantastic causes. People power is so amazing. You just have to trust and reach out.' I could've mentioned that Brownlow and I have loyal followers too, albeit still in the low thousands, but I didn't, because frankly when you do the job we do, you see both the best and worst of people. I didn't entirely buy into this social media world of fluffy, lovable people. Someone somewhere out there was probably trying to buy Rouki's Cockers as we spoke.

'My chief concern,' I tried to explain, 'is that if you're asking millions of the public at large to play detective, you could make the kidnappers panic. The dogs were out with your walker. The thieves may not have realised until now that they are high profile animals. They were probably planning to sell them on for a few thousand pounds, but now their net worth has increased dramatically, but they've also become a liability – too hot to sell. If they show them to a prospective buyer, the person may well recognise them.' Rouki sighed impatiently. She clearly still didn't understand the implications of her actions and thought I was the one who didn't know what she was talking about.

'£300,000 is a lot of money to ordinary people. I think it will make the robbers get in touch and want to hand over the dogs.'

'It might make them get in touch. But it only takes a quick look online to see your net worth.'

'The figure they quote isn't an accurate one.'

'They won't worry about that. If you're willing to pay 300k for your dogs, what's to stop them asking for five hundred grand, or a million say? People tend to think anyone in the public eye is loaded, whatever the truth of the matter.' She did look slightly worried at that. 'Plus, you've just made dog theft even more lucrative. If you pay a ransom, how many other owners will find themselves having to face the same thing in future?'

'It's not a ransom, it's a reward.' Rouki said this patronisingly slowly and with an eye-roll, but I wasn't letting her get away with that when she was the one who didn't know what she was doing.

'Really?' I snapped. 'And the police know and have agreed it's a good idea, have they?' She said nothing. It sounded like it was going to come as a nasty surprise to them too. 'You hope the money will go to an innocent person who finds your lost animals, but in reality the person who contacts you will be a middle man or woman working on behalf of the kidnappers. They'll say they happened upon the dogs somewhere, blah, blah, blah, and you will just have rewarded the criminals who shot your employee and stole Mr Merrytrees and Lady Champignon.'

'I won't pay out until I have them back.' Clearly she wasn't listening to what I was saying, or if she was, the moral position didn't bother her. I gave it one last try.

'If the kidnappers return the dogs themselves, or through a third party, for the reward and get away with it, they'll do it again and again. And so will others like them. I'm sure you don't want to encourage a spate of kidnappings and animals held for ransom. Particularly as many people won't be able to afford to get their beloved companions back.'

'They could appeal online and set up a charitable page,' Rouki pouted.

'But again it could snowball. Pretty soon all the funding sites will be full of people trying to get their pets back, and not enough donations to go around. It'll be a circus – people with the cutest animal photo and saddest sob story will get the cash. Someone else whose dog is less attractive, and doesn't have winsome kids to pose with tear-stained faces, will lose out.' Rouki Bennett simply shrugged.

'I don't see it as my responsibility. My loyalty is to my babies. And well it's done anyway. End of.' 'End of' it certainly was. Every dog owner, walker, groomer, along with the rest of the country would already be out there playing amateur sleuth, trampling evidence and causing untold chaos and confusion. The poor missing dogs, in all likelihood would never be heard of again. Rouki might well have killed her pets with her attempt at saving them.

Rouki rose. She had to bring our 'interview' as she called it to a close as she had a pet clairvoyant and a pet whisperer waiting in the next room for their opportunities to talk to her. The clairvoyant was apparently 'amazing' and had over a million followers. I left the remains of my Gwyneth tea and stood up.

'So I take it you're not going to hire us, Ms Bennett?'

'If you're as good as you say you are,' she returned, 'you'll be the ones claiming the reward, won't you? It's an incentive – payment by results. And it's a life changing amount, worth a little of even your time surely?' I sensed the atmosphere had soured, despite the cloying sweetness of peach and pomegranate, which I suspected would linger on my clothes for several wash cycles to come.

'And the fortune teller and the crystal swinger?' I enquired archly; offended that she was treating these snake oil merchants as if they were as worthy as of a meeting as us, 'Are you paying them for their time?'

'Oh no. But they can mention on their socials that they're helping me. As can you, of course, if you choose to become involved. As I've explained erm… Sophie, the one who gets my babies back will be the one getting the cash. It's totally fair.' I retrieved the unsigned copy of our contract from the table. They cost money to print, and we'd just wasted several hours of our time.

Before she left Alex to show me out, Rouki instructed me to continue to 'follow the conversation,' on her socials presumably, to 'stay in the loop'. I could DM her too if I 'found any meaningful clues, and someone will respond'. At the door, I glanced down and noticed something. Slipped down behind a quirkily patterned vase that was acting as an umbrella stand was what looked a lot like a half-chewed dog biscuit. It was the typical kind of place a dog will lose a treat it's been chewing, in that it was the kind of narrow gap that even the most skilled paw and jaw coordination would find it hard to retrieve a small object from. While Alex was stroking Brownlow's head and saying goodbye to him, I swiftly stopped and retrieved the biscuit, disguising the gesture with a straightening of the bottom of my trouser leg. This tiny find might come in useful later.

In the Clio, with only Brownlow as a witness, I called Rouki Bennett a few choice names. I couldn't help myself.

'Grr-woof,' added Brownlow, which is his own way of joining in a swearing session. 'Well old friend, it's back to waiting for some normal people to bung us a few quid to find out which neighbour their cat has moved in with.' Brownlow grinned his usual grin, happy no doubt to have escaped the olfactory torture of Rouki's candles. He's the laid back one of our partnership. He doesn't have to worry about the financial side of our operation. The only contact he has with the bills is any he happens to chew up when they drop through the letterbox. I knew we couldn't afford to go looking for Rouki's dogs on a payment by result basis. I'd never agree to those kinds of terms if offered by a client. It was a sad fact however that we could hardly ignore the temptation of that kind of money. Plus, we'd never declined a case of an animal in need. While we are not a charity or an official emergency service, if the client genuinely can't afford to pay, I do waive our fees. We've reunited a homeless man with his dog and a blind woman in sheltered housing with her canary without charging them. We've also accepted a couple of quid and a dog chew for finding a little girl's hamster.

Back home, the answer machine informed me that our only current case had resolved itself. Gregory the cat had had once again returned home of his own accord. 'Ponging of pesto,' Clive, his owner explained in his message, sounding rather put out by the fact. Personally, I like pesto and if my cat returned smelling of something nice I'd see it as a plus. I'm a glass half-full kind of person. The pesto was a clue to solving Gregory's potential next disappearance though, so I checked Street View and found Clive and Gregory had an Italian restaurant in the adjoining street. I made a note to check it out, and in particular to enquire whether or not they had a lockable bin store, that Gregory could have unwittingly become trapped inside whilst hunting for left over prosciutto. Unfortunately, according to Street View, the direct route to the back of the restaurant involved crossing a private back garden, and I recalled being previously unable to access it as the owners were away, and their gate was tall and locked on the inside. That looked like the most likely reason Brownlow hadn't found that cat. An insurmountable physical barrier had blocked the odour trail from the flats to the restaurant. There would be no finder's fee for us on this occasion, but it did at least prove that in our failure to find Gregory, Brownlow was blameless. I was also sure that next time, we'd get our cat.

As I tipped Brownlow's personally mixed and delivered dog food into a bowl, I told him that if our financial situation didn't soon improve, I'd have to switch him from his expensive bags of weekly goodness to a supermarket bargain range. I didn't really mean it though. It would be me surviving on random items from the double-discounted section of the Co-op once again. Brownlow might have started his life scrounging scraps from a dusty Afghan street, but I'd never let him suffer such privations again.

With spare time now on our hands and paws, I suppose we could've joined the gold rush to find Rouki's dogs, but her attitude had put my nose out of joint. It's rarely we visit a prospective client and come away without being hired. If she chose to ignore the fact that we have an impressive and proven track record and instead wanted to listen to the mumbo jumbo of Sussex's finest soothsayers, alchemists and magic bean polishers, then we weren't going to get involved with the search for her stolen Cockers.

Hearing my mobile ringtone of 'Who Let the Dogs Out', I rushed to answer, knocking if off the armchair arm in my haste. Unfortunately, it wasn't a prospective client, but a journalist from the West Sussex Gazette researching an article about dog theft 'inspired by the Rouki Bennett case'. Her first questions were the usual ones about why did I think dog theft was on the increase, what did I think of current sentencing for the crime. Then she wanted a little background about what Brownlow does. Despite the fact I had a microwaved pie and chips going cold, I gave her my time and offered a professional standard photo of us both, which she said she'd be glad of 'as it would save sending a photographer out to you'. I hoped the article might cause a few new cases to come our way. Her final question though, was not one I wanted to answer.

'Are you going to be offering Brownlow's services to Rouki Bennett?' I couldn't very well say we'd been turned down, as it wasn't exactly good PR. Lying to the press wouldn't have been a good idea either, as we were likely to be found out. I blustered something about being in touch with Ms Bennett, but 'That, as I'm sure you understand, I can't say more at the present time.'

'Client confidentiality?'

'Is incredibly important to us at Brownlow And Gorrage, yes.'

'You say 'us' – meaning you and the dog?' I cursed myself for the slip of the tongue. The last thing I wanted was it to be one of those light-hearted, quirky pieces where I was presented as a mad animal lady.

'There are other people with specialist skills whom I can call upon if the situation requires it.' I was meaning Quinn. Over at Weatherall his ears were probably burning.

'And the police? Do you ever work with them?' Again, I blathered some general nonsense about how I'd be happy to liaise with them if they wished to consider utilising our skills and experience. The journalist seemed happy with that and I wrapped up the call, reflecting that among my skills was an expertise in deflection and obfuscation that would come in handy if ever I was asked to be prime minister.

I sat up into the night, on my bed, watching an old black and white monster movie, with a drowsy Brownlow acting as my loyal foot-warmer. Not for us, on our current salary, the joys of Netflix, though I did have half a bag of still reasonably fresh salted popcorn, which helped to make the film at least half-enjoyable. I must've fallen asleep, judging by the popcorn fragments scattered on the duvet, when the Baha Men started their refrain from my phone. It was Quinn's number.

'Sorry to wake you, Soph. Have a look at Twitter.'

'Why? What?' For a horrible moment I envisaged something I'd said in the local paper interview was incredibly controversial, already out there and trending in a very scary way. I've never trended on Twitter, I hasten to add, and I'm not sure my thoughts on any subject you could mention would provoke that kind of response. I realised Quinn was still speaking.

'It's not been verified just yet, but people are saying the rapper Medalsum has been violently carjacked...'

'Who?'

'Medalsum. Topped the charts earlier this year.'

'Oh... I think I know who you mean. The jacket with the medals. The rap about holding a party in a traffic jam?'

'That's him. Been carjacked, like I said...'

'In a traffic jam, by any chance?' I interrupted, slightly irritably, 'Look I'm sure it's very worrying for his fans, friends and family, Quinn, but it's the middle of the night and –'

'They took his dog. Left him lying in the road and drove off with her.'

Chapter Three

I decided that Brownlow And Gorrage should try to do
something, despite the fact no one had officially hired us as of
yet. Brownlow too, I'm sure, would've agreed we needed to
act, if he'd been able to voice an opinion. First Rouki's
Cockers and now Medalsum's Staffordshire Bull Terrier had
been taken. Two violent, celebrity-related dog thefts, one in
Sussex and one in London and only a few days apart – it did
seem probable there was a link. Medalsum hadn't been badly
hurt but had almost immediately posted a photo of himself
with a black eye and a gash to his forehead. I'd need to talk to
him, as soon as I could find a way to, but my first job was, as
Quinn put it, to 'secure the ports'. That meant alerting the
Border Force at Newhaven, Dover and the Channel Tunnel,
plus anyone else I could think of who might have eyes and
ears on the ferries and who was travelling on them.

Unfortunately, I don't have a dedicated line to alert Border
Force to these kinds of emergencies, though it would certainly
be useful for them and me. Instead, I had to email their
offices at the various locations individually. I sent photos of
Rouki's missing dogs and one I found online of Medalsum's
Staffie, Tasha. I mentioned in my message that the animals
could have been disguised by dyeing their coats etc, and that
all animals of the same breeds, whether or not they resembled
those in the photos, should probably have their microchips
and travel documents given extra scrutiny. Quinn spoke to
someone he knew at the quarantine kennels at Gatwick

airport. They'd met when he'd begun importing rescued dogs from overseas. She said she would also talk to the baggage handlers who transported pets and other livestock cages to the aircraft.

Rouki's dogs were probably too high profile to sell in this country and unless they were subsequently abandoned or offered for ransom, then they were almost certainly leaving the UK if they hadn't already done so. We might have already left it too late where they were concerned, but if Medalsum's dog had been taken by the same people, then by tracing her, we would also be on the trail of Rouki's two. The carjacking in London had only happened in the last few hours, so Tasha would still be on UK soil, though possibly on her way down the motorway to one of the ports. The police probably wouldn't do more than deploy number plate recognition to bring about a stop and search where the vehicles of any known dognapper was concerned. It was unlikely though that anyone who had once been caught with stolen dogs in their vehicle would use the same one a second time. Many of these criminals have been involved in other lucrative areas of smuggling in the days before pets became worth stealing. This makes them old hands at evading this type of detection. I didn't have high hopes that a stolen car or otherwise suspicious number plate being flagged up would be the thing that led to the animals being reunited with their owners.

I normally take Brownlow for an early morning walk and I figured he wouldn't mind if we swapped our usual saunter in the park and game of fetch for a wander around to Brighton Marina. If someone is going to need to ship stolen animals out of the country, especially ones that people were looking for, then it's possible you have some obliging yacht or small boat moored up somewhere on the coast. Brighton is the biggest, but by no means only, Sussex marina from which this type of activity could take place. Brownlow's wide grin and shaggy, waggy tail is an asset when it comes to making informal enquiries. A man cleaning the windows of an expensive looking craft was the first to happily stop for a chat and comment on the friendly dog. I told him about Brownlow's history in Afghanistan. That always seems to interest people. The man asked, as others have done, if Brownlow is an Afghan Hound.

My reply of 'no he's more of an Afghan rug on legs' got a laugh and good-natured sympathy for the poor mutt whose owner was affectionately disparaging him. From there it was simple to drop into conversation my reading in the news about the rise in dog thefts and as an owner being anxious about it. 'I wonder what they're doing with them – all the stolen dogs. I suppose they're probably all taking them abroad or something?' The man said he imagined that could be the case, but surely it wouldn't be easy. His partner had given up taking her golden retriever on their Med cruises, as the extra hassle complying with the new EU rules had made it too complicated.

'We used to just take off on a whim,' he said a little wistfully. 'Now you can't be that spontaneous what with having to get a Animal Health Certificate from a vet no more than ten days before you travel. Then when you've got it, it only lasts for four months. The last time we forgot, lingered too long in Nice and then it was a faff to get Jeremy back in the country.' I presumed Jeremy was the dog, but to me being forced to linger in the likes of the South of France would have been anything but an inconvenience.

'You weren't tempted to just swerve the paperwork? I mean there's no passport control here.' He frowned.

'And risk a massive fine? Again too much hassle. It's simpler to pay for the dog to stay in kennels. A nice one mind, it's more like a spa.' We joked about how animals get used to their little luxuries. He gave the impression of knowing a lot of pampered, sea-going pooches, but he hadn't heard of any dog smuggling occurring from Brighton. Before we left the marina, I stopped for a coffee outside a café. While people-watching, I noticed quite a few pedigree must-have breeds with glamorous owners. The humans were focused on either visiting the designer outlets or, like me, enjoying an al fresco beverage. One woman tied her Pugs to a street sign while she popped into a clothing store. I resolved to have a word when she emerged to make her theft aware. It did seem though that Brighton Marina was more likely the kind of a place to steal high value animals from, rather than one to use as an export hub. The affluent village-like atmosphere could lull people into that sense that crime was more likely to happen elsewhere. Hove, on my patch, is another dog snatchers' hotspot, for the same reason. My phone rang; it was Quinn. As a Medalsum fan, he'd tweeted the rapper suggesting my services, and to his surprise received a reply. Even more surprisingly, Medalsum actually wanted to hire Brownlow and me.

I assumed Medalsum would expect us to travel up to London to meet him, but Quinn said the rapper was about to fly out on the next leg of his European tour. I was to send my paperwork to 'his people' and they'd sort out payment. He'd check in with me personally later. I told Quinn he must've done a good job pitching Brownlow and me, but he said the main thing with Medalsum was he wanted results and soon. 'He kept saying 'the feds' as he calls the police, are 'all chat and no action'. He wants 'someone on it and getting results'. His words not mine.'

Whoever designed the latest trains on the London to Brighton line gave no thought whatsoever to dogs' tails. Brownlow is a large chap and even when lying at my feet, nose to the carriage side, his tail has a tendency to protrude into the aisle. First of all it was one of those groups of foreign students who can't decide where to sit who decided to walk up and down with their wheeled cases several times. Twice I had to call out to them to remind them to look where they were treading and wheeling, and the third time I managed to curl Brownlow's tail back against his body. At Gatwick Airport the platform was three abreast with people, with luggage of all descriptions, which is always our worst nightmare on these kinds of trips. I got up and we went and stood against the opposite doors to those serving the platform. We let those tail crushing menaces pass us by. It then seemed our safest option was to stand the rest of the way to London. Those 'dogs must be carried' signs you see beside the escalators on the tube make me smile. Carrying a canine companion as heavy as Brownlow on a sluggish conveyor belt up a steep gradient is not for the faint hearted. Lately I've been getting a bit breathy when I run, so perhaps I'm a little more faint-hearted than I used to be. A lot of the cabs are funny about taking dogs, but a bendy bus with few people on board proved the perfect way to get across town. The area for strap hanging commuters was empty as it was early in the afternoon, and so I could sit on a seat taking in the sights, while Brownlow sprawled out.

A teenage girl in cut-off jeans opened the door to Medalsum's Camden townhouse. She was wearing ear-jacks and holding a phone in her hand. 'The pet detectives right?' she drawled in a sleepy kind of posh voice. 'Saw your stuff on Insta – looks amazing.' She ushered us inside. In a long kitchen-diner, two teenage boys were huddled over a laptop. 'This is our hub, where we're working on the campaign and following the story,' she said. 'Oh, and I'm Skyla, that's my brother Jamal and his friend Milo.'

'Err hi,' muttered both boys, eyes barely lifting from the screen in front of them. 'We had to like force Dad into the airport taxi, didn't we?' Jamal nodded. 'He never goes anywhere without Tasha. She is like his third child. Only we live with Mum most of the time, so Tasha's like his constant companion. Especially since he and Blue split.' Skyla spoke as if I'd know who Blue was and that she and Medalsum were no longer together. In fact, it seemed, despite her introductions, she expected me to know who she and her brother were. Perhaps if I was their age, I would have been aware of all the familial happenings in their world, but I certainly wasn't. I would need to get up to speed on it all later. I gathered that Medalsum had been left winded, concussed, cut and bruised after being attacked, by two people, one wielding a baseball bat. Having been discharged from A&E, he had gone home to start a hue and cry over the theft of his beloved Tasha. This morning he had been scheduled to fly to Germany to continue his tour promoting his latest album. His kids and manager had persuaded him to still catch his flight, arguing that there wasn't anything he could achieve in person, with regards to finding Tasha, that they couldn't be doing in his absence. He'd be back in a few days, Skyla told me.

Skyla offered me a coffee and brought in a bowl of water for Brownlow, which I thought was very thoughtful. 'Would he like one of Tash's biscuits do you think?'

I didn't see why not and neither did Brownlow. Skyla brought a teddy of Tasha's for Brownlow to sniff and an old t-shirt of her dad's that the dog liked to have in her basket. When I asked if I could have details of the location where the carjacking had taken place, Jamal looked up from his screen long enough to say, 'You got it'. My mobile pinged with a message coming in. There was the exact location as a map reference. I had definitely got it.

Before we went off to let Brownlow have a sniff around at the scene of the crime, I asked Skyla if she and the guys would forward anything that might be a possible lead to me. Jamal said, 'On it.' I had no doubt that he was. At the door Skyla asked, 'They won't kill her will they?' As I looked at her face, the poised young woman was for a moment replaced by the child of around fifteen that she actually was. I reassured her that dognappings didn't usually end like that. The truth was though, I had as yet no real idea what we were dealing with. Again, like with Rouki's Cocker Spaniels, my fundamental question was were the dogs stolen because of what they were, or who owned them? If it was the second option, were they to be ransomed, or was there a so-far undiscovered market for the pets of celebrities? If so, did that mean the dog, or possibly cat, of any high profile person was fair game? It was however, hard to see the kind of person who might have felt some kind of kudos in owning the Staffordshire Bull Terrier of a famous rapper, feeling the same about possessing the Spaniels of a decluttering reality star. A very different fan base, you would've thought.

'Skyla,' I said, turning back on the doorstep, 'your dad doesn't know Rouki Bennett by any chance? Personally I mean.' Skyla shrugged.

'I've never heard him mention her, but Dad does know all kinds of random people I mean he's got a friend at NASA and then there's the Duke of whatever. Dad's a connector you see, with his charity work and everything. I'll ask him and get back.'

We took another bus to the spot in east London where the carjacking happened. It was a busy road junction, and not the best place to pick up any hint of a trail. Skyla had given me permission to rip up the old t-shirt. I weighted down a portion of it on the pavement on one side of the road, with one of my stickers explaining what it was there for. If Tash had somehow in the ensuing chaos given her abductors the slip, she was likely to return to anything that smelt of her human companion. It was a technique that had in the past worked for one particular Yorkie who had disappeared on a woodland walk. Three nights later he was spotted loyally sitting on owner's cashmere cardigan, close to the spot he vanished. My poster on the closest tree had given little Jojo's finder the contact details of her owner. It was a great result and succeeded where two extensive, organised searches had failed.

I'd told Skyla to print up some posters with Tasha on and put them up in this area. Like a lot of younger people, she'd thought only of using the internet, but there are a number of people out there whose first and possibly only point of contact with your lost or stolen pet appeal is through a poster. I called in at several local shops and also spoke to passers-by, while Brownlow worked the pavement and road.

There was one particular spot, beside the kerb outside a shop, that drew a strong reaction from him. It was a barber's and unfortunately not one that opened late. The owner said his CCTV did give a partial street view and the police had not asked to see it. When he'd a gap between clients he'd check the footage. He pinned my business card to his corkboard and said he'd ask all his customers if they'd been in the area the previous night. He had a Rhodesian Ridgeback himself he said, and was willing to do anything to help. I DM'ed Skyla and asked her to drop him in a poster. 'On it,' she replied. It seemed to be the family catch phrase. I liked Skyla. Like me she seemed practical and a doer. You read so much about the kids of celebrities who trade on their parents' name and enjoy the wealth without seemingly any ambitions of their own. She didn't strike me as that kind of person. I could imagine her leading some blue chip company or perhaps a global charity in the future. She just had that way about her.

Once Brownlow's hunt for a scent trail had eliminated every side street and other possible escape route a frightened dog might've taken, I was left with a reasonable certainty that the abduction had succeeded. There was a CCTV camera a little further up the street, but only the police would've gained access to that. Because a high profile individual in the shape of Medalsum had been physically assaulted, the Met would've been bound to examine this footage. I kept checking their socials to see if they'd been generous enough to share it, but so far they hadn't, despite an appeal for witnesses and dash cam footage. The carjacking had been just before one am as

Medalsum, who had been driving himself, had stopped at traffic lights. As the street had no takeaways or nightclubs, there had probably been few people about at the time. Skyla had told me her dad had been on his way back from a studio he has had built. In the day it is usually staffed and used to record other artists. At night, Medalsum uses it to record his own vlogs for his YouTube Channel, and then it his just him and a technician. I'd checked out a few clips on my way up. In the ones I watched, Medalsum sat on a comfy-looking old leather sofa, often with Tasha asleep beside him. He talked about the rap scene, new releases that he rated, gave snippets of news from his own career etc. Sometimes he interviewed a guest, who again was usually someone from the London rap, grime or garage scene, past or present. The posted clips were tagged with a date, but presumably that was when they were posted, rather than made. To my albeit non-expert eye, they looked as though they were skilfully edited together, rather than being a live stream. There was not one for the evening before the dognapping, so presumably that was still being edited prior to release. It meant Medalsum's attackers hadn't been able to watch him live online and know he was there and had the dog with him. If it was a premeditated raid, as it appeared to be, then perhaps they'd had him under surveillance before following his car.

I called Quinn. 'As my weapons expert, perhaps you can answer a quick question?'

'A very quick one, I've a hedgehog weeing on my lap.'

'Rouki's dog walker was hit with shotgun pellets, Medalsum hit with a baseball bat. Why not use the shotgun again to hold him up?'

'Shotgun in the middle of London? Any kind of firearm there and you're going to get an armed response. You're going to be treated as priority. Roadblocks, choppers, and carloads of officers with submachine guns hurtling towards you. Use a baseball bat, and it's just one of a number of assaults across the city on any given night.'

'So you attract less heat you're saying?'

'Giving you a far better chance of pulling it off and getting away. Look I gotta go, the prickly little horror's started doing the other thing.'

'Okay, enough information. Thanks, Quinn.' Next, I rang Skyla for directions to the studio. She said it was called Studio 55 and if I wanted to take a look inside I should call Bimpe, the studio's engineer, who lived nearby. She was the person Medalsum made his vlogs with.

Bimpe answered immediately. Skyla had already alerted her via WhatsApp to expect my call. She suggested we meet at her flat, as the studio was tucked away on an industrial estate in Hackney and not particularly easy to find. Bimpe lived on the tenth floor and thankfully Brownlow is okay with lifts. She had her bleached blonde hair in Bantu knots and wore a t-shirt from a festival in Madrid. The studio was in unit 55, though its name was also a pun on the famous Studio 54 in New York, she told me as we walked there. She'd worked with Medalsum for ten years. They'd met when she was the sound engineer on his second album, bonding over a love of 1970s rocksteady and old Ealing comedies. I wanted to know if the studio's location was common knowledge among Medalsum fans. She said the address wasn't widely available online, but it wasn't like it was top secret either. A few people knew where it was, and sometimes fans dropped by. If you wanted to find it, you could, basically. Medalsum wasn't such a big star or particularly controversial, so he had no reason to keep a low profile. His fans tended to be a pretty laidback bunch and much of the time he wasn't even recognised in the street, particularly if he didn't wear the jacket with the medals.

The medals weren't entirely a gimmick, Bimpe continued. They had been his grandfather's and he wore them to pay tribute to an injured war hero who had been shoddily treated by the UK, despite his bravery.

My next question was whether it was common knowledge that Medalsum had been at the studio the previous night. 'Did he always record his vlog on the same evening of the week?' Bimpe said that he didn't. It had to fit around his many other commitments. Because she lived nearby, he might just call her up on the day itself and see if she could spare a few hours. The filming sessions tended to go on very late, as he was a perfectionist. 'Although it was unscripted, if he fluffed his words he'd want to go again. He liked the whole thing to look smooth and professional, even though there was just the two of us putting it together.' She'd usually edit the clips and post them the following day. 'I have his passwords and can post for him. He leaves me to do that, though he does preview everything first.' I said I'd checked his social media for the previous day and to my knowledge he hadn't posted his whereabouts that evening. Bimpe said she hadn't on hers either, though she wasn't, she said with a smile 'a regular user' where socials were concerned. I gained the impression that although she appeared in the vlogs and was a natural on camera, she was happier behind a sound desk or lens than out in front. They hadn't had a guest in the studio for the recording of their latest piece, it had just been the two of them, and of course Tasha, dozing beside them.

'Can I ask about Medalsum's private life? I mean, there couldn't be any kind of tug-of-love over the dog? I believe there's an ex-girlfriend, someone called Blue something?'

'Blue's in California with a Hollywood actor now. Not into dogs, or never really seemed to be at any rate. Have you met his ex-wife?' I shook my head. 'She loved Tasha and she's almost as cut up about it as he is. She and the kids would look after her when he's on tour.'

I left Brownlow to sniff around the studio building on his own. He quickly found the spot on the sofa where I'd seen Tasha sit in the video. We were in the 'green room' though it was actually painted in shades of blue. This was a place to relax, outside of the actual recording and technical areas. It had music memorabilia on the walls, a jukebox, bar seats and pool table. It looked like a fun place to hang out, despite the fact the industrial estate outside was bland and bleak. Bimpe said she always walked home via the main exit as it was well lit. Several warehouses along was a derelict one that had been squatted at one point and used as a crack den at another. I asked if she'd noticed any cars in the car parking areas and she said that at night, with few people working there, these areas were just a vast expanse of vacant concrete. It wasn't a place you'd leave your car overnight if you wanted it to still be there in the morning. Even in the day there had been catalytic converter thefts. Some of the warehouses had CCTV, some not. The studio did, and Bimpe kindly ran the most recent recording for me. As she'd said, the car park outside had been empty the previous night, apart from one car. That car was Medalsum's. I watched the black and white footage as he arrived and let Tasha out. Off the lead, the dog had headed happily straight towards the studio door, as no doubt she had done many times before. A few minutes after Medalsum's arrival, Bimpe was seen turning up, on foot as she'd said. She was carrying a metal case that she explained had contained a new microphone they were going to try out, and 'a few other technical gizmos'.

We were chatting away, about house rabbits as it happened, as Bimpe has one, with the CCTV recording still playing, when something drew my eye back to the screen. Bimpe replayed those few seconds. A white van slowly passed on the private road through the estate. It appeared to be stopping but infuriatingly, if it did, it did so screened by the neighbouring building.

'Aren't the main gates locked to vehicles at that time of night?'

'They should be. With only key-holders able to gain access. You could always still get in on foot. When they mend the fence, someone always tears it down again. But you couldn't drive in without opening the gates. Not until a couple of months back.'

'Why? What changed?'

'Someone brought in a couple of shipping containers and set up a dark kitchen. It's down the front to the left of the gates. It's you know, where they make the takeaway food for big name restaurants and fast-food chains? They operate until late, so it's all delivery mopeds coming and going. They leave the gate open while they're operational and by the time they shut it's morning anyway.'

'I'd like to see if that van appears on anyone else's CCTV.'

'You think M might've been followed by the carjackers?' I think 'M' was her name for Medalsum.

'Certainly possible.' She produced a list of the other companies operating in surrounding warehouses and a map of the industrial estate. I started to call the firms up and ask about CCTV. Several of them assumed I was the police, and while I didn't tell them I was, I didn't say I wasn't either. A number of the people there knew Medalsum and everyone was willing to help if they could. It was going to be time consuming checking that many cameras. I also had an interesting response from a textile company. The guy was very defensive on the phone and wanted to know exactly who I was and what business I had to be asking him questions. Bimpe said she hadn't ever noticed them operating at that time of night, but they did use a lot of white vans. I decided it was worth paying them a visit.

Bimpe called the firm 'Raggers'. I didn't know the term, but she said her aunt worked in a charity shop, and that's what they called the people who buy the unsold and unsaleable clothing donations by the sack-load. The raggers would arrive in a van every week and take the unsold stuff from the shop. At the textile firm's warehouse, staff would then sort it into stuff that was only fit for recycling or landfill, removing the better items, which would be parcelled up to be shipped abroad.

Entry to the textile sorting warehouse was by a main door, but a sign said 'no unauthorised access', and a man, who by his accent sounded like the one I'd been interrogated by on the phone, immediately appeared. I said I'd like to come in and speak to whoever was in charge about possible suspicious activity outside of Studio 55, the night before.

'You cannot bring a dog in here.'

'Why? I was led to believe you're only sorting second-hand clothes.'

'No dogs. It's a rule.'

'If I take Brownlow back to Studio 55, could I come in and speak to someone in authority?' The man crossed his arms.

'Tie the dog up out there,' he offered at last. Of course, I told him there was no way I'd be leaving Brownlow unattended. I told him about the dognapping and my wanting to check CCTV. He said he would only allow the police to check his CCTV and only then if they supplied a warrant.

'But if you've nothing to hide...'

'Of course we've nothing to hide!' he exploded. 'We have no dogs here. Just clothes. Lots and lots of clothes. And our drivers have their own vans okay? So what they do with them when they're not working, that is their business. It has not nothing to do with me. Or you.' His chest was rising and the finger jabbing had started. I realised there was nothing to be gained by prolonging the conversation. As I'd been speaking to the man, I'd been giving the odd quick glance at Brownlow, as any fond dog owner might do at their four-footed companion. I was however assessing his body language. If Tasha had been in that warehouse, he'd have told me. If any other dog had been present, he would've given an indication. Brownlow however stayed neutral, apart from moving between the rag seller and me, and giving me the odd anxious look when the man started to raise his voice.

We left and instead walked around the textile recycler's car park. There were a number of vans parked up. They differed in make and colour, though white was ones were the most common. They did not carry the company's logo and were in all probability, as I'd just been told, privately owned. There was one point where Brownlow stopped and sat for a moment and then stood up again almost immediately. It was an empty parking space. Brownlow looked at me. I could tell he was unsure. If the van that had abducted Tasha had been parked here prior to the carjacking, then he would not have reacted at all. If it had stopped here afterwards and the dog had been removed at this point, I would've expected Brownlow to give a full indication by remaining seated and looking at me, until asked to move. Possibly the van used in the abduction had returned here fleetingly, but without the dog on board. That was a possible explanation, but as evidence it was anything but conclusive.

It was only late afternoon, but already I was thinking it might be worth spending the night in London to see if anyone came forward with any new information we could use. Bimpe was willing to put us up, as long as Brownlow was okay with the house rabbit, which I assured her he would be. Whether the rabbit would be as mellow about him though remained to be seen. Rabbits can be very feisty and territorial. Never assume those 'beware of the bunny' signs you see on people's doors are a joke, they rarely are. I thought it might be an idea to hire a dog-friendly taxi with Bimpe's guidance to follow Medalsum's exact route home. If, say, he had passed a club (which would've had bouncers stood outside) or a particularly busy stop for the night bus, these might be places to return to, to see if anyone had seen a van following his car. It was a long shot admittedly, but I was still about to call a cab, when Quinn rang.

'Sophie, Rouki Bennett has just received a ransom note.'

'What? How'd you know that?'

'She's tweeted it and it made the local radio news.'

'Seriously?' Quinn tends to have the radio on in the stable block to sooth some of the nervier residents. 'But she's not my client, so what can we –'

'The thing is, Soph, I think I know who might've sent it. Take a look. See what you think. You had a case where someone asked for money before. I mean only 2k, not half a million, but the wording looks the same.' I checked Rouki Bennett's account. She had tweeted a screenshot of the actual ransom note. It was the way it said 'Pay Up Or Your Dog Dies!!' That's how it had been before – the identical phrase with each word capitalised and two exclamation marks. Of course, it wasn't proof, but it was enough to arouse serious suspicions in us both.

The email address was from a firm I'd also encountered previously. They advertise as providing anonymous, untraceable communications and as far as I know they live up to their word. If this note was from the guy we'd had dealings with before though, then despite his efforts, he wasn't untraceable. We knew exactly where he lived as on that occasion Quinn and I had visited his premises. It had not been a particularly pleasant experience.

Quinn said he'd meet Brownlow and me off the train and drive us out to Hector Belt's smallholding. Hector was a loner with a nasty temper. Our earlier encounter with him had involved a small-scale and ill-fated pedigree cat snatching and breeding venture. What Mr Belt had not fully comprehended then is that you can't always tell a neutered from a non-spayed female feline. When his cats failed to produce kittens, Mr Belt had kittens himself, so to speak, firing off angry emails to the owners of the stolen cats to demand money. Housing cats in chicken wire runs was never going to work for long and one resourceful Bengal managed to escape and return to her owner. Brownlow then followed the trail to Hector Belt's small, self-built bungalow, and the police were called. Sadly, he didn't receive a prison sentence, claiming that he had been given the animals by someone who had found them 'abandoned in a barn,' and brought them to him, because he loved animals. If that last part had been true the relieved owners would not have received their pets back severely underweight and suffering from fleas and mange. All this happened nearly three years ago and Mr Belt was around sixty then. I don't believe he had actually been the one stealing the cats for his doomed venture, but the actual animal snatchers had not, as far as I was aware, ever been caught.

I opened Brownlow's Tupperware-style box containing his dinner, and poured water from his bottle into his portable bowl. I nearly always travel with a rucksack containing a meal for Brownlow. If I'm out late on a case I can usually find a takeaway or 24/7 store selling something to feed myself, but it's not so easy with canines. I had picked up a packet of sandwiches for myself at Victoria Station and I tucked in as Brownlow started to eat. A woman sitting opposite tutted loudly.

'What?' I shot a scowl in her direction. 'We've been working all day. Eating on the train is allowed you know.'

'The dog food – it smells.' Course it did. No dog would touch it otherwise. I'm not sure you or I would eat our dinner either if it didn't have at least a reasonably enticing aroma. We'd had to board the Brighton service, intending to change onto a train serving Billingshurst further down the line. That was the nearest station to Mr Belt's, and where Quinn would be waiting for us. The woman who objected to the dog food was probably a vegan, I guessed, it being the Brighton train. Don't get me wrong, I've nothing whatsoever against vegans. I tried to be one for a while, for animal welfare reasons, and even now I don't eat meat or fish, and tend to avoid cow's milk. My eggs come from a friend's pet hens, but where certain cheeses and Greek yoghurt with honey are concerned, I'm afraid I have fallen off the wagon. I know some people successfully feed their dogs a non-meat diet, but I haven't tried it with Brownlow. Mind you, as his first six months of life were spent as a stray pup scrounging for scraps on tips and by the roadside, anything I served him in a dish would be a better option. I only give him his posh personalised dog food because sometimes we have to work very long hours, and I want him to be at peak fitness and stamina for that. The woman opposite had her feet on the train seat. Someone that selfish could never comprehend the hardships my poor boy had endured before being rescued and finding a home with me. I bet she had never felt raw hunger and fear of the ever-present threat of a kick, a punch or worse. Brownlow has, and so in the past, though I try not to dwell on it, have I. 'I save it for my therapist' I tell anyone who recognises the subtle signs I must unconsciously give off. That's the therapist I can one day afford to see of course. For the present, the only one I share my most painful memories with is Brownlow. There's a level of understanding between us that only we can feel. It's powerful, it's beyond words and ultimately it may in truth be the only therapy I need.

Quinn wasn't there at Billingshurst station and there were no other passengers waiting for lifts or staff on duty at that time of night. It's a small, quiet station, it was dark and once the couple of waiting cabs had departed with their fares, the area was deserted. I was glad of Brownlow's company while we waited. Hearing voices approaching, we both turned our heads at once. Two men in hooded tops who'd been walking along the road opposite had stopped and were looking at us. 'That's a nice dog,' one called across to me. I noted at once there was no warmth in his voice. Then both came walking across to us. 'Don't suppose you've the time?' I wasn't wearing my watch nor did I want to take out my phone to check it. Instead, I gave them an approximation. 'Got a light?'

I noticed both men's cigarettes were already alight. I told them I didn't smoke. The older one indicated Brownlow. 'Bit of sheepdog in him, I reckon? Bit of German shepherd?' I said I didn't know. The older one was perhaps forty, the younger in his twenties. I was getting a distinctly bad feeling about this. I gripped Brownlow's lead tightly and wished Quinn would hurry up and get there. He's usually a good timekeeper, but if some emergency had cropped up at the sanctuary, I knew he'd have to stop to deal with it first. 'What's his name?'

'George,' I lied. No point in giving them the name my dog answers to. If Brownlow has a fault, it's being way too trusting. It's not one I share.

'He is yours is he?' I nodded, wondering why the older guy was even asking. Just to keep me talking and to put me off my guard was my best guess. 'He looks really soppy. Is he?' For once I sincerely wished he didn't. Brownlow was grinning at the men and lightly waving his tail. 'Only my sister's looking for a friendly mutt for her kiddies. They'd give it the best home in the world. They'd spoil him rotten. And she's willing to pay a couple of hundred. Even for an adult mongrel, which is a generous price.

'He's not for sale.'

'That's a shame. That's a right shame.' There was a threat in the man's voice now. I heard a van door slam. Quinn strode over.

'Can I help you, gents?' If you didn't know Quinn you could still probably tell he's ex-army and not someone to start a quarrel with. It's a kind of gruff confidence that I'm not sure he's even aware of possessing.

'Nah, nah, just admiring the dog. Really nice dog.' The men moved on without a backward glance.

'Trouble?'

'Can we drive past them so I can get a quick photo with my phone?' The men had turned into the next street, and by the time we were in the van and moving, they'd melted away into the darkness. I explained what had happened. 'Not really what you expect in Billingshurst.'

'Expect it anywhere these days,' Quinn replied grimly. 'You could forward their descriptions to Carmichael,' he added.

'I could. But it's probably more trouble than it's worth. Since they didn't actually threaten me or try to steal Brownlow, she'll tell me there's nothing she can do. Then she'll start asking what I was doing out here.'

'Do you think there's anything to link them to Hector Belt?' That was a possibility that hadn't occurred to me. The last time Hector Belt was involved in dog thefts he hadn't been acting alone. It might just be a coincidence that I'd encountered those two acting suspiciously, not so very far from his abode.

'But you think Hector Belt might be involved in Rouki Bennett's dognapping? I suppose we should've guessed. He's the most prolific pet thief or fence that we know of.'

'Can't really imagine rickety old Belt peppering her dog walker with lead shot though.'

'He did threaten to shoot us last time,' I reminded him.

'We didn't see a gun though did we? They published an interview with the unfortunate dog walker earlier.' I said I'd seen it on my phone on the train back.

'Tall, slim, wearing a balaclava. Those guys that were bothering me were both shortish. Neither of 'em slim. And Belt's very tall granted, but he's got a belly on him.'

'He did have. We've not seen him for three years,' Quinn reminded me.

In fact, we saw Hector Belt a little quicker than intended. As we approached his bungalow, we noticed two police cars were parked up, just a little further along the road. Neither was occupied, but one was a 4x4 I knew very well.

'Carmichael's here. And with back up.'

'Seems we're a little late to the party,' Quinn observed, driving on past.

'What are we going to do now?'

'I'm looking for a place to leave the van, that's a little more discreet than behind or in front of the coppers. My birding binoculars are behind your seat. Then all we need is a vantage point for a spot of snooping.' Quinn is a keen birdwatcher, when he gets the time, which isn't often. It's how he likes to unwind and de-stress. When most of the birds you see in your everyday work come in the door mangled or orphaned, he says seeing them flying free and exhibiting their natural behaviour reminds him how worthwhile it all is. It makes sense of feeding tiny nestlings at ten-minute intervals, and helping a vet pin an impossibly fragile wing or a leg. Quinn's not one of those bird-watchers with a tick list of species he's desperate to see. For him it's things like listening to the Skylarks singing on the Downs, watching the first Wheatears of the year arrive on the rocks of Lancing beach, or the Black Redstarts nesting at Shoreham station, which he finds quietly satisfying.

Whatever the police were doing, they were in Belt's bungalow, and crouched behind a hedgerow on the opposite side of the road, passing the binoculars between us, we shared a view that told us exactly nothing. It didn't help that we only had the light of a single streetlamp to see by, and that birding binoculars don't come equipped with night sights. 'Would it be worth popping back to mine for the drone?' Quinn laughed.

'I think the police officers might have something to say about you hovering a camera outside Mr Belt's windows – not to mention Mr Belt himself.'

'It would only be a fine if I got caught...' I demurred, 'And I'd imagine Medalsum would let me charge that to expenses.'

'Even though we're currently looking for Rouki Bennett's dogs and she hasn't even hired you?'

'Same case. Maybe.'

'Have you a single shred of evidence to back that?'

'I'm only a day into my investigations.'

'Fair point, but –' Suddenly the bungalow was brightly illuminated. It looked as though a motion sensor in the yard behind had been triggered, turning on security lights. I grabbed the binoculars from Quinn's hands, even though it was his turn to use them. I could see the tops of the wire runs where Hector Belt had previously held the missing cats. Then I saw a police cap bobbing along behind the runs, stopping every little while, presumably to peer inside.

'It's quiet.'

'Too quiet,' quipped Quinn, tugging the binoculars from my hand and taking another look for himself.

'I mean if there were dogs in any of those runs, don't you think we would have heard them?'

'Yes, probably. Particularly now one of the cops is out there inspecting the runs.' Apart from the occasional car passing down the road in front of us, and the hoots of a distant Tawny Owl, the night was remarkably still. 'For my money the dogs aren't there,' he added. 'Not that it's gonna be safe for us to snoop around now. Even when the police are gone.' He was right. After a visit from the local constabulary, Belt would know he was under suspicion and be on his guard.

'Hang on, they're coming out.' We wrestled for the binoculars. Quinn was victorious but quickly handed them to me. 'It's our old friend Carmichael.' I grimaced. He meant 'old friend' without any irony, as the rural crime officer was someone he occasionally worked with, on wildlife rescues. In fact, he sometimes seemed on quite good terms with her, which gave me serious doubts about his judge of character. It's not that I was jealous or anything like that, before you jump to that conclusion. PC Carmichael has a wife, who's a nice woman who manages the best farm shop in the area. What she sees in Gemma Carmichael I can't imagine but ask her to recommend a seasonal fruit jam or chutney and her taste is impeccable.

Hector Belt emerged from his bungalow, with two other police officers behind him. They must've, I surmised, been the occupants of the second car. Belt walked towards the police cars with them. He wasn't shouting and gesticulating, nor was he handcuffed. I looked at Quinn. 'They're arresting him? Are they?'

'Looks like it.'

'So where are the dogs?' Behind us Brownlow scratched himself and gave a tiny whine. He probably needed to do his business. It was about the time he usually had his evening walk. We watched as one police officer got in the back of the patrol car with Mr Belt, and the other got in the driver's seat. Carmichael had a brief word with them and then they drove off, with her following on. 'Alright Brownlow, you can stretch your legs now.'

I cleared up after Brownlow, then nipped into the hedgerow to relieve myself. Back at the car, Quinn had a Thermos on the bonnet, had poured two coffees and opened a packet of ginger-nuts. 'Are we going in?' he asked. 'While he's helping them with enquiries, it would be the ideal opportunity.'

'It would...' I agreed, 'but what if there were more cops? They could've left someone there.'

'Thought of that. I'll ring the front door. If someone answers I'll say I'd had a call about a fox with mange or something, and ask if I've got the right place. If they ask who I am and run a check, they'll only find out I'm what I'm claiming to be.'

No one answered the door of the bungalow, so we both headed round the back of the high fenced yard. The gate was firmly bolted on the inside. Quinn suggested lifting me up so I could lean over and see if it was a top bolt. I reluctantly agreed. It was dark but we had a flashlight. I told Quinn off for groaning as he lifted me. 'One in my ongoing series of tips: never make a woman feel like a great big sack of spuds.'

'Can the sack of spuds find the bolt?'

'With a padlock on it.'

'See if there's any give in the wood. It looks quite old and flimsy.' It didn't take much to flex the end of the bolt out of its metal keeper.

'I don't feel quite right about this. I mean it's almost breaking and entering.' I meant 'almost' because we hadn't broken the lock, just wiggled the fence and the bolt was loose. 'It is trespass though isn't it?'

'Yeah, we're trespassing in someone's backyard. But if you can't stand the heat…'

'No, the guy's a pet thief. We gotta do what we gotta do.'

Off the lead, Brownlow entered the yard ahead of us. Unlike me he wasn't bothered by the legalities of the situation. He stood and looked back at as both, wagging his tail encouragingly. I realised he was showing little eagerness to approach the makeshift kennels and runs. I encouraged him to follow us over to them, which he did, but with an air of indifference. He wasn't excited about making a find, and so I knew even before I reached the kennels that I wouldn't discover any of the missing dogs there. That's the thing with Brownlow, so often he's ahead of the game.

The runs and kennels were even more ramshackle than they'd been on our visit three years previously. Rusting chicken wire was hanging off two of them, and the other three, although appearing still intact enough to be useable, were also empty. I opened the doors to each in turn and sent in Brownlow. Each time he sniffed around and came out again without giving one of his scenting indicators. When he had finished, I entered one of the runs myself. The water dish was bone dry, and there was no food or bedding. I crawled into the narrow kennel at its back and had a sniff myself. I knew full well if my dog hadn't smelt anything very interesting, I wouldn't either. It might though, give me an idea of when these outbuildings had last been occupied. I couldn't smell dog or any other animal. There hadn't been any animals housed here in a long while.

Quinn was examining a set of large rabbit hutches on the other side of the yard. 'Bunnies?'

'Nah. Empty boxes.' He took out a brown cardboard box and examined it, then sniffed it. For once we were both using our noses as much as Brownlow. 'Ah.' He brought it over for me to smell. 'Cannabis.'

'Just one of these boxes would hold more than someone could smoke in a year.'

'Perhaps he's changed his line of business. Perhaps that's why he's got nicked.' There was a cat door in the back door of Belt's bungalow. I held it open while Brownlow sniffed inside, but he wasn't a drugs sniffer dog and he gave no indication that there were any animals in the house.

Quinn stood beside Belt's bins. 'Which one do you want to do? Rubbish or recycling?' Of course, I chose recycling, but as it turned out, both bins were equally stinking and disgusting. It seemed Belt hadn't entirely grasped that the receptacles were for different types of waste, never mind that the materials to be sent for recycling should be presented in a clean state. I hadn't brought gloves but used a couple of unused dog-poo bags to protect my hands, after I'd tipped the refuse out on the ground. I wish I'd had a scarf to protect my nose. As I coughed and spluttered, Quinn got on with his half of the job in a brisk, professional manner, and Brownlow lay at a safe distance from the pong, grinning at us. At home he had been known to upend the kitchen bin on occasion and root around in its contents. For this he tended to be told off, so perhaps he was surprised or even indignant to find his human colleagues now doing the very thing he always received a scolding for. There were no empty dog food packets or cans in Belt's bins. When we'd finished our root around, we returned the rubbish to the bins. All it had proved, apart from the fact that Quinn has a strong stomach and I don't, is that Belt had definitely not been keeping animals on his property recently. If he'd been involved in the dog theft, the animals had not been brought here, even for a short while.

Back at the car, I checked Rouki Bennett's Twitter account. Her latest tweet said that the police were conducting enquiries into the ransom note and she would be keeping her fans updated. 'There is nowhere u can hide' she had added, a trifle optimistically, I thought. As far as we were concerned, her dogs, wherever they were, remained pretty well hidden. Quinn was also checking his own messages. The sanctuary had just taken in a concussed Muntjac deer that had been hit by a car. At night most of the cases tend to be road casualties. The deer would be kept in for observation. When Quinn got back, he'd relieve whichever of his volunteers was working the late shift. As they headed home, he'd do the final checks, making a round of the place to ensure all his charges were comfortable for the night. While the birds, apart from the owls, would be asleep, many of the fitter wild mammals in the outside runs would be becoming more active, and he'd observe them and make any notes about how they were progressing. Dogs, cats and other pets and farm animals needed a food and water check, whereas the creatures of all kinds in the hospital area had more complex needs. When he finally got to bed, it would probably be with an orphan or two in pet carriers beside him, and an alarm set to their next feeding time.

Unlike Quinn, I could at least get a night's sleep, satisfied I'd done as much as I could for one day. Brownlow decided, as he often does, that he was going to sleep on my bed rather than his own. For that I couldn't blame him. While his does have a generous layer of memory foam, it still can't beat a sprung mattress. I'm trying to get out of the habit of checking my phone before I go to sleep, but lying in bed next to the snoring canine, I couldn't resist lifting it from the bedside table for one quick glance. Skyla had tagged me into a message announcing that her father had hired 'renowned Pet Detectives Brownlow And Gorrage'. There were lots of 'well done Soph' type messages from friends and former clients, and people suggesting Medalsum had been wise in his course of action. As I scrolled down, I then came to this, 'Brownlow is useless. Sophie Gorrage a fraud. Asked for two thousand pounds to find my cat, returned it dead and still demanded the money!' I stared. I'd been trolled before, but it had just been insults and threats, mainly from thwarted criminals or people I've had to report for animal cruelty. Now I have never charged anyone anywhere near two thousand pounds to find a cat. I've never returned a cat dead either. There've been a couple of sad cases where I've discovered the lost animal is deceased, and I've dealt with it with all sensitivity. I've made sure a body was returned to the grieving owner for burial, but I certainly didn't turn up at the door with it. In the cases involving pet fatalities I hadn't charged the owners a penny. I looked at the account of the person who had tweeted that pack of lies. It seemed like she'd only joined twitter that week and this was her first tweet. The profile photo showed a smiling young woman snuggling up to her cat. I didn't recognise either of them. She had certainly not been a client of mine. A few moments later, three new messages appeared from other people claiming to have had negative experiences after hiring us. All the accounts had only been active for a few days. All too had plausibly normal profile photos and names. For the sake of restoring our reputation, I quickly tweeted a rebuttal, saying none of these people had been clients. For good measure I added a threat of legal action, adding that if these people wanted to continue to troll me, they should know their lies would be exposed.

I had clearly annoyed someone or possibly several people. No one knew I was unofficially looking into the Rouki Bennett case, so it must be due to Medalsum's daughter going public that we were working for him. I turned my phone off, but still couldn't sleep, which was no doubt what the trolls intended. By the next morning, messages of support from former clients, along with glowing testimonials had flooded in from our followers and beyond. There was also a request to go on Woman's Hour to talk about pet theft. Any other time I would've done it, but the theft of Medalsum's dog was already all over the news. Extra publicity was always useful, but not as useful as actually working the case. I'd also had an email to my website that needed following up, from a boat owner at Newhaven.

Chapter Four

David Kebbles described himself as a leisure boat owner. He had bought a large, half-cabin boat and trailer with a redundancy payout, intending to use it on summer weekends to, in his words, 'pootle around the coast'. Finding a new job sooner than he'd envisaged, and one that involved a lot of weekend work, meant that David's nautical excursions had up to now been few and far between. The boat itself was not currently even afloat. Instead, it was proudly perched on its trailer, taking up the majority of its owner's garden and almost completely blocking the view from his downstairs windows. When I'd received David Kebbles's email I'd been a little apprehensive, knowing my sea legs aren't the best. I'd immediately consulted the shipping forecast and found the sea that morning was 'moderate becoming rough later'. It had quite put me off my cornflakes and cuppa. Here I was though, sitting in an agreeable kitchen-diner, with a mug of hot tea, and despite the jaunty sea-going theme of the décor, my feet firmly on dry land. 'I'd thought the dinghy had been stolen from the boat's half cabin where I'd stored it,' he was saying 'and as I hadn't lifted the tarpaulin to examine 'Daisy Mae' in detail for some time, I thought it could've even happened some time back. But then I discovered it, roughly folded up and shoved behind the garage. For a moment I wondered if I'd even been mistaken and that I might've moved it there myself. But then I noticed a bit of green seaweed stuck to it, and I thought that can't be right.'

The dinghy was a bright red inflatable one. David had bought it new and hadn't yet used it, so it's opportunity to come into contact with seaweed should've been zero. He kept the outboard motor locked in the garage, as he knew these were often stolen, but he hadn't expected someone to take his dingy, inflate it, presumably add their own motor and then take it to sea. 'I was going to call the police, but it seems so silly doesn't it? When I'd just found it. It's not stolen and it's not damaged.' What it did contain, according to David, was 'animal hair of some kind'.

David had got in touch with me after mentioning the strange hair in the mysteriously borrowed dinghy to his son during a phone call. The son had been watching TV when they did one of those quick entertainment industry catch-ups and had mentioned Medalsum hiring a top pet detective. Looking me up, out of idle curiosity more than anything, he had read my post about checking ports and airports, moments before hearing from his dad about the dingy. The roundabout nature of this possible lead coming my way didn't entirely surprise me. In our line of work a lot of our information and tip offs come via one person mentioning something to another and so forth. 'Well my son said his teacher had lost a ginger cat and then Hannah who I see at yoga says there's one that's started visiting her garden recently. She's noticed its eating the food she puts out for her hedgehogs.' The digital interconnectedness of our world, plus the fact the British like to chat about animals almost as much as the weather, are the pet detective's greatest allies.

I left David waiting in the house, as Brownlow would need to concentrate. He would need to first smell the scent of Rouki's dogs from the dog biscuit I'd taken from her house, and then the interior of the dingy. I'd then try the same thing with the items that belonged to Medalsum's Tasha. The dog biscuit might have belonged to one of Rouki's remaining two dogs, but it had definitely been chewed, and any dog that had lived in Rouki's house would share some aromas, in particular I was thinking of those reeking scented candles. It would hopefully be enough to get a response if one of the Cocker Spaniels had been at sea in that boat. Brownlow was alert and attentive as I unzipped the seal on the polythene bag containing the biscuit. 'Scent, Brownlow!' I said. He knew from the soft rustle of the opening bag what to expect, but I wouldn't usually rely on a biscuit as my scent item. It wasn't ideal. If Brownlow was hungry there was a chance his admiration of the aroma of this no doubt expensive canine treat might make him wolf it down. 'Scent, scent.' I repeated, trying to keep a firm grip on the biscuit. He sniffed at it intensely, then made to take it in his teeth. I whisked it away, and dropped it quickly back into its bag, before pointing at the dingy. 'Sniff! Sniff it out.' Brownlow sniffed. He looked back at me. Nothing. He sniffed again and for longer. His tail started to wave. He sat down.

'Good dog, Brownlow!' That was a strong enough positive indication for me. Normally he'd get a treat for that but on this occasion his work wasn't done. I repeated the activity with the scent sample from Medalsum's house. This time despite Brownlow going back and forth enthusiastically, and giving the dinghy a thorough going over several times, he didn't offer his 'matching odour' indication. Not many detective dogs could do this exercise twice over on the same occasion in the same location looking for different scents. Brownlow however could, or at least I believed he could. The fact he had clearly indicated for the presence of Rouki Bennett's dogs and then given a 'no scent' reaction after smelling another object, made it seem likely if not a provable fact. Rouki's dogs had been in this dingy, of that I now had no doubts. It seemed likely Medalsum's Tasha had not been present. Maybe the dogs from the first theft had already been shipped abroad whereas the Staffie was still in this country waiting for her turn.

Before leaving David's, I carefully I collected samples of the dog hair from the dinghy's sides. Unfortunately, I'd need Rouki's permission to get a test done on it however, as I'd need an uncontaminated sample of both Cockers' DNA. If there had been saliva from the missing dogs on the biscuit, Brownlow had unfortunately and inadvertently contaminated the sample with his own slobber. I wondered if Rouki's dog walker might speak to me. It was worth a try. Meanwhile I got in touch with the Newhaven Port authorities. They could they said check their CCTV for a red dinghy leaving the harbour, but unfortunately they would only disclose this information to the police, coastguard or border force. I was still grumbling about this when I phoned Quinn to update him. 'The beauty of a dinghy is you don't need a harbour to launch it from. They will have used a beach. No cameras.' He seemed pretty sure of this assessment. I don't know if Quinn had experience in launching or travelling in small boats during his military service. He never talks about this part of his life with me.

'Isn't it really risky, crossing the channel in a boat that size?'

'That wouldn't have been the plan. A larger boat would've been waiting just offshore. And you said you thought they must've stolen an outboard motor from somewhere else? If they had a bigger boat waiting, they could've used oars to row the short distance out to it. Oars are practically silent. Much less likely to attract attention at night.' I had to admit these were good points.

'So are you off to France then?' I told Quinn I might well be at some point, but first I needed to get in touch with my cross-channel counterparts. 'Le Chien Perdu' might sound like a restaurant, but they're a group of enthusiastic amateur French dog-finders, who I'm in touch with via my socials. They're mainly Paris-based but have members in various places across France. I DM'ed Sandrine, a Normandy-based owner of three Borzois. She's a music teacher who lives in

Ancourt, which isn't too far from Dieppe, so I thought I'd see if she was able to ask around at the port for me.

A quick check of social media showed Rouki retweeting a message from her dog walker Carl de Souza thanking her for the hamper she'd sent round to him. There was even a photo of him gratefully receiving it. I only retweet thanks if a grateful pet owner gives permission, and it's to serve as a recommendation of our services. Tweeting to show your employee receiving your generous gift seemed however a little self-serving. Brownlow and I have received gifts when we have successfully concluded a case – chocolates and bottles of wine for me, various doggy gifts for him. I always thank the giver personally, not publicly. Perhaps though I'm just old fashioned and the nature of the thank you or get well soon note has changed, to be as much about the giver than the recipient. What Rouki's very public hamper gifting had given me however, was the information her dog walker was out of hospital. He was someone I needed to talk to. The problem was, Rouki hadn't hired me. Medalsum had, but I was drawing a blank with regards to finding his dog.

'What would you do?' I asked Brownlow. He lifted a paw and put it on my hand. I was still grasping my phone. Now I know Brownlow wasn't telling me to make a call, I'm not some wacky pet owner who thinks she has a psychic bond with her dog. Well, actually I do think we have that bond, but it doesn't work quite like that. I can feel Brownlow's moods and emotions. I think he can feel mine. That's a different thing entirely. It's not 'Lassie' or 'Skippy'.

I had already found the company that Rouki's dog walker worked for. They were the pricey end of the market, with perks like a private doggy spa and gymnasium your pet could visit. They would only walk your dog or dogs at any one time, unlike some of the people I've seen trying to exercise a whole group, large and small, with leads clipped to a belt, and the tiny ones struggling to make the pace. This in contrast looked like the kind of reputable company I'd go to if I needed it and could afford it. They certainly were pricey. I had thought of approaching with some kind of subterfuge, such as pretending to be considering their services, but the woman who answered the phone sounded very genuine and friendly, and so I told her the truth. I explained who I was, told her I had been very concerned to hear what had happened to Carl de Souza, Rouki Bennett's dog walker. I let her know I was now working for Medalsum, and that I'd like to talk to Carl to see if he could tell me anything that might suggest there were potential links between the cases. The woman said she'd immediately pass my message on to Carl, and it would be up to him as to whether he got back to me. She didn't know as yet when he was coming back to work, but he was keen to resume dog walking as soon as he was fit and able.

I felt a bit guilty over Medalsum and Tasha. I had near proof that Rouki's dogs had been taken out of the country, but had so far drawn a blank on his case. Since I had watched a couple of videos to get myself up to speed on his music, YouTube had kept offering me other tracks by him as well as other artistes in the same field. The opening frame for one Medalsum track caught my eye. Called 'Streets Alone', the video involved a homeless man walking through the West End in the rain and sitting begging outside a shop with his dog beside. The dog, a blue-grey Staffie, was I was pretty sure, Tasha. She seemed quite an actor, looking mournful and shivering, though who wouldn't, out in the rain, whether real or created by a film crew? I decided to check with Skyla that it was Tasha. If it was, it gave me something more than a photo to share with my eyes and ears on the ground, on both sides of the channel.

Quinn rang. 'I've just had a very angry guy on the phone threatening me,' he said with characteristic calmness. 'Said someone from the sanctuary turned up at his house and told his wife they'd been reported to us for mistreating one of their dogs, and had to hand it over, or the police would be called. When he joined her on the doorstep the couple backed down and left. I told him it wasn't us, it's not what we do.' The RSPCA have the legal right to investigate suspected cases of animal cruelty, but Quinn, as he tried to explain, doesn't. 'The guy didn't seem to understand the difference: that we're just an animal sanctuary, and if any cases of cruelty or neglect are reported to us, we refer them to the RSPCA.'

'But it sounds if someone is impersonating your organisation to try to take animals.'

'The woman said the couple were driving one of our vans. But I only have one van, and I was the only one driving it last night.'

'There's no chance any of the volunteers borrowed it?'

'None at all. They'd all gone home by then.' Quinn gave me the contact details for the people who had been visited by bogus sanctuary staff, but before I could call them, I received a message from Carl, Rouki Bennett's dog walker. He was willing to meet me.

Carl de Souza and his husband Jack lived in a garden flat up a quiet lane in Steyning, with their own dog, June, a retired Greyhound. She and Brownlow took an immediate liking to each other, and trotted out through the French doors into the garden to play chase, while I talked to Carl. Jack brought us coffee and asked if we'd mind him staying for our chat, as he was interested to meet a pet detective. A gin distiller by trade, he was also a writer in his spare time and thought he might gain some ideas. I told him I'd like to turn my pet detecting adventures with Brownlow into some kind of book one day. With a twinkle in his eye, Jack promised not to steal any of my ideas. He was also keen that Carl should receive some kind of justice for what had happened to him. I think he was afraid I wouldn't learn the whole story from Carl, who was perhaps a little too discreet and loyal to Rouki Bennett for his own good. At least that was the impression I gained from Jack.

A pad of gauze taped to Carl's forehead showed where one of the pellets had come close to his eye. The others had hit his neck, shoulders and chest. The neck one had been a little too near to the artery for comfort.

'This could easily have been murder,' said Jack. 'And Carl would've done anything for those dogs. Well he would for any that he looks after.' Carl nodded. It was clear his husband, while a tad over-protective, wasn't putting any words in his mouth that he fundamentally disagreed with. Carl's boss at the dog-walking agency had stressed that he was keen to get back to work. 'Just not for the Bennett woman,' Jack slipped in when I mentioned this fact.

'I don't know...' Carl was clearly less sure.

'Come on, she's treated you like crap,' Jack insisted.

'So Rouki Bennett isn't the ideal employer?' Carl looked at Jack, who shrugged at him.

'Well? Tell her.'

'She's... demanding.' Jack sighed in exasperation.

'Understatement,' he said. 'She's not a journalist, Carl. It's not gonna get back to her Royal Highness. It won't affect that thing... that non-disclosure agreement she made you sign. Totally over the top in my opinion. What was a dog walker going to disclose? It's not as if her Cavapoos were gonna start spilling her secrets.' Carl gave Jack a little smile.

'It's just... well Rouki Bennett doesn't let her dogs... well just be dogs. It's all unnecessary fuss. Dog safety seats, dog mosquito nets, only classical music to be played to them. And you can't say anything about it. She's always so afraid they'll catch a cold on their walks or have a nasty accident. Every tiny speck of mud is a flea or –'

'A sheep tick!' interrupted Jack. 'A tick, a tick! Look what you've let happen! Call Sebastian! Call him now! Instantly!' I hadn't heard Rouki sound this agitated, but he'd got her voice down to a 't'.

'Sebastian is her vet,' Carl explained. 'And it wasn't even a sheep tick.'

'A bit of chewing gum caught in Morris B's fur,' grinned Jack.

'And is that how it is? Over-protective panic?' Carl nodded.

'Munchausen by Proxy I'd say,' said Jack. 'I swear that vet is on call 24/7. And it's not really about the dogs. It's all about her. Everything's about her.'

'So do you think she's less concerned about their well-being than how it looks that they've gone missing?'

'No… I think she does love the dogs. Just not in a very practical way,' Carl said thoughtfully. Jack snorted.

'Never mind that – the publicity must be making her serious money!' Jack challenged. 'I mean a juicy news story means more and better-quality reality show invites.'

'I'm not sure that's quite how she thinks,' his husband contradicted him with a frown, 'I think she's become used to seeing her own life as a soap opera. Everything is always at this Oh My God! It's happening to ME! level.'

'She seemed quite calm when I saw her,' I said. They exchanged glances. Jack seemed about to say something but stopped. 'What? When she told me she wasn't hiring me, but putting out a massive reward instead, she seemed quite calm to me.'

'You're not actually working for her then?' Jack queried, raising a quizzical brow. I realised I'd blurted out something I'd meant to keep to myself.

'Yeas, well I'm actually working on the Medalsum dognapping. He's hired me.'

'To find Tasha,' Jack said, instantly. To my relief both he and Carl looked reasonably impressed, rather than annoyed that I'd given the impression I was officially employed to find Lady Champignon and Mr Merrytrees.

'You know about her – Tasha?' I asked.

'It's pretty common knowledge. The guy's besotted with the dog. He mentions her in all his interviews. She's in the videos, even been up on stage… where was it?'

'Reading Festival? I think,' Carl said. 'It'll be online anyway. Has her on his lap singing to her for two songs. Trying to get her to bark along. But she just looks embarrassed.'

'It's quite sweet or a tad nauseating, depending on your view.' I was gaining the impression Jack was a cynic, rather like me.

'She's his baby. I think it's cute,' Carl said,

'But Rouki, you were saying about her being… well a little hysterical, whereas I thought she was very calm.'

'It does come on prescription you know.' Carl shot his indiscreet spouse a look, but it was to no avail. 'Rouki has a doctor on speed dial, or so you told me. For all the guff she gives about how she only uses alternative this and that, she's a total chill pill junkie.'

I thought it prudent to move the conversation on. I was still a little aggrieved at Rouki for not hiring Brownlow and me, but I couldn't really see how delving into her legal pharmaceutical intake or unreasonableness as an employer was going to help with my investigation.

'So what can you tell me about the dognappers?'

'There were two of them. Dressed in black, wearing balaclavas. One came at me first off. Must've been hiding behind a clump of gorse on the common. It was early and drizzling. There weren't many other dog walkers about.' Now it came to facts about the incident, Carl was quite happy to talk, while Jack sipped his coffee pensively and didn't interrupt. 'The guy – I presume it was a guy, simply because he was taller than me, and I'm 6 foot 3 – grabbed the leads and tried to tug them from my hands. But I held on tight, shouted, lashed out with my foot, and other hand. The other person came out from behind the bushes. Shouted something. Maybe 'hey!' – I'm not sure, I just heard the sound. Not sure if it was a man or a woman. You'd think I could tell from the voice but it was just the single syllable so I'm not sure.' He stopped and took a ragged breath. 'I see the gun, rifle-sized, pointed at me – and then he or she fires. Doesn't give a warning. No 'give us the dogs or I'll shoot'. Just does it. I've blood running in my eyes, down my neck, I think I'm dying. First guy tears the leads from my hand. He's got the dogs and they're gone.'

'Did you happen to see or hear a car or van?'

'No. We were quite some distance from the car park. And they could've been parked on the road or elsewhere. I didn't see what direction they went in. I was on my knees by then.' Jack reached over and gave Carl's hand a supportive squeeze.

'I hear the police have made an arrest,' I said, more to give Carl some reassurance than anything.

'Just some greedy old chancer,' Jack said dismissively.

'Sorry?'

'Rouki texted Carl to say the guy who'd contacted her about paying a ransom was actually nothing to do with the thefts.' Carl nodded.

'Just some nasty creep hoping she'd panic and pay out. Apparently he'd done it before. Claimed to have information on lost or stolen animals for a reward and it had led nowhere. The police searched his place thoroughly but the dogs weren't there.'

I didn't admit that Quinn and I had done the same thing. In fact my first thought was a tiny gloat at Carmichael coming up almost empty handed. Hector Belt though had been involved with fencing stolen animals in the past. He hadn't always simply been a lying opportunist. Pulling him in had been a smart call but it seemed not the right call.

I asked Carl if he would be willing to come to the common with me, to help Brownlow find the trail. He looked at Jack.

'It's left him a bit shook up. Is it okay if we both come?' I said that was fine. I could see Carl needed the support. It must've been a scary thing – to believe you were staring death in the face. It's a situation I've been in only twice myself, but both times are etched on my memory. You never lose those images. The guys said they didn't want to bring June along. They felt she was safer locked up indoors for the time being. Jack said that since the incident he'd only been exercising her with a daytime walk in the High Street. Luckily she was elderly and didn't need a huge amount of exercise, but he'd friends with energetic dogs who were currently despairing with regard to finding a safe place to walk them. 'If they put all dogs on a DNA database, this would all go away, wouldn't it?' I agreed it would certainly help, and it was more reliable than a removable chip. You still have to find a dog to check its identity, and unlike microchips, it's not instantaneous. You have to take the sample and send it for analysis. I knew I ought to let Rouki know about the dog hairs from the Newhaven dinghy, so she could send them to be tested against samples from the dogs if she wished. I made a mental note to contact 'her people' again later.

On the common, Carl, Jack and I walked the route Carl had taken while walking all four of Rouki's dogs. All had been on leads. In the car park, I let Brownlow sniff the purloined dog biscuit from Rouki's house again.

'Let's see if he can find where you parked. Where the trail begins.'

'But by now loads of other dogs will have come this way.'

'He doesn't need many molecules of an odour. He has the best nose I know of.' On his extended lead, Brownlow zigzagged back and forth across the car park. Doubling back for the third time, his tail started to wag to a faster beat. Then he sat down and looked round at me.

'That is where we parked. That would be where the backdoor of the dog walking van was. Where I got them out.' Brownlow whined. He was eager to follow the scent.

'Go on, boy. Sniff them out, Brownlow.' He was off, with a mighty bound, nearly pulling me over. 'Yeah,' Carl confirmed. 'This is the route we took onto the common.'

Walking Rouki's four dogs, Carl had kept to the open areas between the gorse and fir trees, including a sandy patch where Lady Champignon likes to roll and Mr Merrytrees would dig. The Cavapoos had tended to watch on rather than get involved in shifting sand around. There they'd encountered an elderly woman with a Bichon Frise who Carl often chatted to. She tended to walk her dog at this spot at the same hour and her Bichon and Rouki's four all liked each other. The woman and her dog had gone on their way first, with Carl joking to her that he had to stay on the common for another ten minutes, as if he brought Rouki's dogs back even a couple of minutes early, she'd moan about 'my darlings getting short changed on their walk, just so you can squeeze in some other client'. This wasn't ever the case, Carl was keen to stress. Once the dogs had tired themselves out, he didn't see the need to keep them hanging about for an allotted amount of time, particularly on cold or damp days. 'It's not as if dogs wear watches, though with Rouki's dogs, I wouldn't have been surprised to see them kitted out with canine Fitbits.'

As Brownlow and I walked with Carl and Jack towards an area with more gorse bushes and tall bracken, Carl started to slow his pace and looked increasingly tense. Brownlow was happily tail-flagging, nose to the ground on the scent. Without warning Carl stopped dead.

'It was here. They came from over there.' He pointed to a narrow path through the gorse and bracken.

'This is exactly where the dogs were grabbed?'

'Yeah. Fennel got loose and ran amok, yapping. I managed to grab Morris and hold on to him, even after I'd collapsed. The other two were carried off. In that direction.'

I let Brownlow's extendable leash out and let him circle. Even though humans carried the dogs away rather than leaving a trail at ground level, I hoped he might still get some vague scent residue indications, to give us a general direction. He was trained to follow animal odours, and not as a human tracker, though if I'd had a sample object containing the abductor's smell, I'm sure he would have been able to follow them to wherever they had parked. As it was, he lost the trail soon after the dogs had been taken. With Jack and Carl, we continued in the direction of the nearest road. As we did so

Carl suddenly cried out and stooped down to the ground. When he arose, he opened his hand to reveal a small sparkling diamante stud. 'From Lady's collar.'

'You're sure?' He took out his phone and strolled to show a photo of her. Her collar was covered in similar faux jewels. 'Okay, let's get a GPS, and mark this spot. It's near the road, so we could get an appeal out for vehicles parked up in the nearest lay-by or even up on the verge here. We have an exact time for the theft, so people travelling this way could check their dash cam footage.'

'The ideal person to put out the appeal would be Rouki,' Carl said.

'Even though you don't want to work for that witch again?' Jack asked.

'It's the dogs that matter. If Rouki tweeting it gets a result –'

'You're right,' Jack agreed. 'Do it for the dogs.'

'I'll phone her if you like?' I offered. 'Though I've only got the PA's number or the Kazowie people.

'I can give you Rouki's personal number. And yes, it's better if the call comes from you.'

Rouki Bennett answered immediately. When I said who it was, she started to try to fob me off. 'I'm on the common, I've an important clue and you need to put out an appeal for dash cam footage.' She listened then. 'One of Lady Champignon's sparkles. My poor baby!' She then said she'd get right on it and put out an appeal. I told her not to mention the information came from me, thinking I should be careful after Carmichael had warned me off. I also told her about the hair sample for the dinghy and said if she wished I could give her instructions of how to send it and a sample from the dogs to a lab, and which would be the best to use.

'Look…' said Rouki, 'I don't know if you're terribly busy at the moment?'

'Well as it happens, I'm working for Medalsum.'

'Oh my God, I read about that. So awful! I tweeted him immediately. Haven't heard back.'

'He's on tour. But we're in touch.' I couldn't resist adding that. I was still smarting from her not hiring us, more affronted on Brownlow's behalf than my own. I still wonder if I hadn't made a strong enough pitch of his attributes to her.

'I suppose I've left it too late to hire you and your dog myself, now you're working another major case?' I was grinning inside at that; I couldn't help myself.

'We do take on more than one client at a time, Rouki,' I said, trying to keep my tone cool and professional, 'and I do have other resources and people in the field I can call upon to help if required.' There was Quinn and there was Le Chien Perdu across the channel, plus one or two other old friends I could probably persuade to put in a few hours for me if I needed to.

Reader, she hired me. I sent Rouki Bennett through the paperwork via my phone and it came back signed within minutes. She requested that I get the dog hairs DNA tested for her. She didn't mind what it cost. Carl and Jack had been eavesdropping on my call. Carl said he was glad his former client had seen sense and hired us, for the sake of the missing dogs. 'Time for a quick glass of something, Sophie? There's a nice country pub – all inglenook snugs and leather-bound books, just down the road.' That sounded like a great idea, though going for a drink was certainly not going onto anyone's expenses but my own. It's important to have high standards. If the only way to elicit information is taking someone for a drink or a meal, then I would charge the client, but for now at least I'd finished interviewing Carl de Souza. I was having a drink with him and his husband because I wasn't sure what my next move should be, and it was near enough lunchtime for both Brownlow and me.

We each had a small glass of wine. The landlord was relaxed about dogs, which was no surprise, considering the regular clientele appeared to be mostly tweedy types with elderly Labradors. Brownlow snoozed under our table, while Jack showed me how to use the filters on my phone to get a photo of the diamante dog-collar stud that made it really sparkle in the light. The dark wood of the table created a background that showed it off to good advantage. Rouki had DM'ed me almost before we'd sat down – requesting a 'pic' of the stud she could share with her followers as she built 'the story'.

'My Nan knew Barbara Woodhouse,' Carl smiled, relaxing a little now we were away from the scene of the crime. 'Si-it! Probably before your time, Sophie?'

'I've seen her on YouTube. Some of her choke chain action was a little alarming.'

'I read she had quite a following among admirers of S&M,' Carl laughed, 'though I don't think my Nan knew anything about that,' The conversation drifted to 'One Man and His Dog' and the fact the title was never altered to 'One Person and His Or Her Dog' even when women took part.

'What was that they used to say to make them go left or right?' asked Jack.

"Way to me' and 'come by',' I told him.

'You don't use commands like that with Brownlow?' I explained I had words I used to tell him to do certain things, but going left or right didn't matter, as I needed him to concentrate and follow a scent. I didn't tell them all the actual commands I use, simply because I try not to use them when

Brownlow is present but not in action. It keeps those words 'pure' in the sense that he focuses and reacts every time he hears me use them.

'So what do you think of GPS tracker collars?' Carl asked. 'I had an email from my agency this morning saying they will be recommending all our owners invest in them.'

'Brownlow has one. He wears it if we have to do off-lead work somewhere like a forest, or at night. But it's quite chunky so it's obvious what it is and it's easily removed. I might see if I can upgrade to a security lockable one, or with an alarm if tampered with. Ultimately though, thieves will always be able to remove a collar. You just have to hope its visible presence is a deterrent or that it buys you enough time to find out where they're taking your dog.' We were on our second glass, a soft one for me as I was driving, when my phone alerted me to a message. 'Police are here. Trouble!' It was from Quinn.

At the sanctuary's gates, Quinn buzzed me in. In his office, PC Gemma Carmichael was sitting with two officers. Quinn had made them mugs of tea. When I discovered what was going on, I thought it was rather too generous of him.

'Ah Ms Gorrage,' sneered my nemesis, 'I believe you're working for DJ Medalsum now?'

'It's just Medalsum. He's a rapper, not a DJ and client confidentiality prevents me from discussing who we may or may not be acting for.'

'His daughter is tweeting about it,' Carmichael returned, 'to all her 25,000 followers, so I wouldn't say it's a big secret.' The other two officers, a younger guy with sandy hair and an older woman with a severely bleached ponytail enjoyed that riposte a little too much. I sensed Carmichael and I were embarking on one of our little verbal sparring sessions, chiefly on her part, to showboat to them. Maybe they outranked her, which after all was relatively easy as she was a lowly PC, or maybe it was because they were proper coppers from the area car or even detectives, where she was lumbered with rural crime. I felt it might be wise to keep to myself for now the fact that Rouki Bennett had hired me. No doubt when Carmichael next checked Rouki's socials, Rouki would've mentioned the fact, but hopefully Gem and I wouldn't be still sitting in the same room by then.

'Medalsum's dog was stolen in London, and I've had no complaints from the Met about him hiring me. So...' I continued, 'what brings you to Weatherhall?'

'As I've already explained to Mr James, a white van bearing a similar logo to the one he drives was seen in the vicinity of the East Sussex home of two animal trainers, shortly after an attempt was made last night to steal two of their dogs.'

'Similar logo?'

'It was described as having a paw print shape, with the faces of various animals around it.'

'Did they see the name on the van?'

'They only got a partial view.'

'No number plate?'

'No, the van was moving.'

'The thing is,' said Quinn, 'there are probably plenty of other small animal charities with similar logos. 'And the name of ours is fairly prominent.'

'And you do only have the one van?'

'We do, and I wasn't in East Sussex last night. I went out on two calls; to Findon to pick up an injured fox, and then again to collect a stray dog from Littlehampton Beach. And I collected Sophie and Brownlow from Billingshurst station as they'd been to London by train.'

'For work on the Medalsum case,' I chipped in.

'No one else had access to the van? One of your staff perhaps?'

'My volunteers? Everyone would've gone home by the time your night-time incident took place.'

'Why would you imagine Quinn could be involved?' I asked.

'No one is saying that he is. It's just that we need to eliminate that van. Have you recently sold or maybe scrapped a sanctuary van?'

'No. We're currently fundraising for a new one, but at the moment we're having to make do with the old crock we've got.'

'Look, I have heard of cases like this before,' I told the officers. 'There was one where a van was cruising an estate with 'RSPCA' on the side, but it wasn't an official one.'

'Oh? I wasn't aware of that.'

'I've a link to the press report on my website, Gem.' I took out my phone. 'Sending you the link.' She glowered. She definitely regrets sharing her contact details with me.

'We'll still need a list of your volunteers I'm afraid,' Carmichael told Quinn. 'Past and present.' She was, I noticed, working off a tick list on her phone. Personally, when I need to ask people for a number of different things, I train myself to remember them. It looks more professional.

'So Ms Gorrage you and Mr James are friends, yes?'

'You know we are, Gem. It's been nearly four years now. Since I answered an appeal to adopt a dog brought back from Afghanistan. Which turned out to be Brownlow here.'

'He's a lovely looking dog,' offered the other female officer.

'You should've seen him when Sophie took him in,' Quinn told her proudly, 'Skinny, half-bald, covered in sores and without the confidence to even look you in the eye.' This was true, but I'd still maintain that Brownlow had done a lot more for me than I had for him. I might not have been half-bald and covered in sores, and I've never been particularly skinny either, but the other part could've described me as much as it did my companion. I was in a pretty dark place when I got Brownlow. I can't see how I could've moved on from there to where I am now without him. For a start he gave me a reason to get out of bed again, and a need to go out and earn money. Far more than that though, he gave me love – huge, unconditional, all-encompassing love. That had been something I'd never expected to receive again, or indeed give again. Of course, I couldn't share any of this with someone like PC Gemma Carmichael. You can't show even a hint of vulnerability to someone like her. Instead, I just reached down and rubbed Brownlow's ears. I don't need to tell him what he means to me. He knows.

'Would you mind if we took a look around?' The male officer was speaking to Quinn, but incensed that he'd the nerve to ask, I butted in.

'Do you have a warrant?' I snapped.

'It's fine, Sophie, I'll give them the tour.' Quinn stood up. The two ordinary coppers followed him out towards the kennels, aviaries, sheds and stables. The queen of rural crime stayed with me and Brownlow. Clearly, she relished our company a little more than I did hers.

'Hector Belt,' I said. Carmichael's eyes bulged like a toad that had recently eaten too large a worm.

'What?'

'Oh just a rumour I've heard on the grapevine. That you arrested him over the Bennett dogs.'

'I'd be interested to know where you heard that?' I ignored that.

'Hopefully it means you're making progress?' She didn't answer. I took that as a 'no'. 'Look, Gemma, what I'm trying to say is that while exploring certain aspects of my case – the Medalsum one, in London – I've found something, though it may be nothing, that might relate to the Bennett case.'

'If you're withholding evidence…' she began, rather predictably.

'No, Gemma, it's just I've no idea if this has any relevance to the Bennett case or not.' Of course, I was actually pretty damn sure that what I was going to tell her was relevant to Rouki's missing dogs, but I couldn't tell her that.

'Go on.' I could see I had her full attention, a bit like a cat when you dangle their favourite toy from a string.

'I'm talking about an inflatable dinghy, which was taken without the owner's knowledge and returned, having been to sea. When it was returned it had dog hairs in it.'

'Where?'

'Newhaven.' I didn't tell her Brownlow had identified the dog hairs as belonging to Rouki's dogs. 'You wouldn't I suppose, like to have some of the dog hairs to test their DNA? I mean I don't know if you do that with dogs. Even if their owner might be high profile and there's a lot of media interest.'

'Where are they? The dog hairs.' Carmichael growled. 'Newhaven?'

'In one of my evidence bags. Would you like me to drop it in – well I'm not sure which police station you operate out of now. So many have closed.'

'I'll call round yours for it when we're done here.'

'Great.' I'm no actress, but I managed to force a little fake enthusiasm into my voice. If I had my own DNA testing person, working in a lab that would test samples for me for free, that would ideal. If I were a TV private eye, I'd probably happen to conveniently know someone in a lab used by the police. Mind you, in that case, I'd probably be an ex-cop myself, rather than a former retail assistant, but there you are.

I had been going to look up DNA test labs when I got home, to try to get the hair samples tested for Rouki, but if I could get the police to do it free of charge, then that would hopefully impress Ms Bennett and reassure her she'd hired the right person.

Quinn and the other two coppers arrived back from the guided tour. The guy looked bored; the woman was chatting animatedly about how she had been thinking of getting another dog for some time. It seemed a blue-eyed Border Collie had made a good expression. The police officer said she'd speak to her husband. Quinn said to get in touch if they felt they might like to arrange another visit, to meet the dog together. The male cop told Carmichael they needed to be heading off. She watched them leave then turned to me.

'If you're off home now, I'll follow on.' I gestured to Quinn that I'd call him.

All the way home, Brownlow kept looking out the car's back window and grinning at Carmichael as she tailed us. Like I said before, he's not always the best judge of character. Back at ours, Carmichael declined a beverage. Perhaps she'd reached her tea quota for the day, or she didn't like the look of the unwashed, slightly chipped mug. I thought she'd leave once I'd given her the bag of dog hairs but she sat down, on my desk chair, admittedly still the only one clear of clutter. Clearly something was on her mind.

'I can't promise I can get results on this even after I've collected a sample to match it with from Ms Bennett. You have to fill in a form to justify why you're sending a sample to the lab, as it costs money. And there is a priority list for forensics.'

'Missing dogs don't rate than highly?'

'I am though personally very keen to make a breakthrough in the Bennett case.' I ground my teeth in a way I hope wasn't audible. That was my case too – now the paperwork had been auto-signed and returned to me, 'and I hope you can keep me in the loop re: Medalsum.'

'Well I would, Gem, but it's not really in Sussex Police's area is it? And a carjacking in East London hardly comes under the remit of a rural crime officer. I might though, possibly be able to get you a free download of his latest track when it drops or a t-shirt from the current tour?' Carmichael bristled in her patented way.

'I am trying to explain to you, Ms Gorrage, that the Bennett and Medalsum cases may well be related to each other, as may the experience the animal trainers reported.'

'Attempted abduction and a suspicious van? Can you tell me any more about them?'

'Just that they train dogs and other animals for film and TV. Anything from pet food commercials to feature films being shot anywhere in the world.'

'I'm guessing they have some reasonably high-profile animals?' I was blatantly fishing for information.

'So I'm told. There's a dog who was in the last Ryan Gosling movie, a cat who sells kitchens.'

'More animals in the public eye. Is there a pattern emerging?'

'Do you think so?' she asked, clearly fishing too. Any more of that and it would be a full-on cod war.

'Maybe,' I said. 'And if I bring you up to speed on Medalsum, would you allow me, on his behalf, to speak to the animal trainers, if of course they're willing?'

'I'd rather you didn't and I'm not giving you their details… though I'm sure you'll find them easily enough.'

'All over the internet already is it?' Her grumpy expression confirmed this to be a fact.

'Well previously, you did warn us off going anywhere near Rouki Bennett.'

'That came from above.' Clearly 'above' hadn't bothered to issue the same instruction over the pet trainers. 'So share what you've got on the Medalsum theft.'

'Right. Yeah,' I said. 'Suspicious white van activity.'

'And?'

'That's it, Gem. Told you I was drawing a blank there.'

'Any logo? On the van?'

'I only had a partial on CCTV.'

'What else?'

'Nothing – I just said. But hey, I've just given you the dog hairs.'

'They could be from any mutt.'

'Brownlow doesn't think so. He gave an indication. He thinks they belong to Rouki's missing pair.' PC Gemma Carmichael gave me her hardest glare. The one than resembles a gannet crossed with Paddington Bear. I looked away; it's always mildly disconcerting.

'How could he do that, Ms Gorrage, unless he had an item belonging to those dogs?' I cursed inwardly. If only she hadn't seen Brownlow in action, on past cases, and gained a rudimentary understanding of how he works. 'You were warned off.'

'And I'm staying off. Okay?' What I meant was, I'd email Rouki Bennett to ask her not to tweet that I was now working for her. With a bit of luck I'll be in time. 'But I've just given you something Gemma,' I reasoned with her. 'Something that if you can get it tested may give you the breakthrough you need.' She stood up, picked up the DNA sample bag and left. Brownlow followed her to the door wagging his tail amiably. Of course, I'd kept a few of the dog hairs back. If the police refused her request to get them tested, or the results weren't revealed to me, I still had the option of getting them tested myself. I was not born yesterday.

I wanted to talk to the dog trainers. East Sussex based and a Ryan Gosling film were the clues my nemmy had left me. It didn't take long to find them. Melissa and Gavin Randall were based near Polegate in East Sussex. I left them a message saying I was working for Medalsum and Rouki Bennett and could we speak. I was curious as to why they should think the van came from Quinn's sanctuary, and why, even after he'd told them it didn't, they'd gone ahead and contacted the police regardless. I'm protective where Quinn is concerned. I know you could say I'm biased but he is one of the few humans I truly trust.

I'd intended to spend the day in London, doing some more delving into the Medalsum case after first catching up with my old friend Belle Abbot. She is also one of the few humans I feel I can rely on. Belle and I were at school together, bonding over a shared love of animals. She's since married, divorced and currently lives in Balham, with a West Highland White named Shortcake who she adopted from Battersea Dogs Home. She works as an optician's receptionist and in consequence is a great person to know if like me, you're partial to designer frames but can't afford anything near their recommended retail price. Belle had seen on my socials that I'd been in London and had suggested a catch up next time I came up. I'd offered a café breakfast on Saturday. The beauty of getting the train to London early on a Saturday is, for those of you not au fait with the quirks of Southern Rail/Thameslink, that there are no peak-time fares as it's the weekend, plus you can get a third off if you've got a railcard. Also, again if you set off early enough, there's more space for you and your shaggy companion, as previously discussed.

When I'd said we'd likely be with her for ten am, Belle had suggested meeting at the café in Battersea Park. 'It's dog friendly. That's where we'll all be leaving from for the LDBD thing.'

'Sorry?'

'The Let Dogs Be Dogs Protest. You knew it was today surely?' When we were at school, Belle had been the quiet one, and it'd been me being bossy and possibly ever so slightly patronising to her, as she now tended to be to me. Dealing with appointments for folk with long or short sight all day long seemed to have this effect on her. I knew nothing at all about 'Let Dogs Be Dogs'. I couldn't even guess what it was supposed to mean. I mean what else is a dog going to be? If it was Let Dogs Be Chickens say, or even Let Chickens Be Dogs, at least that might make sense to the minority of owners whose pet preferred to hang out with another species.

'We're starting in Battersea Park and walking to Trafalgar Square. There'll be lots of people bringing dogs. Obviously.'

'Obviously,' I dutifully echoed, assuming the role our adulthood reversal had bestowed upon me.

'The exact route is still being planned, as there are two other marches passing through the centre this Saturday, and we don't want to get caught up in those. I think one's about Climate Change and the other's about saving a football club… or was that last week…? And it's the National Health again. Not sure, though if it's the football one, they're gathering outside the US Embassy for some reason or another.' Belle was obviously better informed than me about protests in the capital, though perhaps not quite as clued up as it was possible to be.

'But – Let Dogs Be Dogs? What exactly is that?' I heard her sigh.

'Well you're aware of the basic concept I'm sure.' I was glad she credited me with this knowledge and kept quiet rather than reveal my complete ignorance. 'It's against using dogs for things like hunting and that. I mean the term 'working dog' so often means animals being exploited doesn't it? And at the very least being made to do things they wouldn't do, were they given the opportunity to choose for themselves.'

'Right… things like hunting for explosives and drugs?'

'Greyhound racing – so many dogs just put down when too old or injured. Gun dogs made to endure deafening levels of noise, Jack Russells forced down rabbit holes. Sheep dogs –

made to live outdoors and dumped when they get too old to be useful. Those are just some of the areas where we have serious concerns. We want a law passed by Parliament.'

When I came off the phone, I looked up LDBD. It was an organisation of sorts. Well, a collection of various Facebook sites and hashtags at least. They seemed loosely affiliated to various anti-blood sports and even environmental groups. They seemed to have only formed recently and had so far only held a small march in Brighton, and another in Manchester. Both by the photos consisting of a barely a hundred people

Before I went to bed, I received a text from Belle, 'Don't worry, you don't need to bring a placard or a banner.' Of course, I then worried she was going to bring one for me to carry. I didn't really know enough about this LDBD thing, their aims and objectives or how they intended achieving them. Did they get involved in direct action? And if so what kind of thing might that involves? I envied Brownlow as he slept beside me. Even if I can't live in the moment like a dog, it would be nice to be able to simply flop down and nod off the way they do.

Chapter Five

We reached the café ahead of Belle and found a number of dog owners already sitting outside it chatting over coffee and the breakfast menu. We'd eaten on the train, so I just ordered a cappuccino. I noticed a pile of placards on sticks stacked against the wall. They were facing in so I couldn't read what they said. Brownlow received compliments as usual. 'You here for the rally?' said a young woman with Extinction Rebellion and Black Lives Matter badges on her blazer. I said I was and to meet a friend.

'So who's organising the march?'

'Vicki I think… and Tom, no Dan… is that his name, Cassie?'

'Um I'm not sure. Vicki defo.'

'I've not been to any LDBD events before,' I explained.

'Neither have we. Have there been others?'

'In Brighton and Manchester, I think,' I ventured.

'I'm only here 'cos I know Nat through a WhatsApp group.' I was clearly talking to Cassie and Nat.

'We're basically just dog walkers who know each other. All of us lot.' Nat indicated a group of women on another table. 'We all see each other at either the morning or evening walk.'

'Is Vicki or any of the other organisers here?' Cassie craned her neck to look around.

'I can't see her. Not that I know her in person actually. Just her profile photo.'

'Masses of red hair and kitten-eye glasses? Is that what you call them? Cat-eye – they go up at the corner at any rate.'

'I don't know if she's coming along herself today. She doesn't say if she is or isn't.' Cassie was looking at Vicki's twitter account. 'I mean I don't even know where she's based. Or Tom or Dan… no I'm pretty sure that's not his name… I mean it's happening all over.'

'I think there's a march in Kyoto too today. And Bristol too I think. It's a global movement – Let Dogs Be Dogs.'

'Supporters come from all walks of life, young and old. It's not just a left wing, city-centric or studenty thing. It's got a…' Nat searched for the word, 'a more inclusive vibe.'

On the train up, Melissa Randall had sent me a message saying she could see me late afternoon. That meant we'd have to head back down to East Sussex later. I'd never been on a protest, and I was only going to be able to do the first leg of this one as I had to get on with delving into the Medalsum case, then get over to the animal trainers by four. Still, going on a march would be something to tick off my bucket list, I reflected. This case with its shooting and baseball bat attack was possibly going to get dangerous. This demo at least didn't sound like it was going to involve even 'mild peril', as they say when describing a movie. I couldn't imagine there were many police in riot gear waiting, batons drawn for a dozen or so dog walkers to cross the Thames. A man with short-cropped, grey hair approached our table and handed us each a navy-blue baseball cap with LDBD on it in white lettering. Nat and Cassie cooed with delight over theirs.

'Are you one of the organisers?' I asked the man, optimistically.

'No, I just distribute the merch. We've someone designing mugs, keyrings, t-shirts and dog coats. These are just samples, but it'll all be up on the website by the end of the week. Hopefully they'll get the orders rolling in.'

'How is LDBD funded? It is funded, isn't it?'

'Journalist!' the man shouted out in a booming voice, but not with any malice. Heads turned. 'Got our first newshound here folks, come to sniff out what we're all about.'

'I'm not a reporter,' I told him. 'I was invited along by a friend. Belle Abbot.'

'Oh you know, Belle? Right.' He seemed disappointed he hadn't outed a Fleet Street hack. Perhaps he was hoping a write up in a tabloid would sell more 'merch'. 'Yes, she's texted me to say she's on her way,' he told me. 'Had to coax Shortcake to eat a little bit of cooked chicken before she left the house. He's had a dodgy stomach this past week.' It sounded as if Belle might possibly have found herself a man friend, judging by how acquainted he seemed to be with Shortcake's digestive system. 'But you asked how we're funded – it's by donations mainly. We've a page where you can pledge money. I'm sure Belle will tell you all about it.'

Belle arrived, slightly flustered, and Shortcake and Brownlow set about getting enthusiastically reacquainted. We were all to gather in ten minutes and set off. All the outside tables were now taken, mostly by dog owners. Other marchers and their four-legged companions stood in little groups along the lakeside. Belle waved to a youngish man who was in a pedalo on the water. He had a Border Terrier with him, sitting beside him in the little boat. 'Are all these people coming on the march?' It seemed I'd been wrong about the numbers. As people began to finish their drinks, pay for their food and leave their tables, I realised there were at least two hundred of us. Probably around a third had a dog or dogs with them. There was a woman wearing a drum, hanging from a sort of harness around her shoulders, and lots of people had whistles around their necks. Placards were lifted, banners unrolled and held aloft. 'Let Dogs Be Dogs'. 'It's A Dog's Life'. I noticed that many of the others were wearing trendy and expensive looking hiking boots or designer trainers. I started to wonder whether I should've worn something a little more substantial than my old Chelsea boots with the heels that had started to become lopsided. Several people, including Nat, donned tabards to show they were leading the march in an official capacity.

Brownlow though was enjoying the protest and definitely 'Being Dog' by flirting with a young Golden Retriever, walking alongside of us. Her owner, who was wearing the same baseball cap as me, introduced himself as Jonas. We both laughed as his canine companion made big eyes and whined appreciatively in Brownlow's direction. Belle had fallen back to talk to someone she knew from Shortcake's obedience classes. Jonas asked how I'd become involved in LDBD, and I said, semi-truthfully, I was really just here to support a friend. He said he'd always wanted to work with dogs, but a job at a Greyhound racing kennel had opened his eyes to the hardships and cruelties inflicted on dogs in the name of sport and entertainment. It wasn't just the callous way so many are abandoned or euthanised when their careers on the track are over. It was the whole idea of intelligent and social animals being locked up in kennels. Jonas, it turned out, was the one with the printing and design business who was making the t-shirts, mugs and the rest, 'all at cost of course, so the money goes to the organisation.'

'Are you the one who printed these caps?' I asked pointing to my head. He smiled and said he was also working on a range of coordinating dog coats in every size. As well as the items for Let Dogs Be Dogs, his firm printed other animal themed products. If I ever wanted a cushion or a shopping tote with my dog's face on, he could supply that. He took out his phone and showed me an array of t-shirts that he'd printed up with people's pets on – everything from kittens to tarantulas. I bet even Rouki Bennett didn't have her dogs on a t-shirt. Perhaps I'd send her his details. 'And are you also one of the organisers of today's march?' I asked.

'No, that's someone called Vicki I think?' He shrugged, not sounding too sure. 'I haven't met her personally, but we've exchanged a few emails. I think she might be on the organising committee,' he added vaguely. 'Not sure if she's here somewhere, but if after today, you'd like to come to other events, all the details get posted on the website.'

Belle rejoined me as we crossed Chelsea Bridge. Nat and Cassie were busy at the front, handing out flyers. The drummer was drumming, and we seemed to have acquired a couple of jugglers somewhere along the way. We now also had a police escort both ahead, to the sides and in front of us. The ones in front and behind had motorbikes with flashing, blue lights on. Belle assured me this was all pre-arranged and nothing to worry about. The demonstration had official permission and a registered route, she said. Being in the middle of a protest is, I was finding, easier than dodging the usual sightseers, shoppers and pedestrians that throng central London on a Saturday. The police even helpfully stopped the traffic for us at busy road junctions. If only Carmichael behaved like that. There was a small hold up before we reached Trafalgar Square, as another of the marches was heading through, but we'd still made pretty good time, all things considered. As Belle and Shortcake prepared to try to move forward in the crowd to be in a good position to hear the speeches when they started, Brownlow and I took our leave of them, and headed for the bus stops.

'What's this one all about?' asked an elderly woman waiting for the service for the British Museum. She liked their teashop, she told me, perhaps thinking I'd judge her as pretentious for going there to peruse the exhibits.

'It's against dogs having to work.' Of course, then she laughed and pretended she'd never heard of dogs working. The bus indicator informed me that our bus was still eight minutes away. At least hers was due sooner. After I'd gone to the trouble of explaining the term 'working dog' however, she became more serious.

'My son was on a school trip in the Cairngorms, when they lost their way in a fog. Freezing cold it was. I don't know what they'd have done without the mountain rescue team and their dogs. It was the dogs that saved him, no doubt about it. And I think the dogs enjoy that work don't they?' Before I could answer that I was sure they did she added, 'and what about guide dogs and assistance dogs? Would they be banning those too?' I said I presumed not, but in truth I didn't know. I'd taken part in the march with my own 'working dog' partly to meet my friend, and partly out of curiosity. I believe animals should have rights, of course I do. What rights they are given though does have to be governed by what is in their best interests. I'd have no problem with banning greyhound racing and the use of dogs in any blood sport. Yet I couldn't help thinking that dogs in general were facing much more urgent welfare issues than working. Puppy farming, cruelty, neglect, abandonment and pet theft were the things I'd personally prioritise as reasons to march.

I wanted to have another snoop around the industrial estate that housed Medalsum's recording studio, being as white vans had now emerged as a link where the animal trainers were concerned too. A helpful map gave the location and names of many of the businesses based on the site. I noticed that behind the unfriendly textile recyclers was a warehouse belonging to a firm called 'Every Day Raps'. Now

I'd heard of feuds between rival rap artistes and seeing as another rap outfit was based nearby and sharing a car parking area with the rag merchants, I thought we'd pay them a quick visit. As I rounded the corner to approach the building however, I realised the slightly weather-beaten and graffiti-scrawled map of the estate had led me to get the name of the company slightly wrong. They were in fact 'Every Day Wraps'. I then assumed they made paper to cover birthday or Christmas gifts. The warehouse though appeared to be more of a garage with cars and vans inside. A small poster on a wall explained what was going on. 'Vehicle wraps and decals, designed and fitted'.

Just inside the door, overall-wearing technicians were adding what looked to be coloured logos in what I assumed was a thin vinyl film to the bodywork of a taxi. There was a strong chemically smell to the place that made Brownlow hang back. A man seemed to be delicately sticking a thin sheet to a car door, using a squeegee to smooth it down. Over at the bonnet a woman was using some kind of small heating device to seal the design to the car. Seeing me, she stopped what she was doing and came over. Assuming I was a prospective customer, she offered to take me up to the site office.

Getting decals or vinyl logos on a van was much cheaper than a full wrap, which frighteningly cost more than my car was worth. As we'd arrived on a bus it wasn't as if I could volunteer the Clio for a makeover anyway. I mentioned a friend with a van. He was keen to get some new branding and had seen on the company's website that they designed logos as well as had them printed onto vinyl. I'd seen the website on the bottom of the poster outside the downstairs part of the building. She asked if I knew what kind of design my friend was after. I said he wasn't sure. I was wondering if they might have a few examples, he could see. 'What line of work is your friend in? We do a lot of builders' vans and landscape gardeners'.'

'It's a small charity actually. So a bit strapped for cash, but still looking for something eye-catching, you know?'

'We have had clients from smaller charities and not for profit organisations. If he'd like to come in, perhaps we could sit down and design something together.'

'Ah, that's the thing you see. It's an animal sanctuary. Just a small, local one. I don't suppose you've anything slightly 'off the peg' if you know what I'm saying? Something that could be tweaked a bit to be individual?'

The woman walked over to a computer and searched through a page of files. She opened one and twelve small thumbnail photos appeared onscreen.

'Two of these were for animal rescues, there's a dog one that's quite nice, and these we did for a vet. You've a cat's head silhouette imposed on a dog's head, and a paw print as the background.' Around the logo were the words Warmerton Pet Rescue. The writing and the logo were uncannily similar to that on the Weatherall Animal Rescue van. 'Could you share these with me, so I could show him?' She agreed to send the file to my email. I gave her my personal one that just has me down as 'sophieg@....', rather than my Brownlow And Gorrage one. She forwarded the files.

'I like this one very much,' I said indicating the Weatherall clone. 'Do you think that rescue would mind if my friend used something similar? I mean I don't know what area they're based in? We wouldn't want them getting confused.'

'They're in Essex I think, he said.'

'Would you have their details in case my friend does love that design too and wants to check if they'd mind him having something similar, before going ahead?'

'I can't give out customer details I'm afraid, but I'm sure he can find them online. I mean they're a rescue – they're sure to have a website with contact details.'

The Open Air café in Regents Park was a convenient and convivial place for a spot of late lunch. I forwarded the file containing the decals to Quinn. Of course, I had first looked for the Warmerton Pet Rescue, but I'd been unsurprised to draw a blank. Still wearing my Let Dogs Be Dogs cap, to keep the sun off my head, I reflected on the importance of uniforms and branding. LDBD was more of a movement if you could look like you belonged to it. It gave it authenticity and authority. It was the same with vehicle decals. In my line of work, I keep an eye out for suspicious vans, but those advertising a trade, whether a florist, bakery or gas fitter, I seldom give a second look, unless of course I'm requiring one of those businesses. Now I might be wary of a van in my area from an animal charity I didn't know, and so might Quinn, but that's because of our jobs. The majority of people would, like me with the other trades, just take it at face value.

Checking my inbox, I noticed that half an hour previously I'd received an email from PC Gemma Carmichael. *'FYI: have been given go ahead for the lab to DNA your dog hair.'* Clearly in my nemesis's world 'DNA' is a verb. *'You owe me one.'* I snorted into my cappuccino in indignation at this last bit. I most certainly did not owe Gemma Carmichael a thing. Brownlow and I were the ones who'd put some possibly key evidence her way. *'Let me know the results when you get them,'* I replied, fanning a wasp away from my cheese and tomato panini, *'and you might like to look at this van logo – looks very similar to Weatherall's eh? Fitted on a van near the scene of the Medalsum incident. There – we're even!'* That last sentence was pathetically playground, and I slightly regretted descending to her level, but I still sent it.

Brownlow looked up at me, saw me scrolling my socials and uttered a deep sigh before closing his eyes and settling down for a nap. He's chewed up two of my previous phones and to tell you the truth I feel like doing the same to my current model sometimes, and probably would if I had the jaw for the job. At the next table a toddler was shouting and screeching but unlike me, Brownlow has the ability of screening out that kind of racket. The mother was probably a little younger than me, though still quite old to have a tot of that age. She might've been his grandma of course, if she and her daughter had both bred at a young age. I caught myself using the word 'bred' in my mind. Spending most of my life around four-footed friends I sometimes think in animal terms rather than human ones. I suppose you could say I am glad I've never whelped. Like everyone I come into season occasionally, but I can't say I've ever really felt broody. I paused my musings as I switched from glancing at Medalsum's latest Instagram posts to Rouki's twitter account. '*A time wasting lowlife,*' she announced crisply, had been bailed for sending her what she called malicious and false communications regarding the whereabouts of Lady Champignon and Mr Merrytrees. '*The person who wrote those distressing and evil ransom notes actually had nothing to do with their disappearance.*' This made perfect sense. The police, like Quinn and I, had found no evidence of the dogs ever being at Hector Belt's. Belt had, I suspected, not been sufficiently good at encrypting his emails, or removing the evidence of them from one of his devices. I had mixed feelings about this news. On the one hand, I wouldn't want any animal to spend even a short time in his grotty garden cages, but on the other, if Belt had been involved, he was the type of person who would've quickly admitted his involvement. Sentences for possession of stolen animals are not currently terribly stiff. Plead guilty and Belt would've, as on previous occasions, stood a very good chance of evading custody altogether.

When Brownlow woke from his doze, I tipped his lunch into his dish beneath my café table. Carmichael emailed to say she couldn't find any trace of Warmerton Pet Rescue. '*Have you checked the government's charity register?*'

'Just about to do so,' she replied. Odds on she didn't even know you could do that until I'd told her. I asked her to let me know the result. At least she was doing a little unpaid administration for us while we did the leg work. I sent the photo of the van with the charity logo to Skyla, saying that while I knew her dad didn't recall many details of the attack, could she forward it in case it jogged his memory.

On other tables in the outdoor cafe, people were busy on their phones, tablets or laptops. It made me wonder what they were working on, out there in the sunshine, with only the noisy child to distract them, apart from a few gibbon hoots drifting over from the zoo. I tried to check in with Belle at the demo but her phone went to voicemail. I then noticed 'Trafalgar Square' was trending on Twitter. The police were trying to move on the LDBD so another protest could gather beneath Nelson and a few scuffles had broken out. There were little phone-shot snippets of video footage of what looked like little more than pushing and shoving. The other group were impatient to get where they were going, and judging by a few tweets, the LDBD speeches had dragged on longer than intended. Someone else said the protest had been hijacked by hardliners looking for trouble, but it wasn't clear if they were referring to LDBD or the second group of demonstrators, who weren't protesting about National Health funding or a football club owner as Belle had told me, but about the deportation of asylum seekers. There was another video clip of a policeman and a woman wrestling over a placard, but the poster side was turned away from the camera, so I couldn't see which march she was actually on. I pressed 'play' on the final posted clip and in this one the police were dragging a couple of people away.

One of them was wearing a LDBD cap and as it fell from his head, it looked like it might be the man from the pedalo. I hoped the Border Terrier was safe, but I couldn't see it in the film footage. At least neither of the people being detained were Belle or any of the others I'd talked to. There didn't seem much point in going back down there and it would be unfair to take Brownlow somewhere that, according to the pictures, the occasional flare was now also being lit. He's probably in the majority of his kind in hating bonfire night and the new year celebrations. I'd just have to check in with Belle again later to ensure she and Shortcake were safe.

I scanned the news sites and police force socials for pet crime stories, as I usually do. A Met police report, from the previous day, mentioned a number of dogs being recovered in a raid on premises near, of all places, Catford. They had rescued twelve, for which they had yet to identify the owners. They included various Spaniels, Staffies and Pugs among other breeds, and asked anyone who had lost a dog recently to get in touch. I left a message to say I was a pet detective working on a number of missing dog enquiries, and wondering if I could have further information. At the very least, I offered, I could circulate details of the animals still to be identified to my followers.

I'd promised to meet the animal trainers who lived just north of Polegate at four, so it was time for Brownlow and me to head back to Victoria Station and board the Eastbourne service. On that service, we'd just left Croydon when I received a message from no other than Medalsum himself, wanting to talk. I asked if he could give me five minutes. The train wasn't that busy, but I headed into the empty first class and closed the door, before embarking on the video call. I fervently hoped the train's Wi-Fi connection wouldn't cut out. I couldn't remember if it still worked in the fast-approaching tunnels and I was a bit worried about the guard catching me in first class with a second class ticket. Sometimes I've seen them turn a blind eye, and on other occasions offer someone at upgrade. I've also seen them issue a penalty fare, and not only can we not afford to incur that kind of additional expense, it would make me look very small time indeed in front of Medalsum.

'Err hi, great to meet you at last.'

'Likewise Sophie. And Brownlow there. Hi, boy! Oh look at him – what a grin. Is he for real?'

'You're on tour at the moment, I believe?'

'I'm in Frankfurt yeah. Doing the rounds of the TV and radio stations then the gig tonight. It's pretty full on.'

'I can imagine.' Actually I couldn't. His life was nothing like mine at all. I do tend to gush and gabble a bit in these situations. I didn't grow up with Skype and Zoom and Hangouts and the rest of it. I remember how awkward my Nan used to be on the phone. It's like that for me with video calls. I don't think I'll ever get used to seeing myself in a little box on the screen. My nose always seems so much bigger than it can feasibly be, I have a shiny-face and my hair always seems to stick up like someone's rubbed a balloon on it.

'So listen,' said Medalsum, mercifully taking charge of the situation, 'you sent Skyla that photo of that van and wanted to know if I had any recollection. Now here's the thing – I think I do. That logo looks familiar. But I'm kinda picturing myself seeing it after my head hit the tarmac. And I'd thought I'd blacked out right away. But now in my mind I can see that van with the logo, and Tash being dragged into it.'

'They were dragging her?'

'She's a big girl. And she was growling. Yeah, now I'm chatting to you I can remember that. One of the guys is dragging her into the van by the collar. She's squirming and growling. Warning growl y'know? She ain't mean. Never has been. But she'll let you know if you ain't treating her right. The other guy's still over me, checking I'm not going anywhere.'

Medalsum also told me Skyla had been sent some rather wobbly footage from a cyclist's webcam. He'd emailed to apologise for not getting involved, assuming it was some kind of violent altercation and that wasn't something he felt he could get involved in. Medalsum wasn't too happy that a witness had misinterpreted the car-jacking theft of his dog as some kind of gang related incident. He also felt if the witness had tried to intervene it might've given the dog a chance to escape.

He said Skyla would send me the footage by a video transfer site, after Jamal had edited it down as there was quite a bit of before and after, of the cyclist's journey. In the part that briefly showed Medalsum on the ground, it wasn't possible to see the van. It did give a quick view of both attackers though; they were wearing black and balaclavas. Medalsum asked if I thought Skyla should send it to the Met as well. I said of course she should. We weren't in competition after all, just approaching the case in our own ways, utilising our particular skill sets. I'd tried this line on Carmichael on a previous case and she'd muttered 'bollocks'. I hoped the Met accepted my efforts to help with a more generous spirit.

I realised we were going to be slightly later than intended reaching the animal trainers. I phoned to apologise and ask if there was a minicab rank at Polegate Station. The woman, Melissa Randall answered and immediately insisted on picking us up at the station. I'd been prepared to dislike her for wrongly accusing Quinn and his sanctuary of wrongdoing but despite having one of those jolly hockey sticks voices, she did indeed seem rather jolly and no-nonsense.

On arrival, we couldn't help but notice a middle-aged woman in green wellies, tweedy jacket and a trilby, with a large lamb in a harness, standing on our platform. Several children, waiting to travel, were petting the sheep.

'Ah you brought your dog! Hope he's alright with baa-lambs.' I recognised Melissa by her voice, and she had no doubt seen the photos of us on the Brownlow and Gorrage website. I assured her that Brownlow was gentle around all animals, large and small. Melissa led the way to a parked open topped jeep, like the kind you might expect to travel in on a safari. 'Err if your guy sits in the back, do you think you could manage Nylon on your lap?' Nylon was the lamb. I agreed. That way at least Brownlow and Nylon would be comfortable, though the nearly grown-up lamb was rather heavy and a bit of a fidget.

'Got another four of these back home,' Melissa said, indicating Nylon. 'Named after textiles – Linen, Tartan, Denim and Cotton. All bottle-fed orphans. Going to be in a TV series. Nursery rhyme children have become teenagers and now solve mysteries. It's set in the present day. So Mary is eighteen and the little lamb – a sheep. All five look pretty much identical so they can all play him. Nylon is the calmest, so he's learning to travel in cars, which the character has to do.' At this point Nylon baa-ed at a car passing in the other direction. 'Good boy!' Melissa deftly handed him a sheep treat without her eyes leaving the road.

'Can you feel his heart beating? Is it calm?' I pressed my palm to the warm wool. and said it certainly felt that way to me.

'He's gonna be fantastic. They're severely under-rated, sheep. They're so bright, and all individuals. All that nonsense of being 'sheep-like' if you're meek and easily led. They're pushy, plucky characters with minds of their own believe me. Nylon here, is at the age when – if we hadn't purchased him – he'd be about to meet the mint sauce.' I looked at Nylon. It was true. The majority of lambs aren't allowed to live for more than a few months. 'Course,' Melissa was saying, 'our sheep won't ever have to face that fate. That's the thing with TV. It pays very well.' She laughed. I noticed her watch looked like an expensive one. 'When you think what they have to pay the top stars, well it's peanuts for them to factor into our fee the costs of keeping each sheep for the rest of his life. Nylon and his friends could live for ten to twelve years each, but even with vet bills that's still nowhere near a top actor's salary. We either keep the animals ourselves, and usually find them other roles, or we have several approved homes – petting zoo type set ups where the retired animals' former TV and film careers make them a bit of a draw.' I said I hadn't really given a lot of thought to animal actors, beyond the dogs and horses. 'We don't have many horses – just one or two specific 'character' ones. Other trainers specialise in equines. It's because of the numbers. Some period films and series require quite a few.'

'Gavin is out feeding the multitude,' Melissa told me as we pulled up outside a large farmhouse. 'Would you like the grand tour?' What would have been a farm's fields had been turned into wooden fenced paddocks and other types of enclosure. As we looked at the animals, Melissa told me their individual stories. It was rather similar to a tour of Weatherall, but instead of tales of abandonment or injury, these were tales from showbiz. I realised I'd seen Reggie the donkey in a couple of TV shows without knowing it. Cameron the macaw I knew from an advert. He lived in an aviary next to others containing an owl, a raven, ducks and pigeons. Back in the paddocks were several cows, a pigmy goat, pigs, a zebra and a Shire horse. The dogs, apart from an elderly Sheltie who followed us around, were mainly in the house Melissa said, as were a couple of cats and what she called 'all the smalls'. She preferred her canine and feline actors to live in a home environment, as it kept them fully mentally stimulated as well as being better for their social skills and well-being. I was quite impressed by the whole set up. I'd been a little sceptical, thinking of clichés of circus type trainers and animals being taught possibly quite demeaning tricks. Of course, I hadn't seen Melissa's training methods, but the creatures at what she called 'our ranch' all looked both happy and healthy.

Gavin Randall was in the kitchen, serving up food to a horde of impatient dogs of all sizes, while cats sat eating from bowls on the work surface. 'Would your fella like something?' Brownlow to his shame was visibly drooling at the tempting food smells.

'Err he has a special diet mixed for him and delivered.' Even as I said it, I realised I sounded a bit precious. I didn't want to start morphing into a Rouki Bennett type. It does seem a bit ironic that a mutt who started life scrounging garbage heaps should now have a designer diet, but as I've said, he needs the best nutrition to stay at the top of his game.

'Ours have their dinners individually tailor made too,' Gavin said, opening the cupboard to show a range of packets from the same maker as Brownlow's dog food. Would it be something like this?' He held a bag of food for me to sniff. Dog owners, eh? We do like to inhale a bag of meaty biscuits and declare it smells really healthy, as if we can really tell. Anyway, for what it's worth, it smelt to my human nose, exactly like Brownlow's delivered dinner. Gavin said it was the one he feeds to Lucky, their Newfoundland, who is roughly, he'd calculated, of a similar build and age to Brownlow. I agreed he could have some, and he seemed thrilled with it. Gavin was as cheerful as his wife, but his accent was as Welsh as hers was posh. She told me I was joining them for dinner as it was 'the most convivial way to talk'. Dinner had been heating on the Aga in another, smaller kitchen.

'Having a people kitchen and an animal kitchen – so much easier if you've got the space.' I agreed, though Brownlow and I have to make do with a cramped kitchenette, where he's been known to put his front feet up on the counter and snaffle everything from pancakes to custard creams. While Gavin dished up and uncorked the wine, Melissa offered me a quick look at the 'smalls' room. In here was a snake, a bearded dragon, a chameleon, several rabbits, guinea pigs, and budgies. Here also lived 'Jackie, the superstar rat'. Jackie had been in more films than any of Gavin and Melissa's clients. Melissa opened her spacious cage and Jackie immediately ran up onto her shoulder. 'Horror films and crime dramas. Jackie's an agouti-colour fancy rat – in other words identical to your wild brown rat. It's funny, even these days it's usually women who have to have a rat run over their body or a close up with one next to their face. That's why Jackie is a star. She's gentle and affectionate. A lot of actors are at least a little bit nervous of rats, so we bring Melissa to meet her co-stars, sometimes even stay at their homes or in a hotel, getting to know them for a few days prior to filming.' Jackie nestled against Melissa's neck. 'It's quite stressful for the rat if the human is scared of them, and not good for the human either. I mean let's have terrified acting rather than terrified actors, that's what we say.'

I liked Melissa and Gavin and over dinner they couldn't have been more apologetic about erroneously putting the police onto Quinn. As we devoured a delicious vegetable Wellington, they explained how it had been a genuine mistake, due to concern for their animals.

'Melissa is an overprotective hen,' said Gavin. 'But Weatherall's logo looked so like the one we saw.' I showed them on my phone the decals from the supposedly fake animal charity.

'Yes!' gasped Melissa, 'Yes, this time I'm certain… well I think I'm certain. It was certainly that or something very like it.'

'The thing is,' said Gavin, turning serious, 'we're a little vulnerable here, out in the wilds.' I told him about Quinn installing high fences and an alarm system. The couple looked at each other. 'Melissa has been wanting to get it done for some time, but we've been so busy. One or sometimes both of us is often away, filming. And some of that work is abroad. For some shoots we're brought in to work with local animals. We've done that in Hungary and Romania recently. For others though, if it's an animal that can easily travel, we've flown out with them. Jericho the owl and Jackie the rat have clocked up plenty of air-miles.'

'Who looks after the place when you're away?'

'We have a staff of three part-timers as well as ourselves.'

Melissa brought in the dessert, which involved an upside-down kiwi pudding. This was one of the most enjoyable work visits I could remember.

'The thing is,' Melissa said pensively, as we tucked in, 'we want the best for our animals, we treat them like family, but there are people, people who don't believe in training animals at all.'

'Animal libbers.' Gavin got straight to the point.

'Probably assume we crack whips and shout and bully, where in fact it is all about patience, and the clicker…' She took out and clicked her training clicker and all the dogs were there in an instant. 'That and a lot of healthy but irresistible treats.'

'So,' said Gavin, scooping up a piece of kiwi and double cream, 'have you heard of 'Let Dogs Be Dogs'?'

'Yes. Had a demo in London today I believe.' I didn't admit I'd been there. 'What exactly do they want? That's what I don't understand.'

'Gavin,' his wife said, clearly worried he was going to go into a rant of some kind.

'Yes, I know I've got a bit of a bee in my bonnet about them, but even so? Why do they target us? We're not involved in shooting or hunting. We don't ask the animals to do anything they find scary or unpleasant. In a TV show, our dogs are being dogs. If a scene asks for something that wouldn't be right, we don't let our animals do it.'

'We had a scene where the dog is thrown into a cold river.' Melissa added, 'The director assumed that would just happen. We explained how the actor would hold the dog and appear to throw her, then it would need to be CGI from that point. Of course, the producer didn't want to spend the money on the computer animation, but that's how it is. They could go to a country where things are less regulated and use a less scrupulous animal trainer, or they could do things properly. Thankfully they did the right thing. Usually they do.'

'Yes,' Gavin added, 'but it's the bad apples that tarnish our industry. Then someone whistle-blows. So Let Dogs Be Dogs are probably convinced our animals are suffering. They're probably for the most part genuine animal lovers themselves. But that doesn't stop them.'

'Stop them? Doing what?' I wasn't quite sure what it was Let Dogs Be Dogs were doing to the Randalls.

'Trolling us. Hacking our website. Feeding false stories to journalists.'

'They've done that?'

'Twice that we know of. A Jack Russell was killed in a TV drama. They said we supplied it and let them kill it. In fact the dog, named Cyril, is one handled by us, but has a private owner, who we represent, a bit like an actor's agent. We have some animals on our books that aren't actually ours, but their owners share our ethos. Anyway, we had to take the journalist around to the owner and meet Cyril, so she could see he was very much alive. Claudia who owns him dotes on him in fact.

We were hoping they'd run a story featuring Cyril, but all they did was admit they now knew the death story was bogus and wouldn't be running it.'

I still didn't tell Melissa and Gavin I'd attended Let Dogs Be Dogs. The fact was I wasn't a member. How could I be? I have a working dog. I asked if they would forward me the trolling and evidence of website hacking. I wanted to know how they knew the people who had targeted them were from Let Dogs Be Dogs. 'It all happened in a short space of time, like it was a group of people working together.'

'Or one person with more than one account? That's another possibility,' I told him, 'but why do you suspect Let Dogs Be Dogs?'

'One of the messages ended like that,' Gavin replied. 'Ended with the words 'Let Dogs Be Dogs'. No coincidence surely?'

'Unless,' Melissa said, 'it's more of a call to arms. I mean people wear Extinction Rebellion badges and say they support them – I'm thinking of actors in particular here. But not all of them are actually part of the movement. For everyone like Emma Thompson who will sit in a giant boat in Oxford Street, you get many who just call themselves supporters, but aren't actually members in the truest sense.'

'When did this thing start anyway? I certainly hadn't heard of Let Dogs Be Dogs,' Gavin insisted. 'Not 'til the site got hacked last week and then there was that phrase being used. So I did a search on it. But it doesn't look like they've been in existence very long. A couple of months maybe.' I didn't say, but I was thinking, that it sounded as if it was one of those things that catches the imagination and snowballs. These days movements, conspiracies, protest groups can form so vast, build like a snowball on a slide and then as quickly meld and shape-shift into something else. All kinds of foreign influences and political powers are out there vying for our attention and trying to persuade us that their truth is the only one.

We were sitting in the spacious sitting room having coffee as it grew dark outside.

Gavin was scrolling his phone, looking for what he called 'the latest antics' of Let Dogs Be Dogs. He was worrying at the subject like Brownlow with his squeaky chicken, and I was gaining the impression that Melissa rather wished she'd had the foresight to clicker train her husband. 'Click-click – Gavin, leave it!' I found myself smiling at the thought. 'Oh marvellous,' he declared, as Melissa rolled her eyes, 'Marvellous. They're going to hold a vigil. Guess where? Melly?' We couldn't guess. 'Greyfriars Bobby's Statue. In Edinburgh. What has a dog who sat by his master's grave to do with it? Eh?'

At that moment a noise outside sent a pack of six dogs of all sizes, including Brownlow racing, barking to the door. As they ran from the room, various cats leapt onto the furniture, hissing and bristling at the stampede. Gavin strode out into the hallway to see what was wrong, but he could see nothing there. When he came back in, with five dogs, including Brownlow trotting back from their impromptu bit of house guarding, none of us immediately noticed anything was amiss. It was only when Brownlow and I were on the point of saying our farewells and Melissa went to get my coat and Brownlow's lead, that she noticed something was wrong. 'Is Bianca there with you?' she called back to Gavin. 'Err no. I've not seen her since before dinner. Perhaps she's in the laundry basket.'

'No, she's not. I've just looked.'

'Bian-ca! Bian-ca-!' Other dogs pricked up their ears or opened a drowsy eye, but no Bianca appeared.' I heard Melissa run upstairs and then back down again.

'Which one is Bianca?' I asked Gavin.

'The white Chihuahua.'

'Oh God, where is she?' Melissa now looked anxious.

'Relax, she must be in the house somewhere. I mean nobody's been outside since I gave them their dinner and she was definitely here then.' I nodded, remembering marvelling at how tiny and delicate she was even for one of her breed. She was the star of a children's TV series, where she plays a dog that, through a mistake in a will, becomes the ruler of a fantasy kingdom. I'd actually seen a few episodes on those workless days when I'd been sitting at home twiddling my thumbs. It wasn't that bad and so far it had run to six series. It had spawned a number of spin-off books, not to mention a range of lunchboxes, pencil cases and mini-rucksacks, all adorned with Bianca's head, wearing a mini tiara.

Ten minutes later, after a search of the whole house, Bianca still hadn't been found. 'Did you lock the back door when you came in from the feed round?' Melissa asked Gavin.

'As always. And all the windows are shut.'

'She's been taken!' Melissa wailed. 'I know she has.'

'From a locked house? It's impossible,' Gavin reassured her. I suddenly felt a shiver of dread though. I'd come in the front door with Melissa, and I hadn't given the back door, which was in the animal's kitchen, even a cursory glance. Now though I jumped to my feet so suddenly that all eyes, human and dog, were on me. From our chairs in the sitting room, we'd all supposed the dogs had run to the front door barking, but they might in fact have actually run to the back one.

'Do you have a cat flap?' I asked. Melissa cried out, clearly realising exactly where I was going with that thought. We all rushed to the back door. The cat flap was small, but big enough for a Chihuahua to squeeze through. This was no locked room mystery. Not when it concerned a dog who was smaller than a small cat. Gavin threw open the back door and called Bianca's name into the darkness beyond.

'But she never uses the cat flap,' Melissa was saying. 'It only opens for our cats. Their micro-chips unlock it.'

'But the cats have been coming and going freely all evening?' I asked, knowing the answer.

'You think she followed one of them outside? Then why isn't she coming now? She'd never just wander off.'

'I doubt that she's wandered off,' I said. 'There have been similar cases I've read about. The thieves lure the dog to jump through the cat-flap for a tasty treat. In this case, they might've have needed to lure a micro-chipped cat out first to unlock the flap, again with a treat. They'd then let the cat go but hold the cat flap open. We were all chatting and some way from the door. They could've called Bianca softly. We wouldn't have heard a thing. But all the dogs clearly did.' Gavin swore and slumped against the wall.

'She's a very special dog. Very vulnerable…' Melissa couldn't stop the tears. 'She is on medication for her heart and needs her eye drops twice a day.'

'They've got maybe a ten-minute start on us, but it's still worth searching. 'Call 999 and take your jeep and have a drive around. Have you got one of her toys for him to sniff? I'll see if Brownlow can get a scent.'

Brownlow did follow a trail, but it was only around the paddocks, and I suspected Bianca's owners had walked her that way earlier in the day. For my money, she'd been picked up and bundled into a car or van that had quietly pulled into the secluded drive. She was probably long gone. When I got back to the house I'd ask about CCTV. With so many potentially valuable animals in residence I felt sure Gavin and Melissa would have it covering their premises. We were about to retrace our steps when I noticed that a wooden gate in the perimeter fence surrounding the paddocks was open. Carelessly leaving a gate open didn't strike me as something the couple would do, particularly as this one had a wire mesh on the bottom, presumably to stop smaller dogs or some of the other animals vanishing into the woods, when let out of their enclosures. Beyond the Randall's 'ranch', a muddy track led off between the trees. I'd put my rucksack on before leaving the house, and it contained my handy head torch, an essential for such situations. Brownlow was on his extendable lead, and as we approached the gate, he suddenly indicated getting a scent again. Melissa and Gavin weren't there to ask, but I was pretty sure they must regularly walk their dogs in this wood, so a scent here could mean something, or it could mean nothing. Nevertheless, we set off along the tree-lined path. The track was narrow and partly overgrown by brambles. It was also muddy and at various points split off in different directions. Brownlow was pulling me along, so I wasn't given a choice of direction at any of its junctions. Intently focussed on his work, his nose occasionally lifted in the air to sniff something undetectable to me. Perhaps the dognapper was still in the vicinity, but at some distance, upwind of the dog. Onwards we went, deeper into the woods.

I froze upon hearing a sound, or perhaps thinking that I had. I couldn't be sure. I managed to bring Brownlow to a halt and used the hand gesture for sit. Brownlow knows a few of the basic signs used in training deaf dogs, as when stalking a nervous lost animal, sometimes we need to be extremely stealthy. He turned his head to look at me, eager to be told or 'signed' to get on with the pursuit. I heard the sound again. It was definitely a noise made by an animal and that animal was, in all probability, a dog. It sounded like a kind of whine of complaint. I was suddenly fairly sure that someone with a dog was only a short distance ahead of us. I motioned to Brownlow to continue following the odour trail. I tried to walk very quietly now, looking where I was placing my feet in order to avoid snapping any twigs, or rustling the brambles. Brownlow of course could not be told to walk more quietly. His breathing is always quite loud when he is following a scent. A dog has a vomeronasal or Jacobson's organ between the roof of the mouth and the nasal passage. Cats have it too, as do horses, deer, sharks and snakes. It's hard to imagine how a sense we don't have works. It's designed to detect pheromones and works in conjunction with the sense of smell. The dog's mouth is slightly open as he walks drawing air over this organ, but it's a noisy process, even when the animal isn't actually starting to pant. If you own a cat and his or her soft purring briefly turns to a harsher, raspier sound, that again is the animal drawing air across its Jacobson's.

As I'd tried to explain to Rouki Bennett, Brownlow's tracking skills are due to him having a top of the range nose, and that includes the work of this finely-tuned sixth sense. Even without this extra super-power, my nose is kind of a waste of space on my face compared with Brownlow's. Humans have five to six million scent receptors in our noses. Dogs have around a hundred million, and the best ones at following a trail, including breeds like Bloodhounds, have three hundred million. Some like Brownlow, despite being a mongrel, clearly have the same genetic advantages as the hunting hounds bred to follow a trail. When the signals from his nose and Jacobson's organ reach his brain, the area for processing smells is forty times larger than yours or mine. So while I was inwardly cursing Brownlow for making a noise like a steam engine building up a head of steam when ideally we needed to be silent, I also knew that without his scent detectors and processing core, we wouldn't be closing in on our quarry.

My head span round. I'd heard a voice. I was sure of that. It had been somewhere close, a few metres behind us, a short urgent whisper. I turned back to see the direction Brownlow was looking in, to pinpoint the sound. Something hit me. It hit my head hard. I heard Brownlow yelp. That was all.

Chapter Six

'Brownlow, where's Brownlow?' A man in an emerald-green uniform was shining a light in my eyes and asking me something, but I couldn't focus on that. His voice echoed and kept going far away though his slightly fuzzy outline remained. 'Brownlow? My dog? Brownlow?'

***

I was in a wheelchair, clutching a sick bowl in case it was needed. The paramedics were chatting to colleagues. We were in some kind of queue in a hospital corridor. I wasn't even sure which hospital. I tried to stand, and by gripping the wheelchair arms managed to, but then the world started to spin. Hands grabbed my arms and brought me back down into the chair. Someone was saying something about needing to do a few tests. I thought they'd already done plenty of those in the ambulance.

'Where are we?'

'Eastbourne DGH'. I groaned. If there is something guaranteed to make my head hurt worse than it being hit with a heavy object, it's an acronym.

'You're at A&E.' At least I understood that one.

'Brownlow? My dog?'

'I already told you, Sophie. There was no dog with you when you were found.' I tried to stand. 'I need to find him.' Again, they held on to me.

'You need to see a doctor. When you're discharged, then you can find him.'

The doctor wanted to keep me in overnight. The brain scan hadn't showed anything untoward concerning either my brain or my skull, but he still insisted I was concussed and in a confused state. He kept asking about my vision and did I still feel sick. In the ambulance, I'd struggled with the number of fingers being held up, and knowing the day of the week, but that wasn't a problem now. I was sitting in a waiting area while they tried to find me a bed I didn't need. I'd been asked if they could call someone to let them know where I was, family perhaps. The thing is, I don't do family. Mum left when I was seven. Dad found my brother and me a burden, and his girlfriend definitely wasn't the maternal type. My brother's okay, but he works as a joiner on Stornaway, so it wasn't much good calling him. Instead, I'd asked them to call Quinn. It wasn't his friendly but concerned face, I could now see coming through reception to find me. It wasn't a friendly or concerned face at all – it was my ruddy nemmy.

PC Gemma Carmichael did not appear particularly concerned about my health and well-being. She didn't even begin by asking how I was feeling. Briskly, she took out her notebook, no doubt to convince the watching nurse that she was a proper serious crime investigating copper. 'Why don't you start from the beginning,' she droned.

'I don't want to give a bloody statement, Gem. I want to get out there and find Brownlow. The dognappers have him.' Carmichael sucked the end of her pen.

'No, Weatherhall have him.'

'What?' I sat up and immediately retched again. Carmichael moved back to protect her uniform leaving me to fumble to find the sick bowl myself.

'They were called to a dog running about loose in a country lane near Polegate after it was nearly hit by a car. Your friend Quinn attended and identified the animal as Brownlow.'

'Is he alright?'

'The dog?' I grimaced. Of course I meant the dog. 'Apparently.' I slumped back in the chair in relief, mercifully without vomiting in front of Carmichael. The release of tension at knowing Brownlow was safe made my thoughts immediately clearer.

'Gem, they've taken another dog. It belongs to Melissa and Gavin Randall who –'

'I know,' she interrupted, 'I've spoken to the Randalls. So like I said, start at the beginning.'

I answered Carmichael's questions which all concerned my visit to Melissa and Gavin and events prior to and after the theft of Bianca. I then asked two of my own. 'Do you have a DNA result for the dog hair in the dinghy yet?'

'Not yet.'

'Did you find out if that animal charity logo was bona fide?'

'There's no charity with that name. We've alerted other forces and the public via the media to look out for a van with that particular logo. Unfortunately, it is quite close to Weatherall's design, and now their vehicle has been in the area of both the assault upon yourself and this latest suspected dog theft, as they had to collect Brownlow.

This means it will have to be discounted from witness accounts of any similar vehicles seen in the area.' I supposed she was just telling me the facts how they stood, but it sounded as if she was blaming me, Quinn or even my hapless hound.

'Suspected dog theft? Actual dog theft you mean.'

'No one as I understand it witnessed the animal being taken. You were telling everyone when you were brought in that your dog had also been stolen, whereas in fact he was found wandering, not too far from Randall's property.'

'Still wearing his collar and lead?'

'You'll have to ask Weatherall's for the exact details of where and how. What I'm currently focusing on is the violent assault on you, Ms Gorrage. 'You mentioned a voice, possibly male, shortly before you were attacked. You didn't recognise it or hear the words?'

'It was a kind of hushed whisper – I mean even if it was someone I knew or had met previously, I don't think I'd have recognised it.'

'Is there anyone you do know who might possibly have been following you? Have you offended anyone lately?'

'Me?'

'Is there someone involved in one of your recent cases who may believe themselves to have reason to assault you?'

'No. Not at all… unless Michael Davison…' Davison had been a donkey rustler. We'd recovered the donkey and he'd threatened to 'do in' Brownlow and me. Fortunately, when he was charged over the donkey he'd been on parole, so had been sent back inside, before he could attempt to act on his threats.

'Checked Davison. Still serving his sentence. Anyone else?'

'Not that I can think of. Most of my recent cases have been recovering lost pets. Grateful owners, no criminal element.'

'But you are now working for Medalsum which is fairly high profile.'

'Why would that make someone target me? Unless of course they wanted to frighten me off my investigation.'

'That,' said Carmichael with a grimace, 'is unfortunately something I'm sure is unlikely to happen.'

'Damn right,' I said.

I never did get a hospital bed. I was feeling better anyway, so by the time Quinn, who has a key to my flat, had turned up with my pyjamas, some grapes and a puzzle book, I'd been given the all clear to go home, with the proviso that someone would be willing to stay with me. Quinn said that was fine. He'd make me some supper and stop over. He'd already asked a volunteer named Kyle if he minded sleeping over at Weatherall. Kyle had been only too pleased, as he was studying nocturnal wildlife as part of his degree course. He quite fancied staying up and observing Weatherall's recuperating foxes, badgers and hedgehogs, rather than sleeping between care shifts.

At Quinn's van, Brownlow burst out, jumping up at me. I winced as I tried to stroke his head. My neck and shoulder were feeling stiff now. I imagine I must've jarred them when I fell. Quinn surveyed the back of my head.

'No stitches but your scalp looks bruised under your parting.'

'How big is it?' He moved my hair and had a good look. My head felt very tender, even though he wasn't actually touching it, just my hair.

'Tennis ball size.'

'Definitely wasn't a tennis ball. But the person wasn't right next to me. So it must've been something long and quite heavy. Probably not a baseball bat. I mean Medalsum only took a glancing blow from that. If I'd got that on the back of the head, I doubt I'd be standing here now.'

'Yeah, you're lucky it's not a lot more serious. Whoever's taking those dogs doesn't mind risking lives. You can't hit someone over the head with a heavy object without being sure the blow or the fall won't kill them. The same with blasting the Bennett dog walker at close range. He could've been blinded or worse.'

'There were at least two of them, I think. I heard one speak. So it's not one rogue individual.'

'Unless it was one person on the phone?'

'Didn't sound like that. Don't ask me why. It just didn't.'

'Okay, so what about the two who you thought were trying to snatch Brownlow at Billingshurst Station?'

'They seemed... a bit well... more half-hearted about it. I mean no one was around until you got there. If they'd been prepared to use violence, they'd have done it.'

'You've reported that incident and given their descriptions to Carmichael?'

'No.'

'Soph... I know you and Gemma don't always see eye to eye...' We were in the van now, heading towards my place.

'She pretty much accused you of being involved, Quinn. Just over that look-a-like van. Is it any wonder I don't confide in her?'

'Gavin and Melissa called me personally to apologise. I said they didn't need to. They'd done Weatherall a service in a way, by making us discover some crooks are using a similar logo. I've put a big notice about it on the front of our website. Basically, saying that if anyone approaches you, saying they're from any animal charity or even the police, and they need to take your dog for whatever reason, refuse to hand it over, until you've verified their credentials with the organisation they say they represent.'

'I let a dog be taken right under my nose,' I said ruefully.

'You were attacked, Sophie! From behind.'

'But I was slack with the Randalls. Instead of inspecting their property, I just sat around like a star-stuck kid listening to their showbiz anecdotes and scoffing their food. The poor little dog was grabbed while I was sitting in an armchair having coffee.'

'You weren't to know.'

'It's my job to know, Quinn. And I didn't do it. I should've given them security advice on arrival. I should've clocked that flipping cat door and alerted them to the dangers.'

'You can't protect every dog.'

'Quinn - I couldn't even protect Brownlow.'

Quinn slept on the sofa, as he didn't want his phone waking me if it rang to alert him to a pet or wildlife emergency. Inevitably, on the few nights we've managed to spend together over the last few years, that has happened on nearly every occasion. I always smile in those TV dramas where the cop or detective's spouse is on at them for working an all-nighter or being called out. You'd have thought he or she would have realised what the partner's job entails before getting involved. I can't imagine anyone telling a chef 'you always come home reeking of food' or a vicar 'we never get a Sunday to ourselves!' Quinn and I don't stress about this kind of stuff. If he's called out, it's because at that moment an animal needs him more than I do, and the same applies if it's the other way around.

All the same, in the bedroom with Brownlow sleeping beside me, and a couple of paracetamols calming my still throbbing head, I couldn't help scrolling my phone. I added Gavin and Melissa's appeals for news on Bianca to my own socials and forwarded it to all my contacts. I discovered a recent message from Belle in reply to mine, saying she and Shortcake had left the Let Dogs Be Dogs rally when things had started to get a little heated with the police wanting people to move along. It had been all over by around four o'clock, however. She mentioned a guy called Harris, who was the man from the pedalo, being manhandled by the police, as I'd seen on the posted video. They had threatened him with arrest for obstruction, but eventually he hadn't been charged anything, perhaps according to Belle, because his sister was actually an MP. Both he and his Border Terrier were okay. Belle wasn't sure that she'd attend another march as the events at the end had rather put her off, but Let Dogs Be Dogs were planning to have some fundraising stalls at public events and she thought she might get involved in that side of things instead.

The next message was from Rouki Bennett. She had forwarded a dashcam shot of a van – it was the one with the fake logo we'd been looking for. One of her followers had spotted it passing them and grabbed a quick shot with his phone and sent it to Rouki. It was a bigger van than Quinn's and the number plate was partially visible, in terms of the fact that you could make out a couple of the first letters quite clearly. I sent it on to Carmichael to check out in case Rouki hadn't yet shown it to the police. The van had been snapped in the Lewes area the previous day, so it was possible it had been used in the theft of Bianca from the Randalls and the abduction of Brownlow. Whether Brownlow had escaped from the dognappers or whether, upon discovering he was a mongrel and a very distinctive looking one at that, they'd chosen to callously dump him, I had no way of knowing. Of course, Brownlow might've been released by the thieves for a different reason. Bianca was a TV star and Tasha, Mr Merrytrees and Princess Champignon had celebrity owners. If there was a collector out there willing to pay top money for famous dogs, Brownlow, despite our healthy number of followers, was certainly not 'A' list.

Continuing to scan my most recent messages I noted that Sandrine of Le Chien Perdu had sent me two covertly taken photos of blue-grey Staffies her members had spotted in Dieppe. To my eye, either could have been Tasha. I sent them on to Medalsum, who would certainly be able to ID his own dog.

The rising breeze threw a squall of rain at the window. Prickling with goose bumps, I tugged at the duvet, but Brownlow's weight stopped me from being able to bring it up around my shoulders. He's always such a bedcover hogger. On that occasion though, I just felt grateful he was there at all, and angry at those who had risked his life by letting him free in an area he didn't know in the middle of the night. Snoring peacefully though he was, he must've been very frightened and bewildered indeed at the time. As the rain outside grew heavier and the wind continued to rise, an image forming in my mind of a delicate Chihuahua in a dinghy crossing the choppy sea. I got up and wandered into the sitting room. Quinn was asleep under the sofa's throw. He'd put all the files and other junk that had been occupying its cushions in very tidy piles on the floor. He's methodical and neat where I'm messy and chaotic. Opposites do attract they say. 'Quinn...' He muttered something that didn't sound very polite but didn't wake.

'Quinn,' I said more loudly, 'I think we ought to go to Newhaven.'

'Wha... what?'

'We need to go to Newhaven tonight. They might be taking Bianca over to France.'

'In this weather?'

'It's only breezy... well and raining admittedly. But it's not like 'The Perfect Storm' or anything.'

'You can't go out again, Soph. Not tonight.'

'But...'

'They told you not to drive as you have a concussion, and I'm not going out on some wild goose chase. If they were taking the dog abroad, they might've already set off. Besides, as you said before, with a dinghy they could launch from almost anywhere.'

'I know, but the harbour or nearby beach is still the most likely, given that the first dinghy was stolen from a Newhaven address only a few streets in from the coast.'

'Sophie?'

'Yeah?'

'Go back to bed.'

Reluctantly back under the duvet, I rang Sandrine. She said something very grumpy in French, so I imagined I'd woken her up as well.

'There's a little Chihuahua called Bianca and I'm afraid she might be smuggled across the channel tonight.'

'No, not tonight, I think. There is a blockade. At every port. The fishermen are striking. Anyone coming over is risking attention. Plus, the weather in La Manche is very bad.' I noticed she didn't call it the English Channel, even though she was speaking English.

'Je suis desole de vous avoir reveille.'

'All part of the service, honey,' she cackled throatily. 'Bon nuit. Jusqu'a ce que nous nous rencontrions a nouveau.'

'Night, Sandrine,' I said, 'and whatever else you said too.'

I put my ear jacks in and played the latest shipping forecast. For 'Wight' and 'Dover', it was wind south to southwest 5 to 7. Sea state was moderate, occasionally rough. Visibility good, occasionally poor. If I'd been taking a dinghy out, I'd want the sea state to be 'slight,' but then I always chucked up on ferry crossings. For all I knew the dog thieves and possibly smugglers were veterans of the sea. Certainly, after my run in with them in the woods, I knew they were organised and ruthless. A hand reached over and took my phone.

'I'm leaving it in the lounge. Get some sleep,' said Quinn.

The scalp at the back of my head was a mixture of purples, blues and yellows. I checked it myself using a hand mirror in front of the bathroom one.

'Worse than last night or better?' I asked Quinn.

'Worse. But that's what bruises do. More importantly how does it feel?'

'Well, I don't have a headache… Tender scalp I can live with.'

'Witch hazel.'

'Not sure I can put it on my head. It'll make my hair really pong?' He laughed.

'It's only me and Brownlow who'll be in the van with you and we're not fussed. I'll collect your car later on, by the way. Presumably it's still at the Randall's place.'

'Yeah, it's not like anyone'll nick it.' I said.

'Well then, as the weather's improved a bit and the French fishing blockade appears to be over, shall we take a ride along the coast before the morning rush hour begins?'

'Let's do that. I'll bring my drone.' Quinn got the box down from the top of the wardrobe.

'Batteries charged, are they?'

'Of course.' In fact, it was pure luck they were, as I'd been preparing to use it in the hunt for Gregory the cat, before his latest return had, for now at least, resolved the case. As well as my drone, I fetched my binoculars and put Brownlow's waterproof coat on, as it was still drizzly and grey. Quinn made a Thermos of coffee and packed a packet of Rich Teas for us, as well as some dog biscuits.

We started by driving over to Shoreham Beach, where it's easy to park and you can scan the coast from Worthing Pier to Brighton Palace Pier. There's a telescope, which is actually free to use, so Quinn used that whilst I squinted through the binoculars. We were standing on the walkway that allows wheelchairs and baby buggies to access the shingle. There were lots of dog-walkers taking their pets for a walk before work, some turning it into a jog too. Visibility wasn't crystal clear, but it was good enough to let us see the wind farm, a couple of trawlers and a dredger out at sea. As we watched, another fishing boat emerged from the harbour. We zoomed in from our vantage point, looking for any suspicious activity, but the crew could've been fishermen from central casting. I know we're supposed to call them 'fishers' now as there are women and trans people who fish, but these were guys of the strictly Captain Birdseye variety, all oilskins and grizzled beards. I'm not saying that should've given them immunity to suspicion in terms of dog smuggling, but they did genuinely look like they were putting to sea for the purpose of not Letting Fish Be Fish for much longer.

'Fancy doing any droning here?' said Quinn. Since I had taken the drone flying course, he had referred to my using my little remote-control copter as 'droning' – making it sound like I was droning on. I'm pretty sure 'droning' it isn't a verb for flying a drone, at least not yet. That probably meant he was being slightly sarcastic in a way he does when he isn't entirely sure of the merits of a course of action. Quinn's possible scepticism was enough to, despite the still rather breezy conditions, make me decide to put the drone up and put it through its paces. My weather app told me the wind speed was around ten miles an hour, which its instruction leaflet insisted it should be able to cope with. With that in mind, I set it down on the shingle and stood well back before making a vertical take-off. It zoomed away out over the sea, sending live pictures back to my laptop. 'If it crash lands in the drink, you do know we've no way of retrieving it?'

'It's why I learnt to fly it properly,' I snapped back. The course had been a revelation, as had the people on it. There had been a would-be wildlife camerawoman and an architect, keen to get an aerial view of would-be development sites. Then there was the guy who said it was just a hobby, but who we all pretty much knew was a spy, and a woman in her sixties who was upfront and honest about the fact she was an eco-warrior and wanted to use her drone to cause some unspecified disruption. The guy we knew was a spy spent most of the course trying to befriend her and find out her plans. He did though warn her of the dangers and penalties of using a drone anywhere near an airfield. He seemed to know an awful lot about the subject including 'anti-drone technology'. The eco-warrior was no fool and enquired how he knew all of this stuff.

'Just must've read it somewhere,' he muttered.

'Course he did,' winked the architect.

Unfortunately, although I managed not to make a landing in the briny, my first drone flight on the Bennett-Medalsum-Randall case went a bit like that old song we used to sing at nursery school about a sailor who went to sea, sea, sea. Fortunately, it wasn't the bottom of the deep, blue sea I saw, but the top of it, waves and more waves, enlivened by the odd piece of kelp or driftwood. It wasn't blue either, but a dreary grey. I had to constantly battle with the drone too, to stop the wind knocking it off course. I executed a perfect landing on the shingle, which with Quinn looking on was a relief. My drone might not exactly impress him as the nifty bit of kit it was, but at least I'd proved myself well able to handle it. It wouldn't have cost him much to say 'well done' or commented favourably on my piloting skill. Quinn though merely opened the Rich Teas and handed me one. I supposed I would have to make do with that.

'Above Brighton Marina for our next vantage point?' I nodded. From there we could see everything from the row upon row of moored yachts back to the east side of the Palace Pier. It had started to rain again, and that meant the drone's camera lens would be unlikely to show us anything useful. We'd have to rely on binoculars. If there was anything going on down among the yachts, we could always take a closer look. With the rain driving into our faces and blurring the binoculars, we soon retreated into the van for the solace of coffee and Rich Teas. Someone rang from Weatherall, unable to find the daily weight lists for the vet. Young animals that were being reared were weighed daily as well as some of those that were unwell. Quinn directed his volunteer to drawer three of the filing cabinet. The only new arrivals were a couple of gerbils, which had been left in a plastic fish tank outside the gate. Quinn said he'd only had a request for gerbils a couple of days before and had to tell the person wanting them that the sanctuary hadn't any at present. It didn't surprise me, him being as organised as he is, that he knew exactly where his volunteer might find the gerbil fan's contact details.

Quinn had just come off the phone when 'Who Let the Dogs Out' started its familiar refrain. I really would have to change that ringtone. I'd started to find it less than amusing.

'Gorrage, its Carmichael. We've lost a police dog.'

'When you say lost…'

'Stolen. Stolen, it looks like,' she growled. I asked for more details, but Carmichael said brusquely that she'd rather talk face to face. To be honest, I was a little surprised about her even letting me know. I thought the first I'd know of something like a police dog being nicked was in the media. Carmichael asked me to come to Brighton police station, 'if you're recovered enough'. I said I was. Quinn would drop me off then carry on towards Newhaven with the boat scout, checking out Eastbourne Marina on the way.

Carmichael met me at the main doors of Brighton police station and took us upstairs to a large open plan office. It was an ugly building, dating from the 1960s or 70s.

'Are you partially based at this hot desk now?' I enquired, 'Brighton seems a bit urban for the rural crime team.'

'Sit,' she snapped, so sharply that Brownlow immediately obeyed, even though the command wasn't aimed at him.

Carmichael sat beside me and turned a computer screen to show a photograph of the dog – a black and tan German Shepherd.

'Oh Gosh – I was expecting it to be one of the sniffers, a Lab or Springer.'

'Why?'

'Because they're the ones that are mostly taken – for breeding or selling on. Sheps aren't so popular currently. I mean they still have a fan base but a Spaniel or a Golden Lab would probably be worth more. Also, a German Shepherds not an easy steal – a formidably trained animal and the breed is known for its loud bark.' I looked up. Carmichael had taken out her notebook and was taking this down.

'Can you give me a few more details?' I asked hopefully. Carmichael sighed, ran her hand through her hair.

'Okay. It was at Burgess Hill.'

'Right. On your rural patch.' She gave a tiny nod. Clearly, she had been assigned to do something about it. 'Taken while working or off duty?'

'From the kennel in the handler's garden, sometime after midnight.'

'Did the dog bark?'

'Apparently not.'

'Unusual for a police dog.'

'And this dog in particular. She's called Rita. Been with Sgt Hasan for six years. He was shocked someone could've broken into her kennel and taken her. She wouldn't have gone quietly or willingly.'

'Yet she did.'

'So it seems. They used bolt cutters to reach her. So had gone equipped for the job. Premeditated.' I nodded. I'd guessed this much.

'At least she looks like a huge dog. That's a good thing.'

'Oh, in what way?' Carmichael looked at me quizzically.

'I'm guessing, unless she was somehow drugged, she was led rather than carried away. Not easy to carry a dog that size any distance. Like with Brownlow. I look at those 'dogs must be carried' signs on escalators, and know we need to take the lift or the stairs.' She wasn't amused. 'The thing is though, Gem, with a big dog that can't be carried far, it makes it easier to get a good scent. Presumably though, you're going to deal with it in-house?'

'Well…' Carmichael didn't look too happy at what she was about to say. 'My guv'nor did suggest we brought you in on this one. In a strictly limited capacity of course.' I wondered idly if the police would be willing to reveal their use of Brownlow and myself publicly. It would make a nice endorsement on our website.

I told Carmichael I didn't have my car, as Quinn had been going to drive me over to Polegate to fetch it. She said she'd take us up to Burgess Hill in her van. 'You still don't look too good,' she said as we set off. It wasn't an expression of concern, just her usual brand of not so passive aggression.

'Those look like bags for life under your own eyes, Gem. Long night in the Ginger Pig?' I wasn't being especially offensive. That is actually PC Carmichael's favourite local.

'FYI: I'm currently working a double shift, Ms Gorrage. While you were all safely tucked up in bed, I was attending a suspected deer lamping incident in Tilgate Forest and preventing poaching with ferrets on private land near Bramber.'

'Vans…' I mused. 'If you or the area cars spot a van parked up on a country road at night, I expect you start to suspect wrongdoing? At the very least you do a number check.'

'So?'

'Having a logo on the van – saying it's an animal rescue, parcel deliver, posh nosh provider whatever – that would be less likely to draw your suspicion?'

'Normally. Though we've now circulated the photo of the bogus animal welfare logo.'

'It's cheap and easy to get your vinyl decals replaced with something else. Quick and easy to change. Doesn't even damage the van.'

'Meaning you could even use a different hire vehicle each time too,' Gemma nodded, seeing where this was going. Then her eyes narrowed. 'They're one step ahead for now, but it's not gonna stay that way for long.'

'You're not the only one wanting to end this now,' I told her. 'After they abandoned Brownlow on a roadside…'

'Not dog lovers. Not animal lovers of any sort,' she said. I agreed.

'So tell me,' Gemma said, as we passed the sign telling us to drive carefully through the Burgess Hill, 'what you know about Let Dogs Be Dogs?'

'Not a lot to be honest.' Gemma pulled in to park in a leafy street of semi-detached houses.

'Only you were on their London march yesterday morning, I believe?'

'Yes, I was. But who told you that?'

'I've looked at the footage posted on their Twitter account. I recognised you despite the cap. Brownlow is unmistakable. So, are you part of their organisation or do you just sympathise with their ideals?'

'Gemma, you're sounding a bit like you want to sign me up to the 'Prevent' programme. LDBD aren't a banned organisation, and so far, I've not discovered anything particular sinister about them. I went along because I was curious more than anything. But no, I can hardly claim to be a member. I do after all have a working dog, which seems to be the thing they're campaigning against.'

'So you are investigating them, Sophie?' She only used my first name once in a blue moon. It was slightly less hostile than her usual way of addressing me, didn't mean we were becoming Cagney and Lacey or anything like that.

'Not really. I couldn't find much to investigate. I didn't even get to meet the organisers. I'm not even sure they were there. The people I talked to all seemed very nice and normal.' We got out the car and I put Brownlow on his lead. Carmichael still wanted to discuss Let Dogs Be Dogs.

'The usual 'turn up at any protest leftie student or eco types, were they?'

'No. Mostly middle-class Metropolitan dog owners in Boden cagoules, eating blueberry birchers in Battersea Park before setting out.'

Sergeant Hasan came out of his house to meet us and led us down his back garden to the wooden chalet and attached run where Rita had lived.

'Forensics finished here?' Gemma checked before ushering Brownlow and me into the run. I wondered how many times forensics had previously attended a dog theft.

'So how much is a police dog worth?'

'We pay around three thousand pounds for a pup, a fully police-trained German Shepherd like Rita is worth ten thousand upwards.' That was an impressive figure.

'And could I, if I wanted, buy a fully trained police dog?'

'Possibly. A few regional police forces train dogs and sell them.' This was news even to me.

'Sell them to who?'

'Other governments, private security firms and individuals.' As we talked, I was letting Brownlow sniff around in Rita's enclosure. Her bed looked very comfortable.

'She doesn't always sleep out here. Some nights we let her stay in the house, depending on what we're doing, and my shifts. She's treated as a member of the family.'

'Presumably Rita will have had real odour training?' I asked.

'Yes. She's a trained search dog.'

'And not the only one in the area surely. So why call us in?'

'They can't spare the search dogs this morning. There's an elderly man gone missing from a care home at Lewes, so all our dogs are currently over there,' Sergeant Hasan replied. 'And as you know with scenting, time is of the essence.' Brownlow had sniffed around Rita's pen and was impatient to lead us on. With no more ado we all duly followed him.

I had expected Brownlow to take us back up the garden path and out the side gate into the street. Instead, nose to the ground he was leading us the other way.

'That's slightly unexpected,' I admitted. I would've thought they'd have taken her straight out the front, to a waiting vehicle. It's the quickest route.'

'There's CCTV back and front.'

'I know, I clocked it,' I said. I sensed the dog handler was observing Brownlow and me with critical eyes. I was a self-taught trainer; with a dog I'd trained myself. The police had German Shepherds, Springers, Malinoises etc. I was a quirky looking civilian with questionable dress sense, accompanied by a shaggy mongrel. I could see why they'd be sceptical. As I'd told Rouki Bennett though, Brownlow in an expert in what he does. He doesn't apprehend criminals, manage crowds, or search for drugs or explosives. His focus is completely on following an animal trail and as a specialist in one field, like an elite Olympian, he excels.

'The thief probably took her this way to keep his or her back to the camera,' said Sergeant Hasan. We were in a narrow alley now behind the back gardens.

'Yes, I expect we'll come out somewhere they could park, away from your property.'

'You pinpoint where they were parked, and we can get on with looking for witnesses and seeing if any other domestic cameras overlooked the spot.' The alley made a right-angled turn and emerged a little further up the same street. Brownlow walked along for a moment and then stopped to sniff close to the kerb, circling back on himself then walking to the garden wall behind and sniffing that.

'Does he need a pee break?' I glared at Carmichael.

'Possibly Rita had a quick squat here. If she was with an unfamiliar person, it's quite likely nerves would have made her try to pass water. They may not have let her of course.'

'I still don't fully get this,' Sergeant Hasan said. 'She was not a meek and mild dog. I find it hard to believe she would've gone willingly and without protest.'

'The thief or thieves definitely knows dogs very well.'

'A dog whisperer? Someone who has a lot of experience with larger breeds?' Carmichael mused. 'Someone with a dog handling background, maybe in their job? Police, border force, military…'

'I wouldn't disagree,' I said. 'I could get my own dog out and into a van silently, but I wouldn't feel at all confident at doing so with a police dog. I would expect lots of barking – at the very least.'

'Rita is a barker,' Sgt Hasan confirmed, 'more than many, I'd say. I mean she'd give voice when you wanted her to, and when you didn't either.'

'Someone took Ms Gorrage's dog here earlier yesterday evening. Different circumstances. She was with the dog and knocked unconscious,' Carmichael told Sgt Hasan. 'But he either gave them the slip or was dumped a little later.'

'Uninjured or traumatised? That's something. But what's he like with strangers?'

'Pretty soft actually. I would've hoped he'd have stuck up for me or defended himself, but I've no idea what happened. He heard my assailant alright. But that's all I know.'

'Apart from the fact it sounded like a man. Possibly speaking to a second person,' Carmichael added.

'Why do you think they let him go?'

'Probably because unlike Rita, he's all but worthless,' Carmichael answered. I glared at her.

'Worthless, is he? Well, we'll see what your guv'nor says about that when we put in our expenses.'

Brownlow now waited at the kerb and looked back at me to be permitted to cross the road. Further down the street was a large lime tree, which had grown up partially obscuring the streetlamp. It made sense when Brownlow stopped there. It was the end of the scent trail. I gave him a treat.

'Good dog.' Sergeant Hasan scratches his ears. 'That's given us exactly what we needed from a tracker dog.'

'I'm just sorry there's not more we can do at present.'

'There might be,' PC Carmichael replied. Sergeant Hasan and I both looked at her. 'I mean in terms of it linking to your other three cases. I checked in with Ms. Bennett earlier and she confirmed she has now hired you. As I believe have the Randalls who are animal trainers and the rapper Medalsum.'

'You think Rita's dognapping is related?'

'Don't you?'

'Not sure yet,' I said. 'They were all small breeds. Well unless you count them temporarily taking Brownlow.' Sergeant Hasan was filming the street with his phone. 'And there's a TV or celebrity connection with the other three cases,' I added.

'Stealing a police dog is still reasonably high profile,' Sergeant Hasan said. 'You're going to make the headlines by doing it. In fact, two papers and the regional BBC news have already been in touch. We've put them off coming down until you're done, so as not to corrupt the odour trail, but we'll give them the full story later in case a member of the public saw something or recognises Rita.'

'The profiles of all the dogs, including Rita, make people more likely to be looking out for them or report sightings.' I think Carmichael was thinking aloud rather than trying to win an award for stating the obvious. 'Ms Gorrage here thinks they may be being taken abroad. I'm going to look into where dogs such as these fetch the highest prices on the continent. I'm guessing possibly Paris.'

'I've colleagues in France already reporting possible sightings,' I said, adding that unfortunately Medalsum had viewed the photos of Staffordshire Bull Terriers that Le Chien Perdu had sent, and neither was his dog, Tasha.

'I think we should definitely keep liaising on this one,' Sgt Hasan said. Not one to contradict a superior, Carmichael didn't say a word, but I was pretty sure this was anything but music to her ears.

Chapter Seven

I'd been hoping to get a lift home with Carmichael, but she had a call about some beehives that were in the process of being stolen and went off to deal with that, leaving Brownlow and me to make our own way home. At the station, I spotted that a train going to Eastbourne via Polegate was due in ten minutes. At least that would give me a chance to collect the Clio myself, if Quinn hadn't already done so. Quinn answered his mobile, apologising for the mouthful of biscuit. He hadn't, as I'd guessed, got as far as Polegate to pick up my car. He was at Newhaven, watching the Dieppe ferry depart. So far, he hadn't found anything to report there. He had however been approached by a member of the public, with an interesting story, back on the cliffs above Brighton Marina. The woman lived in a flat just behind Brighton seafront. She'd approached Quinn because she'd seen his van parked up and wanted to ask his advice. Twice, when taking her Weimaraner for a late-night run on the beach, she'd seen the same man, walking a dog. That wouldn't have been odd in itself but the thing she'd noticed was that both times it was a different dog. The first time it was a Staffie, the second a Chihuahua. I sat up straight on my station bench at that. She had wondered if maybe one of the dogs wasn't his and the explanation was simply that he was walking it for someone else. Perhaps, she'd reasoned, this dog didn't get on with his own dog, so they had to be exercised separately. She had also wondered if maybe he was a professional dog-walker, but she used one of those services herself, and they didn't work nights. She'd then read a news story about the spiralling increase in dog thefts, though not one that specifically mentioned the cases Brownlow and I were investigating.

'A Staffie and a Chihuahua – did she say what colour?'

'The Staffie she wasn't sure. She was relying on the streetlights on the prom. Probably greyish. The Chihuahua was white.'

'So why did she approach you?'

'My natural charm and charisma? No seriously, Soph, she said it was one of those situations where she didn't know if what she'd seen was suspicious or not. Like I said, she didn't know about the specific thefts of Tasha and Bianca, but just found the way the guy was hanging about in the same spot on two nights in the same week slightly suspicious.'

'The last time being last night with the white Chihuahua?'

'Yes. About eleven pm. And she only really thought about the situation when she got home the second time. It was the fact that both times the guy was standing there with the dogs, as if he was waiting for something or someone. Rather than walking them. She didn't know if it was something she should report to the police, the RSPCA or someone. That's what she said. She thought the police wouldn't take her seriously.'

'Probably would now they've lost a dog themselves.'

'She'd been going to see if she could email the RSPCA, but then saw my van and thought since it's an animal charity she'd ask my advice, see if I'd heard of any kind of suspicious activity.'

'Sounds like you were just in the right place at the right time. You did take her details in case I need to talk to her?'

'Naturally.'

'You know I hate it when it's you who make an important breakthrough, rather than me.'

'I do! I love it! Brings out my competitive streak.'

'Not that we know it is a breakthrough yet.'

'Oh come on, Soph. A Staffie and a Chihuahua...?'

'So it looks like we'll be on a Brighton beach stake-out tonight.'

'You will be. Some of us are on call, babe. I can't keep asking volunteers to cover my shifts, particularly the anti-social ones. In fact, I need to get back to Weatherall now. I've an owl coming in.'

I phoned Carmichael as I had promised to keep updated on developments. She answered but there was a loud buzzing on the line, and I couldn't hear her.

'Hello? Something's wrong with your phone. Too near your radio maybe?'

'It's bees!'

'It's what?'

'Hives!'

'Hives, yeah I get this kind of rash.' The penny dropped. 'Oh, beehives, stolen beehives, I remember. You've recovered them – clever you.' I told her about the man on the beach and the possibility he might be waiting there with a police dog that very evening. Carmichael swore loudly. 'I thought you'd be pleased to receive this kind of information.'

'Just been stung! I'll call you back.'

Carmichael did indeed ring me back a little later, to tell me to send her the details of the exact time and location. She would try to be there. I reminded her it was several miles of beach we'd be watching. I was hoping that several police units at least would join us, being as we were trying to prevent a police dog being smuggled out of the country.

'I've asked, but we're mounting a large-scale op tonight elsewhere involving a number of locations, so my guv can't spare anyone.'

'Seriously?'

'It's a series of coordinated raids and they're taking TV cameras along to various premises across the county. I can't tell you any more.

'If it's not about animals, it's of no interest to me. You're still coming though, Gemma?'

'I hope to.'

I sensed Gemma really did want to be involved if she could and was taking one of my tip-offs seriously for once. Two women and one dog could not really mount this operation alone. My drone was all but useless at night, and we had a long area of beach to keep an eye on. More eyes definitely needed to be on the waves. If it was just Gemma and me, if the smuggler saw us looking on, and suspected we might be watching him, he could easily move further along the beach. If we followed, it would certainly give our intentions away before we could catch him in the act and lead to the arrest of more of his gang. It must after all be a gang if he was waiting for a boat.

The problem with Brighton beach is the coast road and prom rise up from Hove on a gentle gradient of cliff, until they are a considerable distance above sea level. Steps and ramps at various points access the beach, but there are plenty of doorways, awnings and other places on the lower level where one can avoid the gaze of those on the prom above.

Ideally there needed to be a group of us, all out of vehicles, skulking around on the lower level, or perhaps at the flatter Hove end, hiding behind the long row of beach huts. There isn't a single vantage point, well apart from the i360 viewing platform, and that would be closed. Even if we were able to commandeer it for our operation, the glass pod descended so slowly that the suspect could be halfway to France before we got our feet back on the ground. A room upstairs in the Grand Hotel would be a stylish way to look below, but again the view it would afford would, due to the aforementioned geography, be severely limited. I haven't actually stayed at the Grand Hotel in case you wonder. It's not just the money – outside of emergencies, nobody stays at a hotel a few miles away from their home, do they?

Ordinarily, when I need extra bodies for a pet search, I put out a public call, but this could've easily alerted the dog smugglers to my intentions. Instead, I contacted Skyla, Carl, Melissa and Belle. Skyla said she and Jamal would catch the train down and would head immediately over to their mum's office, to scrounge the fare off her. Carl also answered promptly, telling me I could rely on him and Jack. 'Maybe you should also let Rouki know?' he added. I said I hadn't because I was a little worried she might alert her followers. He said he thought she was slightly more sensible than that. I was sure I heard Jack say 'ha!' to that in the background. Carl added that he'd call her himself, but that it would probably sound better coming from me. She tended to speak to him like he was in his words 'the hired help' and he wasn't particularly wanting to revisit their working relationship. I said that was fine, I'd call her. He had no objections to being involved in the surveillance operation with her, though he'd prefer to be in a different search group if possible. That could, I said, be arranged.

Alex the PA answered Rouki Bennett's phone. Rouki was currently filming, but she'd relay my message to her when she was next on a break. I collected the car. Melissa and Gavin were also out on a film set, but by then I'd already had a voicemail from Melissa saying she and Gavin would be free to help us with our nocturnal beach vigil. Belle was sorry she and Shortcake couldn't join us as she'd promised to visit an ailing aunt in Luton. If the beach watch stretched to a second evening, then she'd come along after work, again like Skyla and Jamal, travelling down from London. She said she'd just ordered the brand new 'Let Dogs Be Dogs' coat for Shortcake. It would be perfect for keeping him warm and dry on the beach at night. She thought Jonas the merchandise guy had already made some in Brownlow's size as there was a photo of his own Retriever modelling it.

She offered to order one for Brownlow, but he has a hi-viz jacket with the words 'pet detection dog' on it, so I wasn't sure it was something he needed. I told Belle to keep our operation secret, but she immediately asked if she could let the LDBD What's App group know. 'Some of them lived nearer to or in Sussex, and they might be willing to help.' I considered this, as from what I'd seen of the LDBD crowd, they'd seemed a nice bunch, and unlikely to be connected to the dog theft perpetrators. However, I was still wary about sharing the information that publicly. Conceivably it might only take one person in the WhatsApp group to, in a well-meaning way, publicly mention what we were doing, and the information might be widely shared, or even picked up by a journalist. I needed my surveillance to be at least as professional and reliable as a police operation. This was vital as the team would involve one police officer that didn't exactly respect our methods in the first place. Also, I had to consider the fact that the dog we were seeking to rescue was the property of the local force. The reputations of Brownlow and me were definitely on the line. With this in mind, I told Belle to keep the information to herself. I knew I could trust her to do that. I also, in truth, had slight reservations about LDBD involvement, when we were using one working dog to help find another. At the march there had been disapproval voiced, albeit quite mild, polite disapproval, at the use of canines by law enforcement and the military. Perhaps a few of the group's members might even imagine Rita needed rescuing from the police as much as the kidnappers.

I allowed both Brownlow and myself an afternoon siesta. Quinn had said the dog walker had spotted the suspicious activity around eleven pm, which according to my online tidal information had been approaching high tide. Despite living on the Sussex Coast, I am not actually in any way an expert on tides, or on anything nautical come to that. I just figured that if a boat were waiting to whisk dogs off to the continent, it would probably be at high tide. BBC Weather provides tidal information for Brighton. The previous night's high tide had been 11:19 pm, and on this evening it would be 11:51. The night after, it would be around half an hour later again. I assumed a dognapper wouldn't want to risk running aground in a shallow sea, so would probably adjust their time of arrival accordingly. However, as I said, I know nothing about maritime matters. Even that pedalo the guy was enjoying on the Battersea Park lake involved a little too much water for my tastes. Brownlow likes to go jumping into the sea or sometimes the river Adur at Shoreham on our walks, cheerfully splashing around before rushing out to shake himself all over me. Like me though, he doesn't really go in for swimming. I don't think I've ever seen him go in deep enough for that kind of doggy paddle.

I was rudely awakened from my slumber by the Baha Men barking. As I fumbled blearily to answer the call, I resolved to finally get around to changing that ruddy tune. What had been hilarious three years ago when I'd bought the phone was seriously beginning to grate on me. Perhaps a piece of music by Bach might be a subtler alternative.

'We need a boat.' Carmichael got straight down to business without so much as a 'hello'. 'Do you know anyone?'

Presumably she meant did I know anyone with a boat, rather than more generally, though she did make it sound like I was Sophie-No-Mates. I said I'd assumed there might be a police launch or perhaps the rescue service volunteers or the coastguard might be willing to help if the request came from her. She snapped that those services were there for 'genuine emergencies'. It wasn't as if I'd suggested launching the lifeboat or asked for an aircraft carrier. This was hardly 'Sink the Bismarck.' I think she was just miffed that she didn't have the authority to request official assistance. As it was most of her fellow officers were going to be involved in the secret operation that was being filmed by a number of news crews. I know the TV stations like showing shouty officers putting door-smashers to dramatic use, but it wasn't something that would make the nation's dog owners sleep any easier. Filming us going out on a police boat to look for pet smugglers would in my opinion have been far more worthy of airtime.

I needed to obtain a boat and someone to pilot it from somewhere. I thought of David at Newhaven, but his boat was in very dry dock in his back garden and judging by the ivy growing up the wheelhouse, it had been like that for some considerable time. Even if he was willing to get involved, I had serious doubts about his craft being seaworthy.

I could imagine Carmichael's gloating face if a boat I hired for our first marine operation started taking in water, let alone went the full 'Titanic'. I wondered instead about the friendly guy I'd chatted to with a boat in Brighton marina. I wish I'd taken his details at the time. For all I knew he'd now set sail and was cruising around the coast. The one thing I couldn't do was tell Carmichael my contacts in the yachting set were nil. True she was in no position to feel superior about that, but this was mine and Brownlow's operation. It might not involve door smashers and shouting, but we were the ones running the show, and there was zero chance of PC Gemma Carmichael taking it over. So I told a fib. I told Carmichael,

'Yes, I have contacts in the boating world. Leave it with me. I'll have one standing by this evening.'

Brownlow and I immediately drove down to Brighton Marina. Out on the jetties, I recognised the cabin cruiser belonging to the sailor I'd talked to previously but unfortunately, he wasn't onboard. It's unfortunate that boats rarely display any kind of useful contact details. I suppose it's understandable. They're not like vans. They're mainly leisure craft unless they're used for fishing. You'd have to live somewhere like Venice for your plumber or electrician to arrive by this kind of craft. We wandered up and down the boardwalks, in the hope of some inspiration. After about twenty minutes, I spotted movement on a jetty adjacent to the one we were checking out, and we hurried over. A woman was touching up the paintwork on a modestly proportioned motorboat that was dwarfed by the surrounding luxury cabin cruisers. She had grey, curly hair tied back from her face with a scarf and wore a blue and white striped Breton top and red jeans. As we approached, a small dog yapped and appeared from the cabin. It was a Dandie Dinmont, a breed of terrier you don't see every day. My terrier expert friend Dr Gomez Dwight once told me the breed got its unusual name from a character in a book by Sir Walter Scott. The boat though was called the Dandelion, which sounded as if it might have been named after the dog breed, unless of course the owner had a fondness for common garden weeds.

I called out to wish the boat owner a good afternoon, being careful to wait until she had removed her brush from the boat's surface. It's never a good idea to startle someone who is painting, particularly if you're intending to ask them for a rather large favour. An acknowledgement that I'd spotted the connection between her boat name and her rare breed of terrier was all it took for Brownlow and me to be invited aboard. Annie was a retired solicitor and listened with interest to my tale of stolen dogs and the possibility they were being smuggled to France. She was keen to help if she could but stressed the fact it involved putting to sea at night, did add complications. These seemed chiefly to involve navigation lights. She had them but hadn't used them for years and would need to check the bulbs and wiring. She was bandying around terms like 'masthead' and 'stern light'. I just nodded and tried to look like I understood. I think she said something about red on the port side and green on the starboard, but I can't swear to it. I was only interested in knowing if she thought her craft could be shipshape and ready to put to sea by eleven pm. Annie was becoming enthusiastic now. 'It would be an adventure!' she declared, making me think of posh schoolgirls escaping from a dorm. If she had any problems with her lights, she had a number of boating 'pals' with names like 'Foggs' and 'Weasel' who she could call. For all I knew they were fellow female boat owners, but through lack of imagination I found myself picturing Captain Birdseye or Pugwash types, shouting 'splice the main-brace' or even less likely 'there she blows!'. Like I said, despite being born and still living on the coast, the ocean remains many, many nautical miles outside of my comfort zone.

Leaving Annie to her light checking, I went in search of a camping and outdoor activity store. With our expense accounts with Medalsum, the animal trainers and Rouki Bennett, I could afford to equip my surveillance team with decent flashlights, emergency alarms and a pair of night vision binoculars. The man in the shop was intrigued enough by my bulk buying to offer to show me something called a multi-spectral imager. I hadn't a clue what it was, but he told me to leave Brownlow tied up by the camping gear and come into the back room of the shop. The store was otherwise empty and as soon as we were in the back room, the man flicked a switch, plunging us into semi-darkness. The large cardboard advertising boards of the window display blocked out most of the natural light from the street beyond. The imager was pressed into my hand. 'Hold it up to your eye.' Suddenly I could see Brownlow very clearly – as clearly as if he was in good light. 'Like to try a thermal imaging device too?'

'Don't mind if I do.' My employers were certainly going to have some expenses to meet. Still, it was worth it if it helped my team of spotters locate the dog smuggler, and I admit, to make PC Gemma Carmichael green with envy. I was willing to bet the police with their budget cuts didn't furnish her with vital equipment like this. Never again would she be able to roll her eyes and sneer at my clients, 'ah, I see you've hired PAW Patrol'. As I put my purchases into the Clio, I'm afraid I went as far as telling Brownlow that we were 'The Canine SAS'. Never one to puncture my ego when it self-inflates to ridiculous dimensions, he just wagged his tail.

I chose a late opening and usually quiet coffee shop, tucked away behind the seafront, for the ten pm rendezvous with my team. I picked a café rather than a pub because I didn't know how old Skyla and Jamal actually were. I rather suspected Jamal at least was under eighteen, and that meant I needed to be seen as a responsible adult. I do actually keep my DBS certificate up to date, so in theory I was legally covered to supervise young people who happened to be minors. My reason for having a Criminal Records check was because Brownlow and I are occasionally asked to go and demonstrate our work to schools and youth groups. Sometimes we're even paid a small fee for our time, and it spreads the knowledge of our work in the community. On one memorable occasion we turned up to a primary school to find we would be sharing the stage with PC Gemma Carmichael, with the subject being 'animal related crime'. Carmichael was asked to speak first, no doubt with the uniform bagging her this honour. She then proceeded to litter her talk with barely disguised jibes about 'well-meaning amateurs' and 'people who advertise in the back of local newspapers'. I resolved to be the better person and let it all wash over me. In my part of the talk, I made no reference to rural crime officers at all. Even when we reached the question-and-answer part of the event, I let Gemma take all the questions. Politely, I waited for the kids to stop raising their hands to speak to her. Then I asked a question of my own. 'So, is it okay, do you think, to call the police if your guinea pig disappears from his or her hutch overnight? Well? Anyone?' Gemma cut in sharply, saying that it was not appropriate to phone the police over a lost small pet.

'But what if it's an emergency?' a little girl piped up. 'A fox could eat a lost guinea pig!' There were general murmurs of agreement on this point. Carmichael muttered something about possibly contacting the local force via their website.

'They might even give you a crime number if you do,' I added sympathetically.

'But will you come out and help?' the girl persisted with her grilling of Carmichael. That child will probably be a campaigning journalist one day. Carmichael had squirmed and tried to explain about being under resourced and extremely busy, but she'd lost the debate and her young audience. As we both headed back to our cars, faint applause following us from the hall, she ended up tripping over the nature garden's log pile in her haste to get away. After the way she turned the air blue in the hearing of the deputy head, I'm not sure she'll be invited back to conduct their next mini-beast safari.

Skyla and Jamal were the first to arrive at the cafe, at around a quarter to ten. With them was their mother, Valerie. Warm and friendly, with a polished appearance and a strong South London accent, she bought a round of coffees. Valerie said that when she heard her kids were heading down to Brighton that late in the evening, she had told them that she was very definitely coming too. 'At least it's not a school night,' she added, directing this at Jamal, who scowled. I thought it best to show her my DBS certificate to let her know everything was above board. Valerie talked about how she and Medalsum had bought Tasha as a puppy, and then he'd promptly gone into the studio to work on an album and left her and the kids to train the puppy. Unlike her ex-husband who'd grown up with dogs, Valerie had never owned one before, but Tasha had quickly found her way into her heart. Although the former Mrs Medalsum was on 'barely speaking terms' with her ex-husband, she was keen to help find Tasha and reunite man and dog. 'He was a bit of a rubbish husband, but great with kids and dogs' she grinned.

As I started to explain my plans for our late evening operation, Jamal was eager to see my new spy gadgets, so we got up to go out to the car. As we did so, Melissa and Gavin arrived, and I introduced them to Valerie and Skyla. They said they'd look out for Rouki and Alex, while I was showing Jamal my night vision binoculars, spectral imager and thermal image camera. While Jamal was examining the tech and gratifyingly appearing very impressed by it, my phone rang. It was Annie. The boat was ready when I was. As we spoke, it became clear she expected me to be the team member who'd be joining her on the boat. I had hoped to ask one of the others to volunteer for this assignment. Belatedly I realised it sounded a bit odd and bad mannered to delegate, when I was the one who had enlisted Annie's help in the first place. In the end I told her I'd be down the marina and ready to put to sea by half past ten, once I'd briefed my team. As I finished the call, I spotted Carl and Jack approaching. They, like Jamal, were eager to peer through the various surveillance devices. Jack volunteered to furtively skulk with Brownlow in a dimly lit doorway further up the street, pretending to be our dog-stealing quarry, while we spied on him with the devices.

The thermal image was quite startling. The hotter parts of man and dog – their heads – glowed red, while Jack's puffa jacket and Brownlow's thick fur kept their bodies a cooler yellow. The downside was that the luminous scarlet head could belong to anybody. This didn't give much in the way of facial recognition. It wouldn't help pick out a suspect in an identity parade. Although they were some twenty metres away up the street, and in a doorway not covered by a streetlamp, the night vision binoculars gave a pretty good view of Jack and Brownlow. Both were identifiable and details such as the logo on Jack's jacket were, though not crisp, defined enough to merit a description. My favourite device however was spectral imager. It gave me clear facial features of both man and dog and their expressions. It recorded video too, which would be great for gathering evidence. It was well worth the exorbitant expense, that in fairness I'd share equally between my three or possibly four client accounts. I wasn't yet sure if the police had officially hired me or not, though I would certainly, if optimistically, be invoicing them for our work on their case so far.

I hope my talk of money doesn't make me sound too mercenary. I am a pet detective to help owners and their animals, rather than profit personally. The expensive kit I had purchased for this case would be used on others, with less well-off owners getting the benefit of a well-equipped service. If Brownlow and I came out of this case, with its VIP clients, with any profit at all, that would soon be spent on a replacement for our Clio and upgrading the computer in our home office. I'm definitely not someone who desires the kind of designer bags or trainers both Valerie and Rouki Bennett were sporting. While both women had selected the correct kind of footwear for a shingle beach, I hoped they were aware of the damage salt and tar can do to even the costliest leather. I was wearing wellies, which I hoped was the correct attire for our boat trip. I suppose I should've checked with Annie, but I didn't want to appear a complete novice.

Jack and Brownlow were walking away from my imager to let me judge the point when they became invisible, when I felt a sharp tap on the shoulder. I knew even without turning it was Carmichael. She does, for some reason, nearly always reek of TCP disinfectant. 'Spotted something?' she hissed.

'Nah, Gem. Just testing the tech while we were waiting for you. Now everyone's here, I'll give my briefing.' My nemmie's angled eyebrows raised at this announcement. I wondered how often in the past, this had been her reaction to some statement of mine. Usually, her cap was crammed too low to be able to see them, but tonight, she wasn't in uniform, so I was treated to a view of her entire face and its gamut of critical, sceptical and downright mocking expressions. I'd told her it was a covert op naturally but had forgotten to spell out that she needed not to stick out like a sore dewclaw on the beach. Fortunately, Carmichael had decided to go smart casual in a pair of boyfriend jeans with a claret leather jacket and a pair of Converse high tops. Perhaps this was the correct attire for a boat trip and my Wellington boots were a massive faux pas, but I had no way of finding out without showing my ignorance.

When I'd mentioned briefing my team, Carmichael had been clearly irked to be reminded that this was not her operation. I suspected she'd rather be out with the door smashers, lifting the lids of unsanitary toilet cisterns to look for packets of crystal meth and gurning for the cameras. I took her in and made the introductions. Rouki Bennett made a pointed remark about how she'd have imagined the police could've sent more than one representative to take part in such an important operation. She might mention it to the Police and Crime Commissioner, who she'd already been in touch with about Mr Merrytrees and Princess Champignon. Carmichael grimaced.

There were few other people, apart from my team, in the coffee shop. A group of noisy, selfie-taking language students were sat in a window seat and a couple of older women were discussing what looked like some kind of creative writing project at a table towards the back. I felt a little exposed addressing the assembled company in front of these strangers. How I wished Brownlow And Gorrage had a spacious office or even a bigger maisonette, situated in a conveniently central location, which I could've turned into a briefing room for the occasion. Still, I had made a few notes on my phone to glance at, and I intended to keep things short and punchy. I could do without the whiteboards and pinboards of the TV detectives. There were twelve of us in total, including Brownlow of course. I've organised larger groups to go out searching for lost pets, but this was the biggest team I'd ever assembled for a specific crime-related incident.

Before I split my group into small teams and allocated areas along the beach for them to watch, I asked for one volunteer to join Annie, Brownlow and myself on the boat. I deliberately avoided PC Carmichael's gaze as I made this announcement, and my heart sank when it was only her voice that spoke up. 'I think there should be a police presence on the water, not just because of the health and safety concerns. You do, I presume, have lifejackets for us?' She said this in a slightly snide way, with the insinuation that I almost certainly would've overlooked something this crucial. In actual fact, she was partially right. I hadn't even thought of something so basic, but Annie had, in conversation, told me she'd enough on board for a crew of four. As it happened there was only going to be three humans and one dog on board, and while a canine life jacket would've certainly been a good idea, if I'd thought of it, I was pretty sure Brownlow would be able to swim ashore in the event of an emergency. We also had, Annie told me, some 'mayday flares', which were fireworks you set off if your boat was in trouble, rather than a fashionable spring trouser. She had showed me the short-wave radio set and let me know that my mobile phone would still work, as we weren't going to be too far offshore. That was a relief, as I needed, as the coordinator, to keep in touch with all of my volunteers on the beach, and as a landlubber I had just sort of imagined that everything would be the same as on land.

Carmichael suggested she travel with Brownlow and me down to Brighton Marina in my Clio. She said it was because her vehicle bearing a police logo might alert our suspect or suspects. I had a feeling however it was more to do with the way she'd noticed Brownlow had shed a few hairs in said vehicle on our trip to Burgess Hill. I gave my briefing, putting my land crew of nine into four teams and allocating each a strip of beach to patrol. They all dutifully signed in to the dedicated WhatsApp group that would keep us all in briefed on any developments. Jack and Carl would be the farthest west, patrolling Hove seafront, Valerie, Skyla and Jamal would be just west of the remains of the West Pier, with Rouki and Alex taking the stretch between that and the Palace Pier. East of the Palace Pier would be Melissa and Gavin, who had the longest stretch to patrol. With this in mind, I'd given them the night vision binoculars. Carmichael and I would take both the thermal and spectral imagers with us on the Dandelion and Brownlow would be coming with us.

I'd felt quite confident aboard our boat while it was still tied to the jetty and the water below was causing only gentle undulations. I'd decided to take no chances with my sea legs once we'd left port however, even before I knew Carmichael was coming along for the ride. I'd bought anti-sickness pills and taken them in the café loo on arrival. I was also wearing anti-sickness bands on both wrists and both ankles. How these worked or even *if* they worked, I wasn't entirely sure, but puking up over the side wasn't a good look for our team leader, even if I managed to plump for whichever direction wouldn't blow my vomit straight back in my face. I'd checked the weather app and the shipping forecast more than once in the previous few hours. Winds were meant to be light and the sea calm. As Annie switched the engine on and we began to move slowly from our moorings, the coffee in my stomach started to slosh from side to side. That was when we weren't even out of the sheltered waters of the Marina. I was hoping Carmichael was feeling the same, or in truth, considerably worse. To my dismay, as she stood beside Annie at the wheel, she started to chat about her childhood sailing club adventures and how she had once considered training as a lifeboat volunteer. It was just my luck.

I sat on the seat at the stern beside Brownlow and tried to distract myself from the up and down motion by looking at my phone. Hardly a sensible idea as it turned out as looking down made me feel even worse than gazing out across the waves. The teams on dry land were following instructions and getting in their respective positions. Notifications pinged in from each pair or trio telling me as soon as they were in place. A stream of messages kept coming from Rouki, who seemed to be doing her best to build the drama, even when nothing was happening. '*I can hear a gull screaming. Could it have spotted the criminal's boat?*' was one. '*It's terrifying to think of those ruthless smugglers, lurking in the dark nearby.*' I wished she'd save the unnecessary commentary for her next interview, and I didn't need a notification of every thought that crossed her mind. A few of her comments were questions such as '*why don't we have a team on the pier?*' Fine to ask I suppose, but the Palace Pier closes to visitors, locking its gates at eleven pm. Before that it is patrolled by security.

Annie kept us on a steady course from east to west, intending to turn the boat in a wide u-shaped bend just before we reached the eastern arm of Shoreham Harbour. Brownlow sat watching the sea much as he watched the scenery pass by when we were in the car. Nose up in the air, ears and fur blowing in the breeze, anyone who didn't know him could've mistaken him for a seasoned old sea dog.

I picked up the spectral imager, as I could see Carmichael had a mind to grab it. It made the horizon lurch even more wildly, making me feel like we were in 'The Perfect Storm', but unfortunately without George Clooney. I swallowed back the bile rising in my throat and took another look. There was something out there ahead of us.

It was like that moment in the movies where the cabin boy in the crow's nest spots an enemy ship, an island, a mermaid or something equally momentous. Only I didn't trust myself to shout out. I wasn't entirely convinced it would only be my words emerging from my mouth.

I handed the imager to Annie. 'Yes, there's something there alright,' she said after a few moments of peering intensely into the gloom. 'Those are navigation lights. Off Hove, I'd say. Doesn't appear to be moving, or moving very slowly. Could just be someone night fishing. That's quite likely the case, in fact.'

'Can we get a little closer, without raising their suspicions?' I asked. Annie said she'd bring us forward as far as she dared.

'There's no reason for them to expect we might be watching them.'

'No, but if they're up to no good they're bound to be wary.'

I contacted Jamal, as he, Skyla and Valerie formed my second most westerly group. 'Any action, your end?' Jamal said he could see the boat, but without binoculars couldn't tell me much about it. It was further west than them. He was up on the prom, his mother and sister were down on the pebbles, casually skimming stones like they were tourists. I asked if they could all go up on the prom and walk in the direction that would put them in parallel to the boat. 'I think it might be opposite Hove Lawns.'

'I'm a Londoner, right? What does that look like?

'A long stretch of grass, the opposite side of the prom to the beach. You're not that far from it.'

'Do we like run down there or keep it at a stroll like nothing's up?'

'Stroll.'

Carmichael thought we should edge our craft a bit nearer and use the thermal imaging camera. Annie chugged us along, and Carmichael took a look.

'Can't see anyone above deck at the moment.'

'No one onboard? What is it? The Marie Celeste?' I joked, to try to sound like I was feeling better than I actually was.

'If they're below deck, they're not likely to be line fishing. Far too small to be a trawler of course. So what exactly are they doing out here?' The Baha Men started their barking from my phone. I could see my ringtone really irked Carmichael, so ditched all thoughts of changing it. It was Jamal calling me with an update.

'Hove Lawns,' he said, sounding slightly breathless. 'There's a van with a small boat on a roof rack just parking up.'

'Number plate?'

'On it. Mum's walking over to the litter bin, where she can get a look without being made.'

'Carmichael – standby for plate check.'

'Make and colour too if possible.' I let Jamal know. In moments we had the number plate, the colour, and although Valerie was not yet near enough to see the make of the van clearly, a decent photo from her phone that Carmichael could enlarge.

'Mum can hear a dog! No, wait… I can hear it too. Definite… Big dog barking in the van, probably. Alsatian or something. There's someone getting out. Two people getting out. Looking around.'

'Tell your mum to stay put, make it look like she's putting something in the bin and waiting for Skyla. Tell her not to watch them. She's too close.' I called Gavin and Melissa.

'Okay, we've got some possible action down at Hove. Can you get mobile and park up at the eastern end of Hove Lawns if there's a space. If not go past as far as the flats – err Courtney Gate I think they're called.' I decided to leave the other two teams in place for the moment. Both could quickly return to their vehicles to follow on if they were needed for back up. Carmichael received her vehicle check. The van was not registered as stolen. It was registered to an owner in Croydon, who it seemed was also not a person of interest to the police. While we bobbed about like a goldfish with swim-bladder issues, Jamal sent me a photo of two people wearing hoods and baseball caps taking the rowing boat from the van roof. It was not a dinghy this time but looked like a small, wooden or fibreglass boat. Carmichael said it was the kind of rowing boat you used to access larger boats, if they were moored just offshore in the sea or on a river.

Unfortunately, the two people with the van had their backs to the camera. I could've asked Jamal to cross the road to risk getting a picture from that side, but that might've aroused suspicions. I would have to be patient. It looked like they would have to move to the roadside of the van anyway to finish unfastening the boat from the roof rack. 'Definitely suspicious, they're in caps and hoods,' I remarked to Carmichael.

'I don't know. It is getting quite chilly.'

'Gemma. They are our perps!'

'You can't jump to conclusions.' I could, actually. The evidence was there.

'Do you want me to move any closer to the larger boat?' asked Annie.

'Wait till we get a look at the dog,' said my nemesis, forgetting whose operation this actually was.

'Jamal will send a photo the moment he sees it,' I told them both, feeling the need to sound in control, of our nocturnal activities, if not my stomach. Brownlow whined. It's a sound he makes when bored. I knew he'd rather be on shore, where he could actually be of some use.

'There are oars in the rowing boat,' Skyla confirmed. 'One of them is just taking them out.'

As the team co-ordinator, I sent Rouki and Alex back to their vehicles, and then got Carl and Jack on the move too. '*The chase is on!*' messaged Rouki. That wasn't exactly what I had in mind. I wanted enough people parked up at Hove Lawns so that they were ready to move to try and block the van in, if the dognappers grew suspicious and decided to call off the sea crossing. 'Sophie!' It was Skyla. 'I'm nearer than Jamal is to them now and I can see the dog. It's still in the back of the van, but it's a German Shepherd. Photos coming.' I waited, heart pounding. If this was a false alarm and it was another dog my credibility was going to take a bit of a knock.

The first photo arrived. Carmichael rudely peered over my shoulder as I clicked to open it.

'That's Rita!' Carmichael confirmed. It was the first time I'd heard her voice sound unsteady, possibly caused by a hint of excitement. Immediately she switched to her radio and started calling for back up, saying she had visual confirmation that the missing police dog was in a vehicle parked up at Hove Lawns, and giving the number plate etc. The way she told it, you'd have imagined it was her that could actually see the dog and had obtained the vehicle plates. What she had not noticed, as she gabbled away with her jargon full of foxtrot limas, was that the motorboat ahead of us had started to move forward slightly.

'Do we follow?' asked Annie. I hesitated, looking through the imager. The boat was indeed starting to head off.

'Something's up. Think they've made us. They've shut the dog back in the van.' It was Jamal. 'Yeah, they're looking towards the people in the jeep.' He meant Melissa and Gavin. 'Think they've spotted him using the night vision bins.'

'Gavin, put the binoculars away,' I ordered. 'Drive on. Get out of there.'

'They're getting back in the van. Leaving the rowing boat on the ground.'

'Jack?'

'Yeah, Soph?'

'Get ready to follow the van. Think they might be leaving.'

'10-4. Ready for pursuit.'

'Alex? Can you in any way try to block the van if it pulls out?'

'We can try.'

'Sophie, the motorboat's taking off – fast.'

'Let's get after them!'

Bounce, bounce, judder bounce! The prow of the Dandelion was rising clean out of the water as we cut through the waves. I pulled Brownlow into the cabin and clung to the wall, as we roared full speed ahead. Carmichael was still jabbering into her radio.

'Tried to stop them pulling out but they just cut across us,' gasped a breathless Alex, over the phone.

'We're right behind them, heading west along the coast road,' Jack reported.

'Direction?' Carmichael bawled at me.

'West! Look you talk to him,' I shoved the phone into her hand and let her liaise between Jack and the police cars which were apparently finally approaching from Worthing and Shoreham. Through the spectral imager, I could see the motorboat in front becoming smaller on the horizon.

'Far more horsepower than us. I can't catch her. We're going full out and I can't force the engine to keep this up much longer.' Carmichael returned the phone to me, seemingly baffled by the multiple callers and simultaneous messages. It's alright for her. The police have the luxury of control rooms and command units, not to mention their own radio system. I have to run everything from an ageing Android with a cracked screen and dodgy hash key.

Jack messaged, cursing the traffic lights that had put space between him and Carl and the van. Gavin and Melissa had taken a detour inland, hoping to head off the van, but the one-way system was costing them time. Rouki and Alex were right behind Jack and Carl. Rouki was filming the chase out of her car window while Alex drove. Unfortunately, she was also live streaming it to her followers. This was a complication we could have done without. I had thought I'd made it clear we were involved in a secret operation. The Dandelion started to make a spluttering noise and Annie said that the engine was choking or something similar. For a panicky moment, I thought she meant we were sinking, and started looking in vain for an object to start bailing us out. What Annie had actually meant was she had to slow up and let the more powerful cabin cruiser ahead speed away. Carmichael said she'd notified the coastguard and Shoreham harbour master though the other craft appeared to be heading out to sea. 'Is there a police launch?'

'Not in this area unfortunately,' Carmichael conformed.

'I suppose calling out the lifeboat –' I pondered.

'Is out of the question,' the rural crime office snapped, 'the Coast Watch volunteers will make a report, though of course that'll be of limited use if it's heading further out in the channel.'

'Going back to France.'

'We'll notify Border Force. They can liaise with their French counterparts.' I'd believe that when I saw it. There'd be too much red tape to be unrolled and polished first. I notified Sandrine at Le Chien Perdu. She was in a bar, judging by the drum and bass music in the background. She sounded like she was smoking, which I think you can still do in French bars. Possibly she had a few glasses of chilled wine too. Lucky her, while I was being tossed around like a ping-pong ball in the National Lottery. Sandrine was however, despite the late hour, willing to mobilise her 'volontaires' to go and keep watch at all the northern ports. I was hoping Carmichael would be impressed by my liaising with my cross-channel counterparts, but as we chugged back to port, she prowled the deck like a shut-in cat desperately needing a wee in the garden.

I had some sympathy with Carmichael's impatience. We were missing out on the action and watching the coast road chase unfold through Rouki Bennett's live stream via my phone was no substitute for actually being in pursuit of the dognappers' van. The footage was a little wobbly and I could certainly have done without Rouki and Alex bickering on the soundtrack. 'Outside lane! Overtake now!'

'I can't, Rouki.'

'Get in front of them! Slow them down.'

'There's no overtaking!'

'For f*** sake It's an emergency!'

'But Rouki –'

'Watch out for that bike!' I was on Alex's side. Making illegal traffic moves while your driving is being scrutinised by a sizeable amount of the general public is never a wise move. Rouki was getting a lot of 'likes' and comments for her real-time documentary footage though, including a message from a 'Steve-the-Dad' who was preparing to use his flat-bed lorry to completely block the coast road at Southwick. It was parked outside his house, so it wouldn't take him more than a minute or so to do so.

'That'll put a stop to them, Rouks! ;-)'

Unfortunately, the roadblock was going to be in the direction the police would be arriving from. If it stopped anyone it would be the cops. I took it upon myself to reply and ask him to stand down but received no reply. I feared Steve was already in his truck.

The van made a sudden turn and headed away north up Boundary Road, the divider between Hove and its neighbouring district, Portslade. Two of our three cars were still in pursuit. The casualty was Melissa and Gavin's Jeep. They had got a bit lost in the maze of streets behind Hove seafront and didn't look like getting into any kind of useful position in time to be of help. Meanwhile, those of us on the boat could only wait while we pulled slowly up to our moorings. Judging by Carmichael's raised voice and expletives, the police cars had been delayed by Steve-The-Dad's flat-bed roadblock.

Meanwhile, the level crossing barriers at Portslade had come down, leaving Rouki live streaming a London-bound train that was passing in front of her and Alex. Carl and Jack had got through before the barriers and were still following the van towards the bypass. Rouki was sending them various messages that she supposed were helpful, but which they appeared to be ignoring. This was sensible in my view, as while Carl was driving, Jack needed to concentrate on navigating, rather than taking advice from his husband's ex-employer who was attempting to back seat drive from another vehicle.

When the van jumped the red light on the Old Shoreham Road, Jack and Carl were left fuming at the junction. Despite Rouki entreating them to *'Go. Go. Go',* unlike the van driver they were not going to risk the safety of others by doing anything illegal and reckless. The van was heading for the bypass with no one in pursuit. The police had the cameras over the dual carriageway at their disposal, their vehicle-bound number plate recognition, as well as three mobile units now involved, though too far behind the action to bring a swift outcome. The cops could not, much to Carmichael's intense frustration, call upon the services of the police helicopter, which was hovering over Guildford on another job.

Carmichael was not done, as far as the operation to apprehend the van containing the stolen police dog was concerned, but there was nothing more my valiant volunteers, Brownlow and I could do. I called my teams and stood them down. It was late, and everyone had done their best. Promising to keep each of them updated with any developments, I let them all make their way home. Valerie and her kids had booked into a trendy boutique hotel, which Medalsum would pay for, but the rest of us returned to our own beds.

It was one of those rare nights where I switch off my phone. Call it sensory overload, or perhaps what seasickness does to you, when your medication or spooky little bands don't allow you the luxury of a good old vomit. I didn't see the operation as in any way a failure. We had gained a useful amount of information about the people we were up against, plus put the police closer on their trail. Quinn's dog-walker tip-off had provided a positive sighting of the police dog and proved my theory about the dogs leaving Brighton by sea. As far as I could see, we'd done everything we possibly could. This time around the dognappers had escaped my team. Whether they would also evade the thin blue line remained to be seen, but that part was not under my control.

I knew I should've put Brownlow straight in the bath, as salt spray plays havoc with his coat and makes him itch, but I was all in. He'd have to make do with an early morning bath. It's not as if he's particularly keen on suds and the tub anyway. I woke up some time before six, grabbing hold of Brownlow and screaming 'You need to keep your head above water, boy! Swim, Brownlow, swim!' Brownlow licked my face until I realised I was still under my duvet and dog saliva was the only water in the vicinity. It was a blessed relief.

Chapter Eight

I didn't immediately switch my phone back on when I got up. I was still feeling a little fragile and needed to ease myself into the day. When the landline rang, I assumed it would probably be a cold caller I could dispatch with a flea in their ear. 'Hello. Brownlow And Gorrage.'

'Your mobile's switched off. I had to get your office number from the website.' It was Rouki Bennett. 'I presume it's because we're being trolled.'

'What? We are?'

'On Twitter. Those ghastly Let Dogs Be Dogs people. Lots of links to historic stories of mistreatment of police dogs. They're talking about your dog being an ex-police dog.'

'What? He isn't.'

'Well, that's what they're saying. And they're saying I used Mr Merrytrees and Lady Champignon on my TV show. Humiliated them by making them perform in front of the cameras. And that's the milder stuff.'

'Oh right. I wonder what's provoked it. I mean I've had a few nasty comments in the past but why now?'

'My streaming of the van chase made the local TV news. Perhaps that's enough. But I thought there was only a handful of those LDBD people, didn't you? We've hundreds of negative comments. It'll be trending by mid-morning at this

171

rate. I think it's probably a classic pile-on – just a lot of bullies and wannabes jumping on the bandwagon.'

'Hmmm. No smoke without fire,' I said.

'Sorry? Meaning?'

'I get what you're saying about pile-ons, but somebody tends to start these things deliberately – they have a motive.'

'Bitter and twisted people.'

'It may be more calculated that that. It may be that we've really rattled the dognappers, by coming close to catching them last night,' I explained, 'Err, unless the police have now caught them?'

'Have you heard anything?'

'I was about to check in with my liaison.' I meant Carmichael, though she wouldn't appreciate being viewed as that. Personally, I'd have preferred to call her my 'useful idiot' but it was necessary to be professional with Ms Bennett. Rouki asked to be let know immediately if arrests had been made. She also advised me to stay off Twitter until the fuss died down, as I might do more harm than good by replying to any of the trolls. I was a little miffed at the presumption that she as an 'influencer' should know how to deal with those sorts of people whilst I, as a mere pet detective, would be out of my depth out there in the wild west of social media.

As it happened, I'd no intention of stoking the egos of time-wasters, pontificators and windbags, well apart from one in particular. I called Carmichael.

'Rural Crime.'

'Hi Gem, Sophie Gorrage…' There was an audible sigh, which I thought rather rude. I didn't relish communicating with her either. 'Err can you update me on where we are with last night's incident?'

'Well, what I can tell you is…' This wasn't good. It's a line politicians use when they're about to dodge a question. '… we contacted the owner of the van. According to him it was parked up the road from his house from five pm yesterday evening. We have impounded it for investigation, but there's nothing at this stage to suggest his involvement in last night's activities.'

'He was sure the van was parked there all night?'

'No. He couldn't park outside, so he can't swear it wasn't taken and returned. That's why forensics are taking a look.'

'But presumably he had the keys inside his house?'

'It's an older model, one we often see falling prey to relay theft.'

'Using a device that's easily bought online?'

'That would be my guess. We should know soon if it did travel down to Hove last night, and if our dog that was in there. We've also got the boat.'

'The boat? The one that got away from us?'

'No, the little rowing boat. It was abandoned with its oars beside Hove Lawns. It's being dusted for prints etc.'

'Oh.' I suppose it would've been polite to hide the disappointment in my voice, but I didn't bother. I sensed though that Carmichael shared my frustrations. We'd lost the dog and the dognappers.

'I don't suppose…' Carmichael hesitated, 'I don't suppose you've any other active leads we could be pursuing?' I didn't know if by 'we' she meant the police, or whether she still wanted to do a bit of moonlighting with Brownlow And

Gorrage. Ordinarily I'd have bluffed and said that yes, I was following up in one or two other promising areas, but I didn't. I was straight with her.

'No, that's it for the moment. I've circulated a description of the larger boat among my French contacts who are keeping an eye open along the coast. But apart from that, I'm not quite sure where we go from here.'

'You're thinking of throwing in the towel where this case is concerned?' I snorted with indignation. I couldn't see how she had arrived at that conclusion.

'Oh no, Gem. Quite the opposite. Brownlow and I are definitely still on the case.'

It was one thing still being 'on the case' but another to be actively moving it forward. I took Brownlow to the park and threw his ball for him. A woman with a Pug approached.

'Are you that pet detective?' I don't know why but I half expected her to start laying into me about having a working dog, or indeed for letting the dognappers escape. Instead, she squeezed my arm and said she was glad that people like me were out there. It was more the kind of thing you might say to Spiderman or Wonder Woman, should you run into them in your local green space, but I appreciated the sentiment. Of course, she then asked for some free advice about making her home dog theft proof, but I was happy enough to oblige. When we were on our own once more, I thought about the thefts and whether there was something obvious I was overlooking. I couldn't really think of anything. I didn't bother reading the online abuse. I knew it wasn't an organisation of dog lovers having a pop at me. The criminals were organised alright, and putting some heat and hate my way wasn't, I suspected, the worst they were capable of, to get us off their trail.

Arriving home, Mrs Maynard from upstairs was standing outside scrubbing the front door.

'Ruddy football fans.' She was trying to remove a squiggly bit of badly painted graffiti off our shared front door. 'Liverpool is that? Or Leicester City?' The 'L' was clear enough but after that the following letters had gone a bit awry. I knew what it was saying: 'LDBD.' 'Vandals, selfish hooligans.' I also knew that anyone who makes a habit of using a spray can on other people's property could wield the thing a little more competently than this. I was also ceasing to believe in the genuine existence of the Let Dogs Be Dogs movement. What I'd seen in Battersea Park was a few well-intentioned people, going along to march for a cause an acquaintance, whether in the virtual or real world, had convinced them existed and was worth supporting. I mean if your cat loving friend asked you to go to an event that in some way connected to feline welfare, and you could meet for a coffee and a natter beforehand, I mean why wouldn't you go? Those people I'd walked with were normal, sociable, rational souls. While it was true that I didn't have the chance to get to know any of them very well, I was sure they weren't a bunch of extremists who'd unite to attack either Rouki Bennett or myself.

I was also pretty sure that the lettering adorning the door was not the work of any kind of activist. For anyone involved in animal rights direction action, Let Dogs Be Dogs would have been unlikely to have been his or her first cause or campaign. Blood sports, vivisection, badger culling, live exports, climate change – any of these were likely to have spurred them into previous action, possibly spray-painting walls, windows or even banners. The still wet paint on the door I shared with Mrs Maynard had not been the work of a member of a protest group, I felt sure. It meant I did need to take a look at the trolling messages.

I left Mrs Maynard thinking a random football fan whose 'L' initialled team were not even playing the Albion that week had damaged our door. That way, she got on with cleaning it off, rather than suggesting it was all my fault, due to the nature of my work. If the graffiti was not removable with good old soap and water, I had the feeling I'd still be receiving more than my half of the bill. She wasn't exactly all heart was Mrs Maynard. I took out my phone and took a look at the messages. I'll spare you the insults, the language and the threats. In truth they weren't what interested me about them. It was the senders. I clicked on the first four and they all led to accounts that had previously trolled about completely different subjects and promoted various unrelated conspiracy theories. There was nothing to suggest these people were tweeting about anything they personally cared about, felt angered by or hated. There was nothing to say any of them were even based in this country or were even real individuals. They appeared to be a sort of fake profile, online rent-a-crowd, perhaps provided by the same kind of business that buys you 'likes' or followers or supplies glowing product reviews and toxic reviews of rival businesses. I'm no expert in that kind of thing. So far, my career as a pet detective hasn't taken me far into the realms of cyberspace. I don't have a hacker friend who can rustle up fake documents when I need them, or gain me access to restricted files, like the TV detectives all seem to conveniently do. I could do with one certainly, but I'm guessing if you've those kinds of skills you're either making a fortune on the dark web or fending off job offers from MI5 and GCHQ. Now I'm not the most grammatical person ever to put inkjet to paper, but I detected among my online detractors a certain disregard for the article. 'A', 'an' and 'the' were frequently used wrongly or absent entirely. '*You are cruel person*'. '*I demand a answer*'. Possibly the poor drudge churning these out had to do so many an hour that he or she didn't have time to check them over, or English wasn't their first language. Now I accept that a few Let Dogs Be Dogs members might have trouble writing tweets in basic

English for any number of reasons, but a large number of them? No, I think I could be fairly sure that Rouki Bennett and I had not made ourselves a larger number of enemies. We just had one, or possibly a couple or so. That made it more manageable in some ways, but more dangerous in others. I wasn't sure if it was more sinister to be the target of largely unfocused vitriol online by several hundred outraged activists who would quickly move on to their next target or have drawn the fire of one or so highly organised adversaries, willing to pay to make our lives difficult.

I still didn't have one cohesive theory to explain all the high-profile dog thefts. All but the police dog had been in the public eye. She seemed the odd one out and yet she had brought the most risk to the thief's or thieves' operation, by the fact she was the property of the local constabulary. I did a search on Rita and her sergeant and at first it brought up nothing. As I continued to search, I found mention of another police dog called Rita. She'd had a different handler, a PC Maskell, and been seriously injured trying to protect him from a knifeman who was high on spice. Both man and dog had needed surgery, but both had survived. In the photos of this second Rita that had been issued to accompany the newspaper reports, she looked remarkably similar to the missing Rita. She'd received an award, a commendation and been on the TV News and several other shows at the time. I called Carmichael but only got her voicemail. It might be she was busy, but there's a certain strip of North Sussex that's the Bermuda Triangle of mobile phone signals. You'll see what I mean if you ever take a train to Brighton or Littlehampton via Haywards Heath and I'm not talking about Clayton Tunnel here. It's a strip of unremarkable looking countryside, but it clearly lacks a phone mast. I left Carmichael a message about the two Ritas. *'Is there any chance they are the same dog, but with a change of handler?'*

Le Chien Perdu were doing their bit across the channel, but as that now looked like the almost definite destination for our stolen dogs, I felt I should join them in their investigations as soon as I possibly could. Before Brexit, Brownlow's pet passport would've meant we could both pop over to France that same day, but the new regulations meant Brownlow needed an AHC – an animal health certificate signed by my vet. They only last for four months before needing renewal, and as we hadn't been abroad for over six months, he didn't have the valid paperwork to travel immediately. If I was going to go to Dieppe that day, I didn't have time to get our vet to sign off the relevant paperwork. It would sadly have to be without my faithful friend and business associate.

I was able to book a late afternoon crossing and still had enough seasickness pills to hopefully cope. The shipping forecast was thankfully still being optimistic about the prevailing sea conditions. I'd need to drop Brownlow off with Quinn before I headed down to Newhaven. I called to let him know the situation, only to hear a seagull squawking so loudly it almost drowned out our conversation. 'Skiving on the beach during work-time, are we?'

'No, someone's just brought in a Greater Black Backed Gull with some oil on its wings. Massive thing like an albatross it is. And it's got loose in reception.' In the circumstances I felt a bit guilty about expecting him to take care of Brownlow, but he said it was no trouble. In the background I heard wings flapping and a woman cry out.

'Oh crap, it's got hold of Clemency. Let me grab the broom. Hopefully we'll have things a little more under control when you arrive.' Quinn is, it has to be said, is unlike that gull, completely unflappable. If you ever happened to find yourself stranded in 'Jurassic Park' he's a guy you'd want by your side.

With my suitcase hastily packed for an all night stay in a yet-to-be-arranged French B&B, plus my drone in its box, Brownlow and I left our maisonette bound for Weatherall. Coming down the front steps, I saw a sight that stopped me in my tracks. A teenage girl was slowly and inexpertly painting a thick wobbly line along a garden fence on the opposite side of the road with a spray can, watched by her friend. It was the same colour paint as used on ours and Mrs Maynard's door. I don't like confrontations and Brownlow is good at diffusing situations before they become too heated, so I took him with me as I approached them. I knew the girls by sight as I'd seen them hanging around previously. Probably aged around fourteen or fifteen, they didn't appear to attend school regularly, and I'd seen them both sitting on a wall smoking roll-ups and drinking cans of beer at times when they should definitely have been at home in bed. Whenever I saw those girls, it took me back to a place I try not to go to. It was a time when I was a different person: angry, raw and feeling 'what is the point' about everything. Dad had left, Mum was living with a violent waster and my younger brother was being brought home by the police every other day. My only friend in the world, our ageing Collie Joey, needed to see a vet, but Brad the waster had drank or gambled away his own benefits and my mum's. I took Joey to the PDSA in secret and there was no one sitting beside me when they told me they could do nothing more for my one true friend. There's a flowerbed in a small Brighton park under which my beloved Joey hopefully still lies, buried in secret after a whole night of digging with a plastic spade meant for the beach.

'Excuse me,' I said to the teenagers.

'Yeah? You want something?'

'Did you spray paint my front door earlier?' The girl with the can aimed it at me menacingly.

'What are you accusing me of something? Wanna say that again do yer? Say it to me face?' Actually, I'd already said it to her face, but I thought it best not to contradict her on that point. Sensing trouble, Brownlow instinctively moved between them and me.

'See the thing is,' I said, 'I'd rather it was you that did it, than someone else. Someone who I think is targeting me.'

'Is it?' The first girl gave my statement some thought. It had certainly piqued her interest. 'So someone's got it in for you then? Like a stalker?'

'Could be.'

'Or is it 'cos you done something eh?'

'Revenge.' Her friend suddenly spoke up.

'Yeah, vengeance. Cos you're like a paedo or you ain't paid for your weed…' She was clearly trying to think of other likely scenarios where someone would get his or her door sprayed.

'Or I've just narked someone off?'

'Well you're narking us off, just by chatting to us.'

'Did he pay you? The guy?'

'Who says there's a guy?'

'Those letters.'

'What letters?'

'On my door. What do they mean?'

'That's for you to know eh?'

'But I don't. So it misses the point. I ain't got the message.' My accent had regressed a few years, roughening with memory. The first girl looked at Brownlow.

'Maybe it's 'cos you're cruel. To him. Maybe that's what it says. Cruel Dog Lady.'

'Cruel Dog Lady would be CDL. It didn't look like CDL.'

'Maybe it's saying it another way. LDA. Is that it eh? LDA? Leave Dogs Alone.' I realised with a start that was indeed what was scrawled on the door in a running hand. The girls had been told to write LDBD, and had forgotten the actual wording, but not the sentiment, by the time they came to do it. Brownlow put his nose forward towards the second girl.

'Don't let it bite me!'

'Nah, he's an old softie,' said the first scratching Brownlow's head. 'You are ain't ya boy.' There was a glimmer for a moment of something almost akin to tenderness in her eyes. I thought of child me, a hard, untouchable little kid – unknowable to all but Joey.

'Come on, boy. We better get on,' I said. I felt both girls' eyes follow me to the car but when I got in and looked back, they had gone. I sat there for a moment, just needing a few seconds of silence and space. Then I drove on to Weatherall Fields.

Quinn was sitting bottle-feeding a black and white kitten. He gestured to the plastic box in front of him containing three more little furry gremlins. 'Do you want to help me feed these a minute? Clem's gone to get her tetanus. We managed to somehow get that gull into a run, but not without a little blood loss.' He showed me the plaster on the back of his hand. I took a kitten and a bottle of cat formula. Watching the out of proportion paws padding the bottle was surprisingly soothing. 'New in, are they?'

'Found on a demolition site in Lancing. I've loaned the contractors a box trap and told them to keep an eye out for Mum.' Brownlow gave the kittens his best doggy smile and lay down protectively beside the box, his eyes concerned for them.

'I sometimes wonder if I should get a cat.'

'How about that little fella?' The kitten's blue eyes gazed soulfully into mine.

'Don't Quinn! I'm tempted, I'm so tempted.'

'Well, you've a few weeks yet before he goes into the homing area. Plenty of time to decide. Or why don't you leave it to Brownlow? See which one he chooses while he's left here with us.'

Brownlow would be staying with Quinn, his two aged cats and, by the sound of it, the kittens in the part of farmhouse he used as his accommodation. The rest housed the clinic and an orphans' room. Quinn's dog Septimus had died the year before, and he had yet to adopt another. It wasn't that he wouldn't, he was too pragmatic for that. It had to be a very special animal though, and one unlikely to be homed elsewhere due to special needs or behavioural issues. Septimus had been an aged Doberman, already elderly and with only three legs when he came in. Quinn's cats, Moon and Cloud were likewise two aged and battle-scarred former strays. Both jet black and with only three eyes between them, the brothers were grumpy, spiteful and inseparable. They didn't like dogs and even Brownlow, who could charm most cats, kept out of their way when he was on a sleepover at Quinn's.

.

My phone started playing 'Who Let the Dogs Out'. The kitten on my lap didn't react. Presumably the wariness of canines is nurture not nature. Either that or the Baha Men weren't that convincing with their impersonation.

182

'I'll let it go to voicemail.' I didn't want to interrupt the kitten's meal, but Quinn reached over and deftly retrieved both infant and bottle.

'Answer it, Soph. It might be something vital.' He was of course, infuriatingly right as usual.

'Sophie. How're you doing?' It was Medalsum. 'Sorry about the background noise. I'm at Schiphol. Flying home in an hour.'

'Medalsum! My friend Quinn here is a big fan of yours.'

'Right, right. Well perhaps I can meet up with him sometime. Now listen Sophie, this might be something and it might be nothing yeah, but here is the thing. Last year I played the Isle of Wight Festival. I was meant to just fly in with my guys, do the set and go, but Skyla, she wanted us to do the whole festival thing. Glamping, she called it. Staying in some fancy Yurt, is that even the word?'

'I think so, yes.'

'Well, you've probably worked out how determined my daughter is by now, despite the last thing I wanted to do was to go camping. Anyway, we did it – we glamped. And the owner of the campsite we stayed at; well, he was in Ventnor yesterday. Shopping in town. And he thinks he saw Tasha. No, he says he knows it was Tasha. We'd ended up staying at his place for a long weekend and his dog and Tasha had buddied up. So he has his dog with him and it sees this Staffie which looks just like her and I mean it reacted. It seriously reacted. Went absolutely crazy, overjoyed at being reunited with her... if it was her. But dogs go by scent, don't they? It's like DNA to them.'

'How near did the guy's dog get to the Staffie?'

'Almost pulled his arm off to get to her. They were sniffing and dancing, you know? Just how they were at the campsite last year. Positive ID you think?'

'What about the person with the Staffie? What did they do?'

'It was a guy. Thirties or forties. Seemed perfectly normal. Called the dog 'Lorna'. My friend didn't want to arouse his suspicions, so he didn't ask too many questions.'

'Did he get a number plate?'

'I think he said they were on foot. I was doing interviews this morning when this happened – he saw the dog about ten am. I was planning to fly home today anyway, but now I'm going to be getting off that plane and heading straight down the Isle of Wight.' I thought of the boat that had escaped the night before and the fact my searchers in France had so far drawn a blank.

'I'll meet you there,' I said, deciding on the spur of the moment. 'With Brownlow.' He wouldn't need a pet passport for this ferry crossing.

In the car, I sang along to the radio. It always lifted my mood, and it still was in need of that. The memories stirred up by the encounter with the spray can girls were not something I wanted to dwell on but were not so easily banished. I believe you can live in the past or move on. If the past isn't a particularly happy place to reside, well I'd recommend moving on, however hard that may be. As I sang, I realised I should probably have asked Quinn to lend me a CD of Medalsum or download some of his tracks, so I'd be more familiar with his work before meeting him. True, I'd watched the video with his dog in it on YouTube a few times but that didn't really count. Medalsum's music was probably a little current for me, as I'm not, as you can probably tell, part of Generation Z. I like a bit of nineties music more than anything. I suppose I'm a pre-millennial, if there is such a thing. Brownlow isn't one of those dogs who starts to howl when a human sings. He takes no notice other than to give the occasional grin, and tail wag. Brownlow was only a puppy when he left Afghanistan, but I did once wonder if perhaps he would prefer the music of his country of birth. I downloaded a few tracks and tried them out, but Brownlow just ignores music, wherever it's from.

I had automatically assumed the stolen dogs would be heading for the continent. This new possible sighting on the Isle of Wight had rather thrown me. The only rule for dogs on the car ferry was they must be kept on leads. There was no need to smuggle a pet to the Isle of Wight, so why go to the effort of using a private boat? It didn't make sense. It wasn't until Brownlow and I were onboard the ferry that I started to realise what had put the dognappers off this method of transport. I'd not been on the ferry with a car before and didn't realise you weren't allowed to stay with your vehicle for safety reasons during the journey. Brownlow and I went up onto the passenger decks to explore. You could sit in a comfy lounge or the sun deck if the weather allowed and buy just about any refreshment you needed. What you could not do was find a secluded spot to hide away. As we entered the lounge a voice immediately called out 'what a lovely dog,' and Brownlow had made a couple of new friends in seconds, who wanted to know if we were also 'having a few days away from it all'. Of course, Brownlow loved being fussed and I'd noticed the queue for coffee wasn't too long and they had a cheese, tomato and pesto panini reduced to half price, so I was happy enough too. I felt more confident about the ferry crossing than I had about travelling on Annie's boat. Apart from being a lot bigger, heavier and sturdier it had plenty of toilets, should the going get rough. Seated at our table, I was however still unable to prevent myself checking the shipping forecast on my phone for the umpteenth time. There was no violent storm brewing over the Solent. I think I've just watched too many movies where, a couple of minutes after the main characters set sail, the hurricane, cyclone or tornado begins. A woman on another table waved to me.

'You've brought your dog too? There're lots of dog-friendly places over there, or so I've heard.' Her name was Ruth and she and her Schnauzer Rufus were hoping to 'walk the island'. She'd brought both a sun hat and a plastic rainmac along because 'you never can tell'. She wanted to know all about Brownlow and if he could have one of Rufus's special biscuits. This was all very congenial, but if it had been a stolen, high-profile animal at the end of my lead, I don't think I'd have been so relaxed about it.

Most of the people on the ferry seemed to be folk who made this trip for work or social reasons on a regular basis. They were less interested in Brownlow, uninterested in the view, and even any accompanying children didn't ask them 'are we there yet?' I wondered how Medalsum was going to arrive. Probably be private helicopter I imagined, though I'd read he was a bit of an eco-warrior, so perhaps he'd travel by catamaran like Greta Thunberg. A crew member passed by, so I buttonholed him to ask how I'd get from the Isle of Wight to France, should I wish to.

'Tourists always ask that,' he grinned somewhat irritatingly. 'You go back to the mainland for a ferry to France. There isn't a ferry from the Isle of Wight, you see?'

'Suppose I had a boat?'

'In that case you'd probably go from Yarmouth, sail round The Needles into somewhere like Cherbourg,' he said. 'That's quite popular. But you have to know what you're doing. It means crossing shipping lanes.' I thanked him and tucked into my panini, which happily was still crisp and fresh, despite the later in the day discount. I'd rather cheekily left Quinn the task of booking me short notice accommodation. He had moaned about it, as he had enough to be doing with the

Weatherall kittens and seabirds with attitude. I hadn't heard anything from him, when an announcement had just come over the tannoy telling us we would shortly be arriving. The journey had only taken around three quarters of an hour and it had passed very pleasantly. As we docked, I started to wonder if I should've delayed my departure and made an accommodation booking myself, but then a moment after we were directed to return to our vehicles, confirmation details pinged in. I'd a dog friendly chalet that slept two waiting for me, just outside Ventnor. It was named 'Sea Mist' and looked perfect. It wasn't too expensive either. Quinn had certainly done us proud. I'd have to find time to buy him a gift while on the island. We drove out of Fishbourne harbour and headed for our base.

Not only was the chalet dog friendly, it was Sophie friendly. The owner had left a plate of croissants and a bowl of fresh fruit, plus there was a rather cute little box of dog treats. Brownlow and I almost never get to go on holiday, so we were perhaps both enjoying things a little more than we should. This was, after all a work trip.

Rouki Bennett was giving TV interviews about being trolled and had posted a teary-eyed video in which she talked about being strong and proud of who she was. I wondered slightly if, like me, she or her Kazowie people had discovered her detractors were a bunch of fake accounts, and she was just milking the situation for a bit of publicity. I was pleased to see that several of my followers had gallantly hit back at those who had criticised Brownlow and me, defending our reputations with their tales of how we'd helped them find their lost animals. Notably, our supporters received no replies, even when they were quite vicious in their defence of us. I firmly believed the trolls, when under attack from members of the public, had not replied because they hadn't been paid to do so. I was completely sure by this time that they were nothing more than an internet service for hire. Probably based abroad, hired through the dark web and with no actual idea who Rouki or I even were. Somebody was trying to intimidate us, and I knew who it was, if not their actual identity. It was a particularly ruthless dog smuggler and one I had to be closing in on, to have reacted in this way.

I thought we'd take a little tour around Ventnor itself, ahead of meeting up with Medalsum. Before setting out, I emailed PC Carmichael, letting her know our whereabouts and the fact I'd inform her if I thought we needed back up. 'You are in Hampshire,' came the snippy reply. 'If you need serious assistance you will need to contact the Hampshire force who I'm sure will be keen to assist.' It wasn't worth even trying to analyse that, though it seemed to contain jibes or mini-aggressions. 'We're on our own, Brownlow,' I said. 'Until Medalsum shows up, that is.' Ventnor High Street had an array of one-of-a-kind small shops I could easily have spent a day exploring if it wasn't already past their closing time. It was still a pleasant place to window shop and that wasn't so ruinous to the wallet. Until we met Medalsum's glamping provider I couldn't pinpoint exactly where in town the suspected sighting of Tasha had taken place, but there were a few streets full of shops, and the town was pleasingly arranged on a cliff slope, so it was easy to meander around without losing our sense of direction. I assumed Medalsum would call when he landed, whether that would be from the sea or the air. I popped into a couple of pubs which were not yet busy with evening drinkers. A quick enquiry at the bar about a Staffie fitting Tasha's description yielded no results. I had of course, no idea if the dog had merely been passing through Ventnor as she was trafficked elsewhere, or whether she had been sold to a presumably unwitting new owner here. It was a fine evening for a stroll with my dog in a picturesque holiday town, yet I felt a deep sense of unease. At the first chance I got, I made a discreet check to see if we were being followed. A little later, I again waited, pretending to peruse the goods in the window of a pet shop, while using the reflection in the glass to keep an eye back up the street. I also kept an eye on Brownlow. When he partially turned his head to glance behind, slightly lifting his tail as if to be ready to greet an approaching stranger, I made sure I didn't look over my own shoulder. We simply waited. No one came past us. I turned as if to retrace our steps. There was someone standing in a pub doorway, maybe eight or nine doors back. I was pretty sure there had been no one there when we'd popped in to ask about Tasha. I could only see the person's arm, or more precisely his or her elbow, suggesting he or she was looking at, or pretending to look at, a phone. As we turned back and approached up the street, the elbow disappeared, and we arrived in time to see the pub door shutting behind someone who had just gone inside. Looking through the smoked glass of the door, I half-glimpsed a face looking back at me. It was a man's face, which I kind of felt I'd seen somewhere before. We went back in the pub and walked through the bar. The same few people were sitting drinking. Of the face I'd just glimpsed, there was no sign. He could've gone in the gents or exited via the beer garden. I took the only option available. There was just one middle-aged woman smoking and drinking a half-pint sitting at one of the tables. She had her head down, picking at chipped nail varnish. 'Excuse me, did a guy just come out this way?'

'Yeah.'

'Can you describe him?'

'Err no. Didn't really pay him much attention to be honest. Seemed in a hurry.' Cocking her head on one side, frustratingly she gave me more scrutiny than she had our suspected tail. 'Not been stood up have yer? You have, I can see it on your face. Thought he was leaving a bit sharpish and all. They're not worth it, love. Any of them, trust me. Come an' have a drink.'

Stopping and having a drink, albeit a soft one, was a good idea, but I could not join the woman in the beer garden to compare notes on disastrous dates. Brownlow and I needed to be alone rather than attempting to be social. A pub in the next street provided the solution. I didn't really care if we were followed or watched going in. The important thing was to try and ascertain if we were being followed or not. Counter surveillance methods are not something I've a great deal of experience in. I sometimes covertly observe pet thieves, but they generally have no reason to return the favour. I thought the first thing to do might be to check for what I call 'ripples in the pond'. If someone was watching us, then that person knew we were on the Isle of Wight. The only people who had been given that information were Quinn, Carmichael and Medalsum. Quinn, I'd told in person. He doesn't like social media much and only uses it to promote the sanctuary's work and to rehome animals or make appeals for donations of things like blankets or cat food. He isn't remotely gossipy and has an ex-soldier's wariness that prevents him opening up until he knows you well. My first impressions of him were of someone monosyllabic, suspicious and unfriendly. I'm not usually wrong about people, but Quinn is one of the few I admit I got totally wrong. Where sharing information that Brownlow and I were on the Isle of Wight was concerned, I knew it was safe to assume that he hadn't told a soul. Next on the 'need to know' list was Carmichael. Now, she was only pretending to be temporarily uninterested in what we were doing, because the case had taken me somewhere she couldn't follow during work time at least, as it was outside her force's jurisdiction. If she happened to have the afternoon and evening off, I wouldn't have put it past her to catch a ferry over to the island and trail me, in the hopes of cracking the case. It wasn't Carmichael's face I'd seen through the smoked glass of the pub door though. It was someone tall and male. The third person who knew our whereabouts from receiving direct information from me was Medalsum, who presumably was still on his way. Unlike Quinn and Carmichael, he could

190

possibly have caused 'ripples in the pond' by telling someone else. That person could've told someone else or shared the news and so spread those ripples wider and wider. I had only glanced at my Twitter account a couple of times since arriving, but checking it again in the bar, I spotted that Skyla had tagged us in a tweet about her dad heading back to Britain. There was no mention of where in Britain he might be headed though.

I still had the nagging feeling someone knew we were in Ventnor and were keeping tabs on us, though I couldn't provide the 'how' let alone the 'why'.

My phone rang and it was Medalsum. He was sorry but he'd been delayed in London 'sorting out a licensing issue'. I presumed he meant for his music, rather than his TV. He added that he'd be catching the morning ferry, so at least I now knew how he'd be arriving, even if he'd made it sound like there was only one crossing before lunch, which was certainly not the case. I'd become quite knowledgeable on the subject of ferry timetables generally in a short space of time. I checked the next day's weather forecast. Rain was heading our way in the early morning along with a moderate breeze. I knew I'd be obsessively checking the Shipping Forecast for Medalsum's crossing the next morning, even though I'd already discovered that there was still no sign of a named hurricane or 'Perfect Storm'. Medalsum, I told myself, was a global traveller and had no doubt experienced far more challenging journeys and climatic conditions. It would not be a good idea to mention my petty meteorological preoccupations to him.

I've given several interviews in the past, where I've soon realised my interrogator, usually a very young local news reporter, has tried to portray me as eccentric or quirky in some way. A pet detective of course, makes everyone think of Jim Carey as 'Ace Ventura' and the TV people do like a light-hearted piece to finish an otherwise doom-laden news programme. Leaving their viewers with something light and fluffy might suit their needs, but my job is a serious one. Any animal going missing or being stolen is stressful and emotionally painful. I know I'm not an altogether conventional person and I do tend to get a bit obsessional now and then, but honestly who doesn't? I have in recent years though made efforts to curb my urge to speak before thinking, and I'm learning not to share everything in my head without employing a filter. This was the biggest case Brownlow And Gorrage had ever taken on and I was starting to feel the stress of it. Thank goodness for Brownlow, who if he does share any of my anxieties is brilliant at hiding it.

We had to follow a path along the cliff to return on foot to our chalet. It was starting to get dark, and although it felt safe enough with a rail on one side in the steep parts, I knew I didn't want to linger. Not that this wouldn't have been a lovely spot to dreamily dawdle, on an evening when clouds didn't hide the sunset or there was no chance we were being followed. Brownlow would of course warn me of anyone's approach, but if they wanted to hurl me down onto the beach, I wasn't sure he'd be able to stop them. As we neared the chalet and I could see the Clio parked outside, I noticed a white van parked up a little further along the private road. Perhaps it belonged to the owner of one of the other bungalows or chalets. As we grew nearer to 'Sea Mist' I could see someone was sitting in the driver's seat. I stopped and took off my backpack. I'd only brought the lightweight night vision binoculars out with me, though the spectral and thermal imaging devices were in the chalet. I focused the binoculars and got a shock. The driver of the van was also looking through a pair of binoculars and they were pointing right at us.

I wasn't immediately sure what to do. If we retraced our steps back along the cliff edge, we were exposed and vulnerable, but if we carried on towards the chalet then a confrontation with the van driver, if that was what he or she wanted, seemed inevitable. I couldn't really call Hampshire Police and tell them someone was looking at me with binoculars, or rather I could, but it was unlikely to result in any kind of rapid response. Instead, I rang Quinn.

'Weatherall Fields.'

'Quinn. We're out in the open. Someone in a white van is watching us through binoculars. Retreat means a quiet cliff-top path or taking an unfamiliar route. The watcher is parked near our chalet. Best course of action?'

'Ah.' There was a pause. He was processing.

'Stay put, stay on the phone,' he said after what seemed like an age but couldn't have been more than a few seconds. 'Can you pace a little, point to him and gesture as you're talking to me?'

'I'm not really a pacer and a gesturer.'

'Just do it. Act. You're putting on a show. It'll hopefully read that you've made him, you're agitated, and you've called in back up.'

'Okay, I'm pacing and gesturing. Err I'm not quite sure what I'm gesturing.'

'Right. Now take a photo of him with your phone camera.'

'It's too dark for that.'

'Doesn't matter. Do it very obviously. You're trying to unnerve him. If it is a him of course? Can you identify the person? Are there more than one?'

'Just one is all I can see. And I can't see a face. His or her binoculars are in the way. But there was a man who was following us earlier, I'm pretty sure of that. Hang on, he's put his headlights on. He's driving off.'

'Go to the chalet. Be careful of course. But if it looks safe, get inside and lock the door.'

'Heading down towards it now. I'll check the windows and doors before I go in.'

'Stay on your guard even when you do. It's a holiday rental – who knows who else has a key.'

I ended the call while I did my perimeter checks on the chalet and didn't call Quinn back until the curtains were drawn and I was snuggled up under the sofa blanket with a cup of cocoa. Brownlow was in the kitchenette making appreciative noises over his supper. 'So tell me about the guy who was following you earlier?' he said.

'Oh did I mention –'

'You did yes.' I told him I thought I'd seen the guy somewhere before but couldn't place him. 'You once showed me your diary app,' he reminded me. 'I said I prefer the traditional paper variety, but I noticed you put a lot of detail down. Can't you go through it and see if the guy's face flashes up when you're reading where you've been and what you've seen?' I tried it, starting from when I'd heard about Rouki's Cocker Spaniels being stolen and got as far as visiting Medalsum's studio before my eyes felt too tired and scratchy to continue squinting at a phone screen.

In the night the wind picked up and rain beat against the windows. I started worrying for Medalsum arriving by ferry in the morning. Before I could stop myself, I was checking the shipping forecast again. 'Moderate, occasionally rough at first, becoming smooth or slight later'. I was glad I'd crossed when the sea was 'smooth'. The wind was predicted to be a 'north-easterly 4 or 5, occasionally 6 at first in the south'. Visibility was 'good'. As I put my phone back on the bedside bookshelf and rolled over, Brownlow stood up and got as near to pricking his ears that their floppiness would allow. 'A-woof.'

He'd heard a sound outside, above that of the wind and rain. I flashed back to Bianca the Chihuahua being lured away through Gavin and Melissa's cat flap. 'Sea Mist' didn't have a cat flap. Few people who take a cat on holiday let it out in an area it doesn't know. Also, while Brownlow might be able to get his head through a cat flap, the rest of him would have been unable to follow. As I strained to hear what the dog had heard, I heard a clicking sound. For a moment I couldn't identify it, but with a sudden jolt I did. It was a key in the front door lock. Then there was a loud crunch. I leapt up and as I did, heard Brownlow barking. His claws skittered on the wooden veranda floor as he rushed outside. I sprinted to the front door. It blew back in my face. Shoving it open again, I took in the empty veranda, and I shouted and screamed into the wind. 'Brownlow! Brownlow! Here boy!' There were no lights out front to see anything by. I heard Brownlow make a half-bark, half –whine, some way off and I heard a voice, at about the same distance. 'Brownlow!' I bellowed into the night.

I heard him before I saw him, running at me, barking again. As Brownlow reached the veranda, I grabbed him as he jumped at me. We both fell back onto the floor, my arms wrapped tightly around the dog as he nuzzled my face. With my still bare feet, without getting up, I kicked the front door shut. After releasing a long sigh of relief and relinquishing my grip on Brownlow, I got shakily to my feet. There was a bolt on the inside of the front door, but it was now hanging off. I started looking around for furniture I could pile against the door, and also to block the back one. As I turned to check on Brownlow who was simply standing watching me, I noticed he had a lead clipped to his collar. A lead that was not his own. That's when I lost it, I really lost it. 'You're not taking my dog! You're not having Brownlow!' I yelled; fists balled defiantly. If someone forced their way in at this point, I'd hit them with a dining chair, or used my basic martial arts. Perhaps I would've swung my night vision binoculars on their strap as a weapon or hurled some of decorative, locally made pottery that adorned the windowsills hard at the intruder. No one tried the door again, so no one felt the raw edge of my rage.

I thought of calling Quinn, but I knew he'd be tempted to come straight over, and I didn't want him taking the ferry on a rough night. Instead, I called my nemesis, whose well-being mattered considerably less to me.

'Carmichael,'

'Gemma, sorry to wake you.' She always answers with a growl or a snarl, so it was difficult to ascertain whether she'd actually been asleep or not. 'Something's just happened here, and I could do with your advice.'

'Here still being the Isle of Wight?' I thought she was going to lecture me on how it was the Hampshire force I should've been bothering, but she didn't. She took me seriously for about the first time ever and even offered to report the incident for me. Since the intruder had not entered the chalet and had used a key, I wasn't sure it could be technically classed as a break-in. I was sure however it was definitely an attempted dog theft. 'You're positive it's not your own lead?'

'Of course I'm sure.'

'That is of course, something that could be seen as evidence of the attempt to steal. Going equipped if you like.' She was not only trying to teach her grandmother to suck eggs, she was shoving them in her mouth.

'I know.'

'Not that arrests are likely be made. As you didn't see the person or persons involved. It's a pity you didn't get the reg. of the van you mentioned earlier.'

'It was side on to me unfortunately. And I didn't think it wise to approach.'

'Will you be staying put?'

'In my chalet?'

'On the island?'

'Yes, until sometime tomorrow at least. Why?'

'In case the local police need to contact you.'

'Oh right. Fine. I thought for one second there, you were going to tell me you were coming down here.'

'It would be in an unofficial capacity, though I'm not working tomorrow…'

'No, no it's fine, Gem. I've got this, honestly. And have you seen the shipping forecast? Not looking good for crossing the Solent I'm afraid.' She laughed, but it was a dry, sardonic laugh.

'See you tomorrow, Ms Gorrage.'

Chapter Nine

I was mightily relieved when it was only Medalsum strolling off the nine o'clock ferry to meet me. In baseball cap and shades, and without his signature 'medals' jacket, he didn't seem to have garnered any attention from fans during the crossing. It seemed he hadn't been recognised. The journey across the Solent had, he said, been 'slightly bouncy', though that hadn't prevented him from tucking into a hearty breakfast onboard. He was on foot, and I apologised for my shabby car, expecting he was used to chauffeur driven stretch limos, but he assured me my car was 'class' compared with the rust buckets he'd owned in the days when he was just another struggling rapper carting his only equipment between gigs. He immediately noticed my nervousness as I double-checked the rear-view mirrors. 'Something been happening over here?' I found myself telling him the whole story.

'Are you being tailed or are you being tracked?' I asked Medalsum what he meant. 'Is there any chance someone could've placed a tracker on your phone? I mean it seems a bit of a coincidence otherwise, that they even know where you're staying.' I told him that I didn't think I'd left my phone alone anywhere but couldn't be sure.

'Who knew of the chalet's address?'

'Just Quinn… err my partner who booked it. He didn't tell anyone else.'

'Have you checked your apps?' As I was driving, I invited him to take a look at my phone. I knew I'd nothing on there that was particularly embarrassing. As you've probably noticed by now, I don't live a particularly racy or scandalous existence. It's not that I judge people who do, it's simply not me. 'Hmmm, it would be quite well hidden. Let's have a little look.'

'Just don't muck up any of my settings. I'm hopeless at putting things back right after I've fiddled with them.' He laughed and kept scrolling, as I drove.

'So how come you're a bit of a phone hacking expert?'

'I'm not, Sophie, seriously I'm not. But an ex once put one of these damn bugs on my cell.' I think he meant 'cell' as in cell phone. His accent seemed to have a slight transatlantic twang to it too, despite my having read he grew up in east London. 'And then she's selling stories, selling photos. I paid out to get this cyber guy onto it. And asked him what to look for. Didn't want to end up in the papers half asleep in my M&S pyjamas again.'

'It could've been worse.'

'Hell yeah. It could've been a lot, lot worse.' Medalsum chuckled. 'But once bitten… Forewarned is forearmed.' He put my phone back on the dash – I mean the dashboard. I think Americanisms may be contagious. 'Yours looks clean to me. What about the motor? Car trackers are a thing, right?'

'I've seen them on fictional cop shows.'

'Me too. Not something a pet detective uses?'

'Not this one.' Medalsum took out his own phone and started scrolling. 'Nice,' he muttered to himself, and 'Yeah, that's a good 'un.' Noticing my slightly quizzical face, he explained he was downloading a few pictures of car trackers. They're quite cheap and available to buy, it seems. 'When we get to Adrian's we'll give the car the once over. At least now we'll have some idea what we're looking for.' Adrian was Medalsum's glamping campsite host who had provided the sighting of Tasha. 'Actually, pull over a minute. Just up ahead.'

We were on a narrow country road travelling inland. There wasn't much traffic, and the point Medalsum had indicated we stop was little more than a gateway into a field of what looked like it might be kale. He got out of the car, and I followed with Brownlow after clipping on his lead. 'We're a little bit higher than the road junction back there – that crossroads.' He pointed. I fetched the binoculars from the car. He nodded approvingly. 'So you're following a dot or whatever on a screen. You're staying back, so they don't make you, right? But then they stop. The dot isn't moving anymore.' I trained the binoculars on the crossroads.

'I'm still impressed you know about this stuff,' I said.

'I don't, Sophie. I honestly don't. But I love a spy movie. Not just Bond and Bourne, stuff like 'Tinker, Tailor', 'The Spy Who Came in From The Cold', any of the Harry Palmers. I'd love to have been an agent. But they don't recruit state school dropouts from Poplar.'

'White van slowing up at the junction.' I handed in the spectral imager.

'Got it. Is it coming on or is it gonna turn? Choices buddy. We're on ya.' The van turned off.

'Could be something, could be nothing,' I said.

'True enough, but shall we do the search while we're not leading anyone anywhere?'

Medalsum looked under one side of the car and I checked the other, after perusing his recently assembled folder of mobile tracking device jpegs. Some of the pictures showed them placed high in a wheel arch and I tried there, running my hand along in the filth and grease. Suddenly I felt something. It was like a little box where I'd imagined the chassis should've been smooth. I tried to get a better look with the light on my phone. 'Found something?' Bolder than me, Medalsum reached into the wheel arch and pulled out a small object. It was a black metallic box. On the underside were two round objects. 'It's got magnets here, see?' He stuck the object like a limpet onto the car door.

'As long as it is a tracker, not some explosive device?' I said nervously.

'Yeah, it's this one. Look at the picture. Exact match.'

'So what do we do with it?' I asked. Medalsum looked at me.

'Well, you know what they'd do in the movies, Sophie?' I did.

'Stick it on another car!' The only trouble was there weren't any other stationary vehicles nearby. Medalsum thought we should temporarily keep it with us rather than dump it, so the people keeping tabs on my Clio would see it moving again and think nothing was amiss. We started to look for a public car park and on the outskirts of Shanklin we found a large one that served a supermarket. I pulled in and parked up next to a Volkswagen campervan.

'Perfect,' Medalsum grinned. 'Let's stick in on the Mystery Machine. Let 'em follow Scooby Doo.' He leant out the car door to transfer the tracker and then we were off again.

'What should I be calling you? I mean do you prefer Mr Medalsum or what?'

'You can call me 'M' if you like. My first name's Emil and everyone's always called me 'Em'. Some people probably think it's 'M' for Medalsum, and it kinda is that too.' We could see the yurts of the glamping field long before we'd reached it.

'I'm not sure I even really know what a yurt is!' I confessed.

'Middle class camping I guess you might say. Not camping like when you and I were in the Scouts and Guides, with leaky little tents and beans on toast.'

'I was never a Guide. But they're based on some traditional design, aren't they?'

'Yeah, Asian nomadic tribes had cone shaped tents. So Skyla said. She seemed to think it was some culturally significant experience. I mean come on – it had a flushing toilet and a power shower – my first flat didn't even have that. And we're on the Isle of Wight – not the plains of Outer Mongolia.' We pulled in and went up to the log cabin that acted as the site office. Medalsum's friend Adrian was delighted to see him and there was much hand clasping and embracing. Adrian said they were in the process of getting ready for a food and drink festival but if we joined him in his office, he'd tell us what he could about seeing Tasha in Ventnor. He kept berating himself about not taking a photo of his dog and the one that appeared to be Tasha getting reacquainted. My phone started to ring. It was Carmichael. I let it go to answer.

'What did the person with her look like?' I asked Adrian, as he poured us some of his homemade elderflower cordial.

'He was slim, late thirties or early forties. Unremarkable sort of guy really. Not someone you'd immediately associate with anything underhand.'

'Tall?' I queried, thinking of the man I'd seen through the pub door, and who I still had some unfocused kind of gut instinct about.

'Not especially.' Adrian himself was tall though himself I noted, so maybe his perception of height and mine would not be in accord. His phone rang. 'Sorry, it's the wife, I better get it.' Immediately he answered he was saying 'What?' and 'Where?' Medalsum and I looked at each other. 'Okay, okay…' said Adrian, 'they're here now actually. I'll tell them.'

Adrian the campsite owner ended his phone call. 'You guys need to go. Hilary's in Ventnor now, having a coffee with friends. The guy with Tasha is sitting outside the Spyglass. Err it's a pub on the waterfront.'

I drove while Medalsum found the pub on a map on his phone and gave me directions. As we arrived, we could see a large terrace overlooking the water, that was covered in tables full of punters. It was certainly a popular spot. I parked up. The plan was to try to identify the dog and then call the police. Tasha however had other ideas. Even before we'd spotted her, her sharp ears had picked up the sound of Medalsum speaking softly to me as we approached the pub's decking, and she immediately recognised that voice. A big, happy blue-grey blur barked once, then thundered through the maze of benches and legs, hurling herself at her delighted owner.

'Tash, oh Tash!' Medalsum bend down and hugged the dog to him as she bounced up and licked his face again and again. Brownlow cocked his head quizzically as if he had never indulged in similar displays of exuberant affection himself.

'Look, Em, shall we just take her and get her back to the car before –' I stopped speaking abruptly. A blond-haired man in chinos and a blue shirt was looking at us. 'Oh you've caught my dog,' he said. 'I thought I'd tied her lead to the bench.' Medalsum looked at him. I looked at him. 'I was afraid she'd run out into the road,' he continued, 'I've only just got her, you see…'

Paul wasn't much taller than me. He wasn't a dognapper either. He bought us both a drink, a soft one again in my case, and we all sat down at a table with a gorgeous view of the bay. The sea still looked a little choppy, but the wind had dropped to almost nothing. Paul had, he said, adopted 'Lorna' as he had recently lost his previous dog to old age and renal failure. He'd been looking to adopt a female English Bull Terrier but then he'd seen Tasha advertised and figured a Staffie would also suit him.

'Advertised where?'

'Oh a friend sent me the ad. It was on a local Facebook page. She's a member, I'm not I'm afraid. Anyway, it was from a small dog rescue charity, based here on the island.'

'Can you show me the ad?'

'It's on my phone somewhere… look can I send it to you when I've had a chance to have a look for it? I've got my email in such a muddle of folders, drafts and spam and so forth.' Paul seemed like a nice guy, just one who wasn't in complete control of his mobile. Where that was concerned, I sympathised.

Medalsum took out his own phone and showed Paul a number of photos of Tasha.

'Oh I'm not disputing she's your dog. The way she reacted just then. My Samantha was just like that. Hadn't eyes for anyone else.' I presumed he was talking about a dog rather than a person, but I didn't ask him to clarify. He gave the impression of being a genuine, decent dog owner, the kind I'm usually working for, rather than against. This was starting to feel awkward.

'Did you have to pay anything for her?' Medalsum asked.

'They accepted a donation. They didn't ask for one, but I thought it the right thing to do.' Medalsum immediately offered to reimburse Paul, but although he was willing to reluctantly relinquish the dog to her owner, he wouldn't take the money. 'I'm sorry it's been so unpleasant for you, having your dog taken from you like that, but I don't think the charity people were to blame. The man seemed very kind and genuine. I asked where they had met. Paul named a nearby park. 'They're only a small concern. The dogs are fostered in people's homes. That's what he said.'

'You weren't invited to anyone's home?' He shook his head.

'What was the man like?'

'Like I said, he was very nice. I didn't really focus on him to be honest. I spent most of my time looking at Lorna, err Tasha. Making sure I'd be right for her and her for me. I thought she looked great. Friendly, happy, very well cared for. I wasn't suspicious at all though. Then why should I have been, as the man wasn't asking for money?' Paul looked at me sadly.

'Have I been very naïve?' he asked.

'No,' I said truthfully. 'I've never come across a case where people have gone to considerable trouble to steal a dog, and then offer to give it away.' Medalsum had after all been carjacked. That made Tasha seem like a very valuable prize. Why on earth would anyone take that kind of risk if there wasn't a healthy profit in it? Perhaps, I wondered, they'd hinted at a rather large donation and Paul had agreed to it or had needed to part company with the dog urgently. It might be that our operation off the coast of Brighton had panicked the crooks. They couldn't of course have known that we'd all imagined they were heading to the continent with the dogs, rather than just across the Solent.

Medalsum still wanted to do something for Paul, as he, like myself, could tell that Paul had already fallen for Tasha.

'If I can help in any way, to get you another dog…?' Paul said that was kind, but he'd try to acquire one at another rescue. He added that he'd make sure he took on a dog that genuinely needed a home the next time around. At this point I chipped in to tell him my friend ran a bona fide sanctuary and that I'd happily put them in touch with him. Paul agreed and we exchanged details.

There was a slightly odd smell in the car as we headed to 'Sea Mist.' Brownlow, sitting in the back with Tasha smelt it too, and sneezed a couple of times, before putting his nose through the gap between the seats to rest on my shoulder.

'Not sure he likes your perfume, Sophie.'

'I'm not wearing perfume.'

'Hang on…'Medalsum turned in his seat. 'Come here girl.' He put his nose to his dog's head and inhaled. 'It's Tash. Some fancy dog shampoo Paul's washed her in I expect. Bet he got drenched, she ain't an easy dog to bath.' There were no suspicious vans hanging around outside 'Sea Mist' but Medalsum insisted on going in first alone to check it out. Fortunately, he found no one was lurking inside and it didn't appear, to me at any rate, that we'd had any uninvited visitors in my absence.

The dogs had just settled down, when a ring of the doorbell sent them both to the door. There wasn't a spyhole or a chain, so Medalsum opened it a crack, his weight behind it.

'PC Carmichael,' said a voice I knew all too well.

'Let her in,' I groaned.

'If you're wondering how I found you,' said my nemesis grimly, 'when you clearly couldn't be bothered to answer your phone, I phoned your friend Quinn James. You hadn't told him about last night's little incident, had you? Didn't want to

206

worry him perhaps?' If Medalsum hadn't been there I would have throttled the woman.

'Yes, that's it, so thanks for that. And for your information my mobile phone provider seems to have distinctly patchy coverage in the more rural parts of the island.' Carmichael wasn't even listening.

'This is one of the stolen dogs, isn't it? And you, sir… are you… um, the London-based musician?'

'Medalsum,' said Medalsum, offering a handshake. 'And Tasha, my dog.' Carmichael took out her notebook.

'Perhaps you'd like to make us all some tea Ms Gorrage, while Mr Medalsum brings me up to speed on this latest development.' I felt like telling her to make it her ruddy self, and to stop acting like it was her enquiry when she'd done absolutely diddly-squat so far. I needed to look professional in front of Medalsum though, so I stepped into the kitchenette to stick the kettle on.

When I came back into the room Carmichael was writing notes. Medalsum was still sat on the sofa with Tasha on his lap, rubbing the dog's head.

'Sophie, come here – give this another sniff.' I put my nose close to the Staffie's short velvety fur.

'Lavender. I couldn't quite place it in the car. But that's what it is. And it smells like the fresh stuff too,' I said. 'We used to have a bush in the back garden only Brownlow kept peeing on it, and it died.' Carmichael made a 'too much information' face.

'PC Carmichael, come and smell my dog.' Now that surely wasn't an offer she got every day of the week. 'Does it smell like it could be like a shampoo or bath stuff to you? Maybe a flea treatment or whatever?' Carmichael came over and without even a little humour, inhaled the top of the Staffie's head. Tash's jaw dropped open in a big doggy grin. As a canine a fair proportion of her life had involved being sniffed or sniffing other dogs, but I was willing to be this was the first time she'd had a communal scent sharing session with humans. I got the feeling it made her feel very special. Perhaps we should all spend quality time sniffing our dogs, rather than saving it for those occasions when they're suspected of rolling in something unpleasant.

'I'm with Ms Gorrage. It smells like fresh lavender, not a perfumed product. My grandma used to use lavender soap and wore lavender cologne. But this smells like the plant when you crush it.'

The same thought had struck all three of us and set us scrabbling for our phones. I knew the other two would be searching for lavender farms on the Isle of Wight. While they were doing that, I called Paul, Tash's temporary owner. He answered straight away and told me exactly what I'd hoped to hear. He hadn't taken her walking anywhere near lavender. He'd only walked her on the beach and in the town of Ventnor. He'd hoped to get to know the dog a little more, and her become used to him, before taking her somewhere more rural where she could be let off the lead. Like us, he had noticed that she smelt of 'something flowery and pleasant'. He'd thought maybe it was some flea or mange treatment she'd been given by the charity.

Meanwhile Medalsum and Carmichael had completed their web searches. The internet was offering us three lavender growers on the island. I went and switched the kettle off. This was no time to sit around quaffing beverages.

'Would you like to travel in my car or Ms Gorrage's?' Carmichael asked Medalsum.

'I'll stick with Sophie and the dogs.' It wasn't until she'd pulled away in front that Medalsum admitted that he'd thought Gemma would be driving a police car. He'd declined her offer as he didn't particularly want to be photographed sitting in the back of one of those. 'Papp that and it would sell, but our covert activities would be well and truly blown.' I explained the Volvo estate was Carmichael's off duty car. 'She's off duty? I assumed she was plain clothes?'

'Gemma? She should be so lucky. She's uniform. And rural crime.'

'Rural crime? That sounds really interesting.' He wasn't being sarcastic either. I decided to stop disparaging my rival investigator. It wasn't big or clever, and worse, it clearly wasn't working.

'Yes,' I said, trying to sound charitable, 'I'd imagine it could be.' If he wanted to use cows stuck in ditches and bee hive thefts in the lyrics of his next album that was up to him.

We followed Carmichael down a narrow lane with tall hedgerows on either side. Then it opened up to give us a breathtaking view of long fields of multi-coloured wild flowers on either side of us. Medalsum wound down the window.

'Can't really smell lavender, apart from Tasha in the back seat. Be a great place to make a video though. Aerial shot of a figure, then panning down.' Hopefully the figure he was imagining among the flowers was himself or even a scarecrow. If it was PC Carmichael, I can't imagine it getting great viewing figures. As we pulled into the farmyard, Carmichael had already arrived, left her car and was knocking on the door of the house. A woman in a long and appropriately floral dress answered.

'Campion House?' Carmichael asked.

'Yes, are you here to collect the wreaths?'

'No, no. I just wanted to ask, about your lavender…'

'Ah, I'm afraid we can't supply lavender. We've chosen not to grow it at all this season. We've diversified into other flowers for drying. This year it's statice, achillea, yarrow, cornflowers, strawflowers and dragon's breath. Last year we had a bad time with lavender beetle...' she explained. 'Plus, there're too many other lavender growers, and with one crop you're quite limited in what you can do with it. We now sell mail-order everlasting bouquets and arrangements, as well as wreaths and wedding flowers.'

'Do you have a card?' said Medalsum. 'If those are your flowers in the field back there, I'd like to call later to place an order.'

We drove off in search of the next lavender farm. It was on the other side of the island, towards Ryde, but judging by their social media, which Medalsum checked while I drove, they were currently still growing it. 'I'm going to get a bouquet of those other flowers sent to Valerie, to thank her for helping in the hunt for Tasha. I'll send it from the dog though. The kind of relationship we have, it'll go straight in the bin otherwise,' he said with a wry smile.

'Lavender beetle,' I said, 'that's a new one to me.'

'Lots of folk from the music biz dream of buying the big place in the country. But it's not for me. I think that just might be why.'

'Slow up, pull in to the side,' Medalsum suddenly insisted. I stopped, letting Carmichael pull further ahead of us. Medalsum got out of the car and put his arm carefully through the barbed wire fence. Beyond was a field planted with purple-bluish flowers. Medalsum got back in the car with a few flower stalks and crushed them between his palms. He inhaled. 'That's it, that's it, Sophie. It's definitely fresh lavender she stinks of.' I wouldn't have called it a 'stink', more of a healthy aroma, but I couldn't argue with his conclusion.

'Tasha's been walked or let off the lead in a field of lavender. In the last few days. Definite.' Carmichael was already inside the farmhouse and had unhelpfully closed the door behind her. She really was doing all she could to completely take over my investigation, and just at the point it might be getting somewhere. It was beyond frustrating.

'So do we just wait in the car?' Medalsum asked.

'Or maybe have a little snoop around the outbuildings while she's busy inside?' We snapped on our dogs' leads and set off briskly towards a couple of barns. A movement caught my eye, but it turned out to be a rather splendid looking golden-feathered chicken, sitting on a half open stable-type door. Inside, were some sacks, hay-bales and a luxury chicken house, around which another half-dozen hens were strutting. They were all large birds, including more golden ones and others with black and white speckles. The hen on the door fluttered down and strutted towards us. Brownlow gave a half wag of his tail, but Tasha cowered behind Medalsum's legs, her tail pressed firmly to her rump, as she showed the whites of her eyes.

'This place reminds me of the magazines they had in the doctor's waiting room when I was a kid. All pretty cottages, chickens and spotted pigs. I didn't reckon anyone actually lived like that then. Thought it was fake, but what did I know?'

'I think the chickens are what they call Heritage Breeds – Buff Orpingtons and Sussexes quite possibly.'

'Orpington chickens? From southeast London? My drummer comes from there.'

'Well, it would've been in the Kent countryside when they were first bred.' Brownlow whined. We, including Tasha and the chicken, looked at him. He had his head up. Perhaps he was catching a faint scent, or sound on the wind. Away in the distance across the lavender field were two smaller buildings, reachable only be a narrow track between the plants. That was definitely the direction Brownlow was interested in. As soon as he saw me looking that way he started to tug at his lead, eager to head that way. I shrugged at Medalsum, and we followed.

The path between the short, bee-covered lavender bushes was single-file and we had to watch our feet to avoid treading on the insects, let alone getting one up a trouser leg or landing on our shirts. Somewhere nearby there must've been a lot of beehives. Perhaps Carmichael should be giving their owners some of her invaluable anti-theft tips. The wind and rain of the previous night had beaten down some of the lavender heads across the footpath and whilst avoiding the bees we couldn't help treading on and brushing against it. 'It won't just be Tasha who's reeking of the stuff time we get there,' Medalsum commented. He was right, but this made me all the more eager to get to where Brownlow was taking us. Tasha wasn't giving any indication she'd been this way before. If she'd been dragged or forced along this path, I'd have expected to see a little uncertainty about her. If she'd been having a fun time or had received some great treat on arrival at the huts, I'd have imagined her pace quickening and some increased tail wagging. Tasha however did not seem to react, but she was not my dog, and I couldn't read her the way I could Brownlow. He was reacting by straining at the leash, pulling me forward, tail flagging back and forth. Brownlow definitely thought this was a walk worth taking and I was happy to go along with that.

As we grew nearer, I could see the buildings ahead were wooden log cabins, with picnic tables and chairs outside and what appeared to be a hot tub between them. They also appeared to be holiday lets, like 'Sea Mist' and Adrian's yurts. The first cabin had thick sailcloth blinds drawn across the windows, but one of the windows was slightly open. As we approached, a dog started to bark from within. By the sound, it was a large animal.

'Hello? Anyone home?' The dog whined and barked. Nervously I put a hand through the window to try to find how to raise the blind. The dog jumped up, and I felt its breath hot on my hand. Pulling my fingers back hastily, I looked around for something to reach into the room with. A group of long sticks supported the hollyhocks and other tall blooms in a planter beside the next chalet. Pulling free a stick, I used it to push the blind aside so I could see into the room beyond. A dog stood blinking in the sunlight. It was Rita, the missing police German Shepherd.

If Carmichael was annoyed it was Brownlow who had made the breakthrough rather than her, she made a good effort not to show it. She paced up and down outside, speaking to Hampshire Police, her boss back at Sussex, and goodness knows who else. A couple had rented the cabin from a holiday lettings website. The man had told the owner, on their arrival, that they wanted to spend some time in seclusion, meditating and being mindful. After he'd collected the keys, the cabin's owner had left them alone. He hadn't even seen the woman. A complimentary basket of fresh eggs and lavender products had not been taken in, and he hadn't seen anything of either of them. The way the little huts were situated at the highest point in the field, meant the nearest lane giving motor vehicle access couldn't be viewed from the farmhouse, so not seeing the tenants hadn't been particularly unusual, especially as the man had indicated they intended keeping themselves to themselves. The poor farm owner, who had his baby son in his arms, looked so worried by plain-clothes (or rather day-off clothes) Carmichael. He kept repeatedly apologising for the situation. I could hardly have imagined him looking more anxious if he'd been faced with an elite SWAT team waving AK47s around inside his holiday let. To be honest, I wouldn't have been surprised if the 'back up'

Gemma insisted were on the way consisted of a solitary part-time PCSO on a squeaky bicycle.

Carmichael only permitted Medalsum and myself a quick look around with the instructions to leave our dogs outside and not to touch anything. In reality there wasn't a lot to tempt us to make a tactile response. The wardrobe doors were open, but it was empty, the bed unused and there were no personal possessions anywhere. The dog had been left a bowl of dry dog food and one of water but that seemed to be it. In the kitchen area there was a kettle, which the owner said she'd provided along with a bottle of washing up liquid and numerous other household bits and pieces. The two white mugs on the draining board that had, by the fact they were upside down, probably been washed up, were the only items apart from the dog bowls she did not recognise as her own. 'I've left some floral ones in the cupboard,' she whispered as if making some heinous confession. The newness of the white mugs was supported by the plain box at the back of the kitchen bench that appeared, had I been permitted to delve, to contain another four identical mugs.

I pointed to the box of mugs as Carmichael strode over. With her blue PVC gloves, she tilted it to inspect the contents, giving me a glimpse of what I'd hoped to see – another four unused mugs.

'Looks like they were expecting company,' stated Carmichael with authority. I turned away, so she didn't see my slight smile.

'Six mugs…' mused Medalsum, 'and they certainly seem to be making mugs of us. Always one step ahead.' I said nothing but had noted two important things. Firstly, that the place was clean. The dog had not had the chance to soil the rugs or wooden floor, so had clearly been taken outside regularly, if she'd been here for any length of time. The second thing I'd clocked were the mugs and I thought I knew a little more about them than Carmichael did. This was not Goldilocks and the Three Bears. The presence of six mugs didn't mean six dognappers were planning to gather there for a nice mug of tea or coffee. Carmichael could run with that idea, but I had a theory of my own. Things were hotting up, and not because of the sunshine pouring in the cabin window.

'Local police are on their way, and this will now become their investigation. I'll hand over to them as soon as they get here. There's no further need for you to stay, Ms Gorrage, or you Mr Medalsum.' I beamed.

'Thanks Gem. That's fine. I'll be seeing you.' I left with a spring in my step and a grin as wide as Brownlow's at dinnertime.

'Em,' I said to Medalsum, as we retraced our steps through the field of lavender, 'Can we get out of here? I need to get back to the mainland pretty sharpish.'

'I'm guessing you've seen something back there that me and Country Cop have missed. If you need to follow it up urgently, I can speak to my tour manager. He's one of the best fixers in the business.'

While I was in 'Sea Mist' packing my bags, Medalsum made the call. We were, he then explained, going to be heading for Sandown Airport, where a plane would be waiting for us. I was a little apprehensive at flying, as it gives me the same kind of queasiness as boats. I wondered whether my seasickness bands and tablets would work for turbulence or whether I needed to buy special ones for flying. As you may have ascertained, I'm not one of the International Jet Set. This did, I assume involve a jet – one of those luxurious private ones. Medalsum and I would no doubt be sipping cocktails in our own flight lounge as we whizzed across the Solent. Maybe there'd be a staff member on hand to serve our drinks and the dogs their biscuits. I went through a spate of buying second-hand airport lounge novels in my local branch of the Dog Shop. After a night crawling around on my hands and knees after some errant cat or rabbit, a bit of glamour and escapism didn't go amiss. That's where my ideas about sumptuous Lear Jets staffed by uniformed flunkeys came from. In those books, famous rocks stars regularly whisked the intrepid heroines off to Greek or Caribbean Islands by this mode of transport. I just wished I'd packed or for that matter even owned the kind of slinky long dress and sandals the women on the cover invariably wore, as they raised a glass to the azure Aegean.

In those books, problems like how to get your car home if you're going by plane, never seemed to arise. Fortunately, Medalsum's manager could, he said, have it couriered back to my place. I told Medalsum I couldn't possibly let him pay for that, but he waved away my excuses. 'I've got Tasha back. The police have got Rita. You need to go find those other stolen dogs. If I can help with a few logistics along the way, that's the least I can do.'

It was a very small airport and a very small plane. It wasn't a gleaming jet like the kind John Travolta might have parked up outside his house. It was red and white with two sticking out wings and a propeller. 'Gonna be a bit of a squeeze. Dogs on our laps probably.' As we bumped along the runway, with engine sounding more like a lawnmower than something that was going to attempt to get airborne, I closed my eyes. Perhaps fortunately, when I opened them again, all I could see was the head of the great shaggy dog who was crushing my knees.

'Is this strictly legal? Travelling like this?'

'Probably not. At least Border Force won't show any interest us, as we haven't left the country.' I'd somehow expected we'd be flying to London, possibly to Heathrow or City Airport, but that's when I was imagining we'd be travelling by jet. In fact, we landed at Shoreham or 'Brighton

City Airport' as they've rebranded it in recent years. It's still in Shoreham, naturally, with its pretty little Art Deco terminal looking like something out of a period drama. From Shoreham, Medalsum had an Uber waiting to take him and Tasha wherever it was they were heading. Brownlow and I relied on the 700 bus to get home.

'Been somewhere hot and exotic?' asked the driver, seeing my suitcase. She was probably someone who read airport lounge novels too. It was, I could safely say, a day of 'Planes, Trains and Automobiles' as we were making at least one journey by each of the above, and the bus too of course.

'It seems like a rather odd thing to be thinking of, in the midst of such an important case,' said Belle, stirring her cappuccino, 'though I suppose promoting your brand is important too.' We'd arranged to meet at the Battersea Park café again. We were chatting while the dogs lounged on the terrace, waiting patiently to be walked around the lake. 'So you're thinking of Brownlow and Gorrage t-shirts?'

'And maybe mugs and key rings.'

'You're going to sell them from your website?'

'Or just give a few away to supporters. Through competitions on our socials. I haven't completely decided yet.'

'I've been so worried about you, you know. All that trolling. So awful. I know lots of people have had those kinds of issues. But you? Totally uncalled for.'

'It's nothing, Belle. Paid-for sentences, badly constructed by some poor soul in a social media sweatshop abroad. It doesn't mean I've got lots of enemies here in the UK. It's just one, or possibly two. The only thing is they may get more desperate and dangerous, now they know I'm closing in on them.'

'Can you tell me more, Soph?'

'Not at the moment. But soon,' I promised. Belle buttered her croissant pensively.

'You know I've left Let Dogs Be Dogs?'

'Have you?' I must've looked a little startled at that.

'Because I thought it was them who were trolling you. Even though everyone I know who was on the march and that assured me it was the last thing they'd do. But I thought maybe they'd been infiltered,'

'Infiltrated?'

'Infiltrated. That's it. By extremists. I mean that can happen, can't it? And you don't know who's behind it, do you?'

'That's just it, Belle,' I said. 'Actually, I think I do.'

We continued to talk as we walked around the lake. Shortcake was keen to chase the ducks, but Belle was very good at distracting him with his squeaky toy.

'You said you'd never met Vicki?'

'Vicki?'

'She's the main person behind LDBD isn't she?'

'Oh that Vicki. No, I've not met her. And I muted them. Because I thought they were the people trolling you. Even though I didn't recognise any of the haters' profiles.'

I decided it was okay to tell Belle I'd been on the Isle of Wight with Medalsum. Although her taste in music tends to be rather more pop related, she was still excited by the idea that a mate of hers had been hobnobbing with a bona fide chart topper. I filled her in on most of what had happened and promised I would be posting some photos from the trip soon. I told her I'd felt it was for the best to keep my visit to the island a secret while I was there, in part to protect Brownlow and myself from the people we were after. She was wide-eyed when she heard about the car tracker and the intruder entering our chalet. 'I won't let anyone know I've met you today, or that you're back,' she promised.

'Is there anyone you know who has been asking questions about me, or shown an interest in any way? Maybe after the march?'

'No. No, I don't think so.' That dented my ego a tiny bit. I'd kind of imagined my quarry seeing me as a worthy adversary and needing to find out every single detail about my dog and me.

Before we went our separate ways, Belle promised to send me Nat and Cassie's contact details, as she was sure one of them would know how to get in touch with Jonas with regard to discussing merchandising needs. He hadn't been in the LDBD WhatsApp group himself, and now she'd left LDBD, Belle had no further contact with Nat or Cassie. If they couldn't help me with Jonas's details, she said, there were probably plenty of people offering similar personalised printing services online.

'I liked him,' I said, truthfully as it happened. I had. 'He told me about his designs while we were on the march and I'd like to put my trade his way if I can. I expect he has a website, but since I've only got his first name and don't know what name he trades under, it's a bit like looking for a needle in a haystack.' Belle said that fingers crossed, either Nat or Cassie would know where to find him.

'But when you say you liked him, Soph… I mean he seems like a nice guy and he's a dog owner… are you saying things are a bit on/off with that other guy, the one with the sanctuary?'

'Quinn. No. We're still together.'

'But not living with each other, or… I don't know, any serious commitment?'

'And that's just how we like it, thank you, Belle. I'm not looking to settle down with anyone other than my dog.'

'Well in that case… if you do get chatting to Jonas, remember me to him, won't you?'

'Belle?' She looked slightly embarrassed. Belle did once have a fiancé that I know of, but it was so long ago, people could be studying him under the subject of ancient history. 'Alright,' I lied, 'If I meet him, I will see if I can subtly drop your name into the conversation somewhere, along with the t-shirts and key rings.' Of course, I had no intention of doing such a thing and she might well thank me for that later.

Back home, I let Rouki Bennett, and Gavin and Melissa know I hadn't given up on finding their dogs. The fact that Tasha the Staffie and Rita the German Shepherd had been well looked after by the kidnappers, and that Tasha had been rehomed with a responsible dog lover, were, I felt all positive signs. Unlike so many stolen dogs they hadn't been sold to an unscrupulous breeder or fallen into the hands of someone with no knowledge of how to care for a dog. Neither had they been deemed too 'hot' due to their celebrity status and abandoned on a roadside or dumped in some remote location.

My theory was that Rita had been left behind by the dognappers, possibly with the full knowledge Brownlow and I were closing in and she wouldn't remain there alone for long. Of course, that might be pure ego on my part, and they had actually left the dog, intending to tell the owner of the holiday let they had to check out early, again as a pretext to prevent Rita starving or suffering in any way. As I'd implied, I had no evidence the kidnappers meant harm to the animals. I also thought I knew why Rita had been left behind, rather than Lady Champignon, Mr Merrytrees or Bianca. Rita was a large dog and a noisy dog. Whether travelling on a public ferry, where small dogs could be discreetly concealed in luggage, or a private hire boat where a larger dog would be seen being taken onboard and possibly barking, taking Rita back to the mainland by sea meant a greater risk of discovery. With Brownlow and me on their trail, the kidnappers would've known that now even making the trip at night, as they'd done at Brighton, risked them being caught out. Shortly after we found Rita, I realised that in all likelihood Rouki's Cockers and Gavin and Melissa's Chihuahua were in the process of leaving, or had already left, the island.

'*Where are you?*' Carmichael's text was brusque and to the point.

'*Home. You?*'

'*Still following up leads,*' she replied, clearly trying to needle me.

'*Much luck?*' She didn't answer. That was a '*no*' then. I suspected Carmichael didn't even have a suspect in her sights. Clearly as far as she was concerned a mug was just a mug. While he might have made a mug of our doyenne of rural crime however, Jonas had not made one of Brownlow and Gorrage.

Chapter Ten

I looked up Greyhound racing kennels, making a note of all those in the Southeast. I thought I'd try calling them first. Jonas had said he'd worked at one, and if I could find a former co-worker, I might find someone who knew where he lived or possibly get some idea of what he might be planning. One thing I was sure of, he wasn't done yet. Judging by the way I'd been followed and the attempt to take Brownlow while we were on the Isle of Wight, he definitely saw us as a serious threat. He knew now that the trolling and the spray-painted door and even the blow on the head weren't giving me second thoughts about seeing this thing through. One way or another, we were now on a collision course.

I called Greyhound racing kennels in Kent, in London, and in Sussex. There seemed to be either a high turnover of staff at these establishments, or else they were so small as to be more or less family affairs. No one remembered a Jonas-without-a-surname, until I called a trainer based outside Brighton. His landline number transferred me to his mobile. 'Jonas Joiner, he practically ran things here for me for a couple of years. I was trying to run an office supply business at the same time, you see? I was overstretched. It was utter madness! But the dogs were my first love.'

'But Jonas, what can you tell me about him?' Why is it people always start talking about themselves. I didn't require the kennel owner's life history. I needed to at least be sure I'd even got the right Jonas.

'Look, I've got a few of mine in a race at Hove today. I'm there now. Can this wait?'

'Not really…'

'Well, can you come down then? I'll be in the bar all evening, schmoozing and maybe doing a little bit of business. If you want to talk to me, that's the place to do it.' I told the guy, whose name was Stewart Prowse, that I'd be right there.

I clipped on Brownlow's lead and headed outside to the car. The Clio was in my resident's parking bay where Medalsum's courier had handily delivered her while I was in London. Unfortunately, at some point after it had been delivered, someone had whitewashed the windscreen. On the white paint, sprayed in red was a single word 'Woof!' I grabbed a squeegee, but the paint was not water soluble. I suspected it was household gloss, with 'Woof!' in car paint on top. It meant a new windscreen and the Clio wouldn't be going anywhere until I had one fitted. No doubt those two girls were responsible, but I knew it wasn't wanton vandalism. Jonas had paid them. Clearly, he felt if he could keep us off the road, he'd stay one step ahead. I called Quinn. Wearily, he said he had volunteers he could leave in charge and would run Brownlow and me to Hove Greyhound Stadium.

As Quinn drove through Hove I called the emergency replacement windscreen people, sending them a screenshot and the address where they could find my car. I hoped to have my car in a usable state by the next day. I'd clearly need to see if I could cheaply rent a garage in the vicinity of our maisonette for it in future. If we were going to be taking on major crime cases our security efforts had to improve. Quinn said he'd never been to a Greyhound race. He'd had unwanted and injured Greyhounds brought in to the sanctuary.

Some owners love their dogs and are responsible, keeping them as pets or homing them when their racing lives are over.

But some just want rid of them when they're no longer winning, and don't care how that happens. That kind of puts me off it as a sport. Like with horse racing there's too much collateral damage where the animals are concerned. I gave Stewart a call when we reached the stadium, and he came down to meet us, giving us lanyards that allowed us to join him in a bar that was reserved for owners and trainers. On the way, we passed other bustling bars and a restaurant, already busy with punters. 'People come for an evening out – you can sit down to a full meal and watch the racing taking place below.'

'But the races haven't started yet today?' Stewart checked the time on his phone.

'No. But my dogs should be arriving about now. I got here earlier to meet a prospective client.'

'Office supplies?'

'No, no I'm out of that line now. No, I was meant to be meeting someone who said he was interested in getting into the sport. He phoned after seeing one of my dogs win here last week. Asked if I'd any youngsters in training he could buy.'

'Is that how it works? You house and train them for the owner?' I checked.

'That's the usual arrangement. I don't think this guy had owned or even part-owned a racing dog before. But on the phone he sounded pretty keen.' He shrugged.

'But he hasn't turned up?' Quinn asked.

'Not yet at any rate. Perhaps something's delayed him.' We ordered drinks and sat down. Around us were pictures of winners. They mainly stood on podiums, in their racing jackets with rosettes pinned to them, proud owner and trainer on either side. We looked down on the track below, where a few staff members were making final checks.

'So, Jonas Joiner?' I said.

'Best kennel manager I ever had. What he didn't know about dogs wasn't worth knowing.'

'How do you mean? Their racing form or looking after them?'

'Everything. Health, nutrition, when a vet was needed, when a simple strain just needed rest. And a dog whisperer. They loved him. Never met a dog that didn't. Even the most highly-strung ones would settle with Jonas.'

'And what was he like as a person?' I asked.

'Quiet. Hard-working. I didn't find out much about his private life. Seemed to want to keep that side of things to himself. He didn't really go out and socialise with the other staff, and even if we won, and we'd all be in the bar celebrating, as like as not, Jonas would be downstairs with the dogs. Even after he'd tended to their post-race needs. I remember him once saying he was raised by dogs. Perhaps that's something of an explanation.'

'Not raised by wolves?' Quinn queried.

'No, you remember Nana in Peter Pan – where it's the dog left looking after the kids?'

'I've only seen the film.'

'That's what I meant. Only it wasn't in some big old house in London. He grew up on a hill farm. Somewhere in Cumbria, I think he said. And I remember after he'd left us, one of the other staff told me that when one of our dogs was sick, and he insisted on spending the night with it in the kennels, he'd said it was nothing new to him. His father was a drunk, mother had left, and he'd tend to sleep in the barn with the Collies. Those dogs were pretty much neglected, judging by what I heard, and so as a kid, was he.' Stewart Prowse looked at Quinn and me. 'But I can't believe Jonas would be involved in this dog stealing racket you were saying about. If you pardon the pun, I think you're very much barking up the wrong tree there.' Neither of us smiled as he went on to elaborate. 'Nowadays I just train a few dogs and breed a few too, but in those days, we had a fair few champions with us. If he'd wanted to steal animals that were worth serious money – and it's pretty easy to ship abroad through the right networks – well, the opportunity was there. But as I said, he isn't that kind of bloke. Or wasn't then at any rate. Not money oriented. Honest, hard-working and good with dogs, that's my assessment of Jonas Joiner.'

'You don't happen to have a photo of him? As he was then of course – what five years ago?' I asked.

'I don't. Like I said kept himself to himself.' He gestured to the photos on the wall. 'Didn't seem to enjoy the whole razzamatazz side of things.'

'What does he look like? Or look like then I mean?'

'Tall, slim. Kind of average really. It's been five years; I find it hard to even really picture him now. Light brown hair, blue eyes maybe... Now, do either of you want another drink?'

Before we could reply to Stewart Prowse's offer, an official approached and drew him aside for a quick word. Returning to us, he checked his phone. 'I've just been told my dogs haven't arrived yet. They're wanting to do the pre-race checks on them of course. They should be here by now. Perhaps they're stuck in traffic.' He dialled a number. 'No answer. She must've left and they're on their way.' We followed Stewart Prowse downstairs and into the car park to await the air-conditioned truck carrying the Greyhounds. As he repeatedly checked the time and made calls that went to answer, Quinn and I looked at each other. Another official approached Prowse and the two walked, having an animated conversation. Finally, the second man departed and Prowse rejoined us. 'Okay, we've missed the deadline to enter the first race. That'll go ahead without my two that were going in it. Pity. It's the first time this has happened. I did remind Vicki she needed to get the dogs boxed and into the truck in good time. She's never had any problems doing it before.'

'Vicki?' I said.

'Yes. Why?'

I offered to Stewart Prowse that Quinn and I could pop in at kennels on our way home, to ensure that all was well, and that Vicki and the greyhounds were safely on their way. He agreed and we set off.

'His kennels are where?' Quinn raised an eyebrow. 'That's not in my reckoning, remotely on the way back to either Weatherall or yours.'

'So?' I replied, as we pulled away, Brownlow with his head out the window, tongue lolling as usual. 'In that case either I've no sense of direction, or I want to get a closer look at that training kennel.'

'I noticed,' said Quinn, without taking his eyes of the road, you reacted slightly when he said the name 'Vicki'. Not much escapes Quinn James.

'Yes, it could of course all be a huge coincidence. Very common name after all. Or maybe I've got things all wrong. Perhaps it's the mysterious Vicki who is said to be the leader of Let Dogs Be Dogs who is behind things after all. Maybe Jonas Joiner has nothing to do with it.'

'And yet?' Quinn mused, there were at least three people involved in the attempt to get the police dog on the boat. Two with the van, one or more at sea. And what about the tall man in the Isle of Wight?

'Well, it could be a ringleader assisted by either criminal associates, or sympathisers to the cause.'

'And what do you expect to find at this Greyhound place?' he asked. I shrugged,

'Probably nothing. Nothing at all.'

I was both right and wrong. When I'd said I'd expected to find nothing, I'd meant nothing linked to the missing dogs' case. I hadn't meant that I'd expected to find a completely deserted premises. I walked up and down the empty runs just to make sure, then I called Stewart Prowse. 'Have your Greyhounds arrived yet?'

'They're putting the competitors into the traps for the second race now. With three traps empty that were supposed to be occupied by my dogs.'

'We're at your place now. All of the kennels are empty.'

'Not all of them – there are plenty of dogs there that aren't racing today.'

'No there aren't, Mr Prowse. I'm pretty sure of that. There aren't any dogs here at all.'

Quinn and I continued to look around, but the silence told its own story. There was no dog transporter parked on the drive either.

'This side gate,' Quinn indicated a tall gate with 'private property' and barbed wire on its top. 'It's supposed to be padlocked on the inside, isn't it? And there's no other easy way in. This place is designed to be secure. We shouldn't have been able to stroll into the yard through an open gate. Mr

Prowse was expecting us to ring the doorbell and speak to someone. This Vicki wasn't supposed to be here alone.'

I was peering through the windows into the detached house but there were no signs of anyone being home. Quinn went around to the front door and rang the bell. From inside the yard, I knocked on the back door. We received no reply. I rang Stewart Prowse back. He said he'd already called the police and was heading back himself to wait for them. I wanted to stay put for him to arrive and unlock the house, which appeared to double up as an office for the kennels. I'd have liked to have had a snoop around to see if I might gain some clues as to whether the Vicki who had been working there, was the same Vicki as the one who was behind LDBD. Quinn however said he needed to get back to Weatherall Fields. They'd had a number of nests of baby birds of one sort or another brought in over the past few days, some – like a group of eight blue tit nestlings – needing feeds every ten minutes or so. Clemency was there and had said she'd have a ring round the volunteer register to find someone else able to give a hand. Nevertheless, all the creatures were ultimately Quinn's responsibility and feeding perpetually hungry baby birds was a fiddly and stressful job. Things could easily go wrong, and casualty rates could be high, as the delicate tiny creatures, still blind and featherless in some cases, had to adapt to an inevitable dietary change from what their parents had been feeding them, as well as cope with a whole different sensory world around them.

If I'd had my Clio, Brownlow and I could've stayed put, but as things stood, we were way out in the country and not on a bus route. The nearest one I knew of only ran once a day, two days a week. It was not one of those days, or the right hour. Reluctantly, Brownlow and I left with Quinn.

The windscreen repairer had left me a jaunty little message on my phone to say my replacement would be fitted within the next two hours. With luck, by the time I reached home it would be done. Quinn understandably wanted to go to Weatherall first to check on the delicate orphans, though promised to run me home from there, once he was sure Clemency and whoever she'd press-ganged into joining her were coping with the feeds. Ordinarily I'd have pitched in myself, making up the protein-packed mixtures and gently inserting them crumb by crumb into little hungry beaks. I could not however just break away from investigating what appeared to be the largest scale dog theft of my career so far. Stewart Prowse had said the kennels had contained twelve dogs and these were all now, it seemed, in the establishment's truck or possibly, considering their number, more than one vehicle, heading to an unknown destination. In fact, it was likely that the racing kennel's own lorry had already been abandoned, with the thieves knowing that number plate would soon be on the Police National Computer. I felt frustrated to be heading away from the scene of this latest and most audacious theft. Of course, it wasn't Quinn's fault or that of the delicate nestlings. I was almost entirely certain that the damage to my own car was all part of the plan, to ensure I could not have been on the scene of the Greyhound robbery until it was too late. Just when I thought I was closing in, the dog thieves had upped their game and stayed ahead.

Quinn unlocked the main gate to Weatherall Fields, or rather he tried. The electronic lock failed to respond. 'Not the first time it's happened. Electronic rubbish,' he grumbled. 'Give me a good old key any day.' He pressed the buzzer for Clemency to let us in. There was no reply. 'Must have her hands full of chicks. Just have to wait.' He took out and checked his phone. 'Oh, she's left me a message.' He played it and frowned.

'What?' I said. He handed it to me so I could replay the message.

'Hi boss, it's Clem. All's well here. I've found someone willing to come in and give me a hand. It was lucky really, she rang up to ask your advice about a stray cat, and as we were chatting, it turns out she used to work here, so she's coming in to help out.'

Quinn tried the intercom's buzzer again. There was still no reply.

'When she says the woman used to work here, I hope she double checked with the list in my desk. That shows the names of all the volunteers we've had, past and present.'

'Have you told her to always double check?'

'Err no. No I haven't. We always just use the contact details of the current people, which is pinned up on the wall behind the phone.' He rang reception. The answer machine came on. 'I'll try her mobile.' I was, to be honest, rather surprised when Clemency answered. She and Quinn spoke briefly and then he hung up.

Quinn looked relieved. 'She said it's a fault with the gates. She's currently talking to the manufacturers, and they'll get it sorted out. In the meantime, she says, I'm not to worry. Suggests I go to the pub and wait. They're managing with feeding all the birds – she and Victoria.'

'Victoria?' Warning bells began to clang in my head.

'So she said.' He frowned. 'But we've never had a volunteer called Victoria. I'm sure of that. Well, I mean unless she's from before my time, when Marjorie was running the place.'

'Vicki – Victoria.' I spelt it out for him. 'Vicki the mysterious organiser of Let Dogs Be Dogs, Vicki who works at the Greyhound kennels and then disappears, maybe only an hour or so ago, along with all the dogs.'

'Yes – the moment you said 'Vicki'. Before that I hadn't made the connection. Now it all seems very convenient – a problem stopping us getting into Weatherall when those dogs are missing, from a few miles away.'

'Could Clemency be part of it too? I mean why would she allow someone to lock us out otherwise?' Quinn shook his head.

'I doubt it. She's leaving next month to start her training to be a vet. Seems very focused on that. I don't think she'd jeopardise it by getting involved in criminal activity or any kind of activism. Whichever this is. Besides… she didn't sound… well quite like her normal self.'

'I don't know what she usually sounds like. Well apart from posh that is.'

'She kind of enthuses…' he struggled to explain. 'She's always upbeat. And in the message, she sounds a little more subdued. Plus, she suggested I go to the pub and chill. We're not near a pub. I don't have a local where I go for a quiet pint. It just doesn't happen. I know this isn't exactly evidence anything's going on… it's just a hunch, Sophie. An instinct.'

'No,' I said, 'it's more focused than an instinct. That call's made you think someone else was present in the background making her spin you the tale about the electronic lock.' He nodded.

'Vicki – Victoria,' he said. 'You're right. It has to be.' He turned the van around outside the gates.

'What? We're leaving?'

'Let them see us go on the CCTV. There's a farm track back down the lane where we can park and head back up here on foot.'

Quinn thought we should take a look around the perimeter of Weatherall before calling the police. The wire fence had CCTV and an alarm protecting it, but although the cameras had only been installed a few weeks, Quinn knew where their blind spots were. 'The thing is, it's trees that are causing the problem. A mature oak inside the perimeter and a row of horse-chestnuts on the outside. I'd have to trim our tree back severely and ask our neighbour to fell at least two of his if we were going to have a clear view of the back of the premises. But I couldn't do that to those trees. I can't imagine it's something Marjorie would've approved of whatever the circumstances. She loved our oak. Said it was over a century old. That's why I've got the entire fence fitted to the alarm system. I couldn't see if someone was breaking in under cover of the trees, but I'd very definitely hear them.'

We made a wide circle to reach the back of Weatherall Fields without appearing on any of the cameras. I wished I had my various long range viewing devices with me, but I hadn't imagined needing them when we were only going to the Greyhound stadium. I'd imagined there'd have been plenty of binoculars there I could've borrowed in an emergency, if I'd needed for any reason to closely scrutinise the track or the dogs.

'If I'd thought to bring my drone, we could fly it over the fence and take a look in the windows'

'Too noisy. We might see who was in there, but we'd give the game away that we know something is going on.' He didn't reckon we needed a drone or optical devices, just our own eyes and ears, plus of course Brownlow's heightened senses. As we crept up to the fence, a few dogs were barking, but the noise didn't increase on our approach. 'That's a hound kind of bark,' I said.

'We do have a couple of Greyhounds, but they've been here a while and are very quiet and settled. That's a more of a lost, bewildered kind of bark. Slightly panicky. Do you think, Soph?'

I concentrated hard, trying to work out how many different dogs were giving voice at the same time. It was difficult. I could definitely hear those Greyhound type higher pitched barks, and the short yap of something smaller and terrier-like. I'm sure there are people who can identify every dog breed by their bark but I'm not one of them. I mean I could tell a Miniature Poodle from a German Shepherd, but German Shepherd from a Dutch Shepherd or even a Doberman and I'd be struggling. Quinn was crouched down, close to, but not touching the fence, edging with small steps along the perimeter. He stopped abruptly, beckoning me to join him but to stay low. I brought Brownlow with me on a close lead, looking at his furry face as I gave him the signal to stay silent. Once beside Quinn I could see what he was seeing. It was a truck with the silhouette of a racing Greyhound upon it. Those dogs were here, inside Weatherall.

'That's it,' Quinn whispered, 'the evidence we need to call the police.' I took out my phone to make the call, but before I could, to my horror it let me know I'd a call, with the Baha Men in full voice. The racket set off pretty much every dog in Weatherall. Large barks, small barks, growls, howls and whines. Quinn shot me a glance as sharp as a thousand daggers. Of course, I knew the first rule of surveillance was to turn your phone off. It was just that with so much else to think about I'd forgotten about it. 'A-woof' said Brownlow, deciding that if the tiny people inside the talking box were allowed to bark, then so was he. With all that noise going on, I decided I might as well take the call. Walking quickly away into the trees, I checked the number onscreen. I didn't recognise it. 'Hello. Brownlow And Gorrage.'

'Hello Sophie.' It was a man's voice that sounded familiar. He was addressing me as if he knew me, yet with a coldness in his tone. 'I was wondering if you'd have a word with Mr James for me. I know he's there with you. What I have to say concerns you both.'

'I see.'

'I passed his van on the way up here, parked down a track. Then I discover that you were sitting in it with him, when you came to the front gate. So what I have to say is this,' he said, coming to the point, 'don't call the police. And tell Mr James not to call them either. We won't harm the animals. We'd never do that. But we have Clemency, and believe me when I say this, if the police are called, then clemency is the last thing she'll receive.'

'Wait? Hello? Jonas?' He'd ended the call. I shouted to Quinn.

'Don't call the police?'

'What?' I could see he already had his phone to his ear, I rushed back and snatched it from him, ending the call.

Quinn said he hadn't got around to giving the 999 operator his details. The dogs in Weatherall Field's kennels had been making such a racket he hadn't been able to hear her properly. He'd still been asking her to repeat whatever it was she'd been saying, when I'd terminated communications.

I tried redialling the number that had just called me. The phone had been switched off. Instead, I tried Weatherall's landline again. This time it didn't go to the answer machine. A woman answered, her voice clipped and rather plummy, like the receptionist of an upmarket dental practice. This I suspected was 'Vicki'.

'Look, what exactly is going on –' I began.

'You'll find out,' she declared smugly, 'soon enough.' She put the phone down and after that all I got was Quinn's voice on the answer machine once more.

'So they're planning something. 'You'll find out, soon enough' she said.'

'Of course they are,' Quinn retorted. 'Otherwise, it would make no sense to hole up in there and get into a siege situation, even without the police involved as yet.'

'Assuming of course they are making rational decisions…'

'They are, Soph. No doubt about that. It's how they've stayed ahead of you and Brownlow. They've a plan, it's just one that isn't clear to us. It doesn't follow the pattern. We assumed, much as anyone would, that they were stealing valuable dogs for profit. Possibly to order. But then you found they'd given Medalsum's Staffie away. I've talked to Paul who had adopted her. He sounds like a nice guy. Of course, I'd have to do a home check and follow up, but he sounds like the kind of person I'd let one of our animals go to.'

Quinn sat back in the long grass. He looked at the fence. 'But we do need to get in there. It's not just the baby birds, the kittens will need feeding too. And I've a fox and a hedgehog who've had surgery and who the vet was coming to check on their progress this evening.'

'If we touch it – the alarm sounds?' Quinn nodded.

'I wish I'd listened properly to what the installer was telling me. How I could have an app on my phone and operate it remotely. You know what I'm like with apps – and I had this vision of setting the alarm remotely and then not being able to get back in.'

'So you never set it up?'

'And I wouldn't know where to start.' I told him I'd an idea. I rang Skyla and let her know about the alarm problem, though not why it was currently an issue. I didn't want the news of what was happening at Weatherall Fields getting out, until we were hopefully more on top of things. Skyla consulted Jamal. She took the name of the alarm company, then asked if Quinn could access his account with them via his phone. He said they'd emailed an invoice and receipt. Both documents had a customer number and other details on them.

'Forward them to us,' said Skyla, 'and we'll get back.'

I assumed that if and when the alarm was disabled, we'd be cutting through the fence. Quinn though said he'd made sure his fence could not be easily breached by someone with a pair of bolt cutters. It would take a power tool to cut through the reinforced mesh. Quinn's idea was that if someone had somehow managed to knock out his alarm, or there'd been a power failure, he or his staff would hear any break-in attempt, if it could only be accomplished by using power tools. It was typical of Quinn to be so security conscious, though not a great deal of help if he was the one currently stuck outside.

'Could we dig under it?' I was grasping at straws.

'I've had it embedded two foot in the soil to deter wild foxes and badgers digging in, with an 8-inch horizontal overhang below ground too. But in theory we could dig under that, as long as the alarm was switched off, as it is touch sensitive.' I thought about who lived near enough to Weatherall to be able to help us. It was Rouki Bennett, her live-in PA Alex, and Carl and Jack, her former dog-walker and his husband. Luckily all were in when I called them, and Jack said there was a hardware shop in Steyning, which he knew stocked spades and shovels. He and Carl didn't mind buying the excavation equipment on the way. I thanked him profusely, but he simply laughed.

'My favourite all time movie is 'The Great Escape'. Re-enacting it, even in reverse, will be a dream come true!'

My phone lit up. It was now, belatedly, on silent mode.

'Hi Soph, what are you up to?' It was Belle. I could hear Shortcake snuffling around in the background. I started telling her I didn't have time for a chat at present as unfortunately I was rather busy.

'I know. I'm watching and waiting. You are a tease.'

'I am? Err what do you mean?'

'Your live stream.'

'My what?' I told Quinn to check on my socials. He rolled his eyes.

'Is it really the time to check your likes and shares?'

'Just do it,' I snapped. An animated gif was playing of words appearing on a screen.

'Dog lovers everywhere', it said, 'you don't want to miss this'. Quinn took his phone back to answer a call.

'What?' he gasped in disbelief. 'Yes, yes, I am. No, I didn't just call your news desk. No, I don't represent any organisation. It must be a hoax, okay. That is not happening.' He shoved his phone back in his pocket. 'Apparently, at six pm, there is going to be a live-stream event from Weatherall Fields by the organisers of the Let Dogs Be Dogs movement,' he said. I gawped at him. 'They will demand the complete ban on dogs being made to work in any capacity. That was the BBC. They thought it was me behind it, as the message supposedly came from the people running Weatherall.'

'Well, I suppose whoever's in there are currently the people running Weatherall,' I reminded him.

'The news reporter wanted to know if I was including the banning of guide and assistance dogs in my campaign. So now they think the sanctuary is being run by a group of extremists. This could really damage us. I think we do need to call the police.'

'But you heard what the guy said about harming Clemency. If they're going to live-stream at six, that's only half an hour away. The police'll soon know all about it, whether we tell them or not.'

My phone screen shone out again. It was Skyla, asking to be passed across to Quinn. He had to download the app controlling the alarm and then insert a pass code the manufacturer would be sending to his phone. That would let him switch the alarm off and on as he pleased, remotely. As soon as I got my phone back, I sent instructions to the digging team of how to reach us. After looking at a map on screen, I was able to tell them where to leave their cars. They would then need to use a public footpath winding through a hazel copse to come out behind Weatherall, where the trees would shield them from the cameras. 'We've a bonus,' said Quinn, 'in that the alarm manufacturers fitted the CCTV too. This app gives me control of it too, separately.' The alarm could be discreetly switched off, but the cameras going dark would be noticed by anyone checking the monitor screen. Quinn said he'd leave the cameras on until we'd managed to breach the perimeter fence.

Although we were still waiting for the shovels to arrive, I encouraged Brownlow to begin digging. It's always one of his favourite activities and to be honest it doesn't take much to get him starting on a hole. It's not like I have some command of 'dig Brownlow, dig,' like they'd have in a 'Lassie' movie. At home, he only needs to see me start clearing a few weeds to try to re-plant my pathetic attempt at a herb garden, and he's there in an instant, big paws ready to start scrabbling. Weeds, herbs, stones and soil go flying, while Mrs Maynard upstairs opens her window so she can tut loud enough for us to hear at ground level. Luckily for Brownlow and me, Mrs Maynard's lease doesn't allow her access to the garden. She has her pristine window boxes of petunias and pansies and has to make do with that.

Beyond the Weatherall fence, Quinn and I started tearing the grass and weeds away with our bare hands. As the fence had been only recently installed, although the grass had quickly grown up again, the soil around it was still fresh and not yet tangled with roots. I'd soon broken a couple of nails and been stung by a nettle, but it was the perfect excavation site for an eager pair of paws.

By the time Rouki, Alex and the guys arrived laden with shiny new shovels, Brownlow had disappeared out of sight. They approached to see me holding a lead that apparently had no dog attached. Even Rouki smiled when, hearing their approach, Brownlow suddenly emerged to grin at them. 'Looks like he's already done most of the hard work,' Carl exclaimed. 'Good boy, Brownlow!' The excavation team had bought spades for Quinn and me too, and I offered to take the receipt from Jack, telling him he would be reimbursed from our expense accounts.

'No, this one's on me,' Rouki insisted. 'If there's even the faintest chance my two darlings are in there...' I hadn't imagined Rouki Bennett would have been such a strong digger, but those gym honed muscles and the physical tasks she'd had to perform on more than one reality show had well equipped her for the task in hand. She grasped her shovel with long gel nails that would've put an anteater to shame. 'Look at that huge worm,' she cooed at one point. 'At least today they're not going to try to make me eat it.' Jack and I exchanged glances.

'Think I missed that show – thankfully,' he muttered.

'We're making good progress, well done people,' Quinn said as he finished his digging shift and handed his spade to Carl. There were too many of us to all dig at once, but we were taking it turns, in teams of two, in five-minute bursts of energy.

'So, what are we going to do when we get in there? Storm in and overpower them?' Alex asked.

'If so, with what?' asked Carl. 'Shovels I suppose.'

'No, I just need to get to the storage shed,' said Quinn. 'It's the end building on the left.' I wondered what he had in there.

My phone screen lit up with an incoming call. 'Sophie Gorrage?'

'Jonas Joiner, I presume.'

'Where are you? Still hanging about in the area I expect? With Brownlow too. Which is convenient really.'

'Why? What do you mean?'

'Bring him up to the front gate and tell him to stay. Then you go.'

'No. No way.' Somewhere behind him, I heard a young woman scream.

'I've someone who wants to speak to you.' The next person I heard was Clemency. She sounded terrified. 'You need to do it, Ms Gorrage. Leave the dog.'

'Clemency? Who's there with you, what are they doing?'

'This man... Vicki let him in, I've no idea... they've been in the clinic, and they've got a syringe full of something... she says they'll inject me... You need to give them the dog.'

'I can't.'

'They won't hurt him. Or they say they won't. They've got that little Chihuahua and those two belonging to the home makeover woman. The missing dogs. And they look okay. I don't think they'll hurt animals… just me. Give them Brownlow, Sophie, please!'

'Quinn, I can't. He's dangerous – Joiner. When he hit me from behind… it must've been him… and Brownlow ended up alone wandering in the road. And he tried to snatch him again when I was at Ventnor.'

'He won't be taking him anywhere this time. Only into Weatherall.'

'But if they're willing to inject Clemency with I don't know that? I mean they're cold-blooded potential murderers.'

'She did say they hadn't done it yet though. It may just be a threat. Look, let them have Brownlow. And allow them to start their live-stream broadcast or whatever it is. It will keep them distracted while we continue digging.'

'But…'

'You don't have a choice,' said Rouki. 'Personally, I'm glad my dogs are probably in there, rather than at some unknown destination, having whatever happening to them. The thieves won't be taking him anywhere. Where are they going to go from here?' I knew they were right, but it didn't make me feel any better. It was particularly unfair to hand over Brownlow, when there was no way I could ask him his feelings on the matter. If he looked back at me with 'don't leave me, Sophie' in his eyes, I wasn't sure I could even do it.

The other humans were resolved that this was the course of action we had to take. Reluctantly I agreed to do as they wished. Quinn told me to take Brownlow on a wide detour, so as to evade the cameras and not give away the digging party's location. I should first go back to his van and drive up to the main gate of Weatherall Fields in that, as if I'd been somewhere else.

'On second thoughts,' he added, 'I'll come with you in the van.'

'What?' I said, flaring up with anger, 'don't you trust me, Quinn? Do you think I won't be able to leave Brownlow sitting there alone?' He rested his hand on my arm.

'I think,' said Quinn quietly, 'you know me a lot better than that. You know I trust you. But if they see us both drive up in the van, they'll think, since Jonas saw it parked up previously, that we had both gone back to it, and driven away somewhere. It'll appear we're returning from some place a van journey away, rather than a location much closer to them, where we're in the process of tunnelling in from.'

My mouth was dry as Quinn, Brownlow and I took the detour across the fields, which would bring us to where we'd left the van, without arousing suspicion. I wanted to tell Brownlow things would be alright, and that we would soon be reunited, but I knew it was my emotions he could best understand, and they'd be at odds with my words. I ruffled his tousled head as we reached the van but said nothing. He jumped up on the seat, eager to begin whatever journey it was we were setting out on, but I could see worry in his huge brown eyes. I still felt like I was betraying him. I know Jonas and Vicki had insisted that they were acting in the dogs' best interests, and they had so far harmed no canines. Now though, they were trapped with a number of stolen animals inside Weatherall. I couldn't see what their next move could be. Surely the stand-off would eventually lead to a siege situation with armed police outside. That was unless we managed to tunnel in and overpower them in the meantime, but that course of action too was fraught with risk, for my team as well as the dogs. I didn't know how fanatical Jonas and Vicki were about preventing dogs from working or being otherwise exploited in any way. Might they choose to take desperate, drastic action to stop the dogs falling back into the hands of their rightful owners? If they truly believed that the previous lives of the dogs they had stolen had been miserable and exploited, involving suffering, might they think it kinder to end the whole thing in some kind of dramatic and very final act? I could hardly bear to think of such things. I knew there were drugs in Weatherall's clinic that could make taking a grim course of action a possibility. If I was going to leave Brownlow outside the main gate, retreat and allow them to take him inside, I had to keep those dark thoughts from my mind.

Quinn waited in the van while I walked with Brownlow to the gate. I wasn't going to press the intercom to let Jonas know my intentions. I was sure he and Vicki would be watching, via the CCTV. 'Sit, Brownlow. Good dog. Now stay. Stay boy.' Only his eyes followed me, anxious and forlorn as I stumbled back to the van. Immediately I was in, Quinn drove off. I didn't even get to see Brownlow taken inside.

Chapter Eleven

'For all you dog lovers out there, who've been following our actions in the media over the past weeks, at last we to get meet you all face to face and explain our actions. These two dogs, Lady and Merry – their names shortened, as dogs prefer short functional names – were humiliated on a TV show, where they had to perform unnatural and demeaning tricks in front of a baying crowd.'

'My little darlings!' Rouki Bennett gave an anguished howl.

'They're okay – look they're okay.' I tried to keep my voice steady. We were watching the live stream on my phone screen. In front of us, Carl and Jack were currently again taking a shift at digging. Jonas was indeed the man I'd glimpsed in the pub on the Isle of Wight. When we'd met and talked on the Let Dogs Be Dogs march, he'd had a baseball cap on, its peak shadowing the top half of his face. That's why the guy in the pub had seemed familiar, but I hadn't at the time been able to place him. For his live stream from Weatherall, he was wearing a black t-shirt with a dog logo and LDBD. A couple of similarly logo-ed mugs were prominently displayed on the shelf behind him, the ledge that normally held the sanctuary's own promotional materials. Jonas was definitely paying attention to his branding, though to what purpose I didn't know.

On screen, a short red-haired woman, who appeared to be in her forties or fifties, had now joined Jonas. She wore glasses with green cat's eye style frames and in her arms was a small white Chihuahua.

'You may remember the TV police drama 'Every Dark Lie' – and the tiny dog who cowered in his basket while a violent fight took place. For Bianca, the punches, the yells and the screams were real. That dog wasn't acting. She was scared – utterly terrified. And her schedule in a current children's TV show is exhausting for so small and delicate a dog, as are the promotional appearances where she is poked and prodded by any number of small, noisy children.'

I wasn't sure I agreed with that assessment. I suspected Bianca had been trained to pull an anxious face and cower. In fact, I seemed to remember her showing a similar expression in a dog food commercial, before the new wonder product was whisked under her nose and she became a tail wagging, lip-licking ball of happiness. The appearance of dogs on TV shows was tightly regulated, and I couldn't imagine an animal that didn't enjoy meeting small children being allowed to be touched by them, in case of a growl or a nip being forthcoming from the animal.

At least I now knew where the dogs I had not yet recovered were, and so presumably did all their owners. I asked Quinn for his phone, and as we continued to watch the broadcast, I called Melissa and Gavin. Gavin answered. Yes, they were watching. It was trending on Twitter and had just made the national news as a breaking story. Gavin said the details of the broadcast had been sent to every pet influencer and animal organisation, as well as being spread widely by every Let Dogs Be Dogs member. Building on the existing news story of the stolen dogs, it hadn't taken much for it to go viral. Jonas was currently talking about the Medalsum video and how they had rehomed Tasha to stop her being used in such a callous way again.

'Our good work in finding a non-exploitative forever home for that Staffordshire Bull Terrier was unfortunately undone by a misguided pet detective, believing she was somehow acting in the dog's interest.'

Vicki nodded intensely, making a serious face to back Jonas up. There was something of the TV anchor team about them, sat on the sofa in Weatherall's reception, surrounded by dogs. They appeared reasonably professional on camera and certainly unfazed by the situation they were currently in. It made me wonder for how long this event had been their plan. Had they, when first stealing Mr Merrytrees and Lady Champignon already had this point in sight?

Of Brownlow and Clemency there was no sign. Many of the other dogs there were walking or running excitedly around. There were Greyhounds galore and also some canines I presumed had been released from Weatherall's homing kennels. Occasionally Jonas had to stop speaking because the din of excitable animals greeting, playing or even threatening each other started to drown him out. He seemed very at home there surrounded by canine chaos, as did Vicki. I noticed none of the dogs were wearing collars. Perhaps to Jonas it was some symbol of oppression or servitude. He was certainly letting the dogs be dogs, at least at present, with the camera rolling. They were I assumed, self-filming, as everything was being shot from one direction, straight in front of them, as if that was where a webcam had been carefully positioned. It was well lit too. Jonas or possibly Vicki certainly knew about slick presentation. He started to tell the story of Rita the police dog, and to make more general comments about police dog training. He then recounted a few documented, historic cases of cruelty and negligence by individual police officers. Then the Greyhounds were brought in, and Jonas moved on to lecturing us all about the treatment of racing dogs.

Jack stepped back from the fence and tapped my arm to make me lift my head from the phone screen. 'We're through! I reckon we can all just about squeeze down and under now.' Quinn took a look.

'Right, I'll black the CCTV and then we'll head in. Hopefully those two will be too busy with their vlogging for a minute or two to notice the monitor going blank.' On my phone Jonas was still talking to camera. I took my ear-jacks out, but then I saw Brownlow's face appear in front of the screen.

'Brownlow's with them now.'

'Well let them say their piece about the supposed sufferings of pet detection dogs or whatever. It'll give us a chance to get in there.' My phone indicated I had a call. It was Carmichael.

'I don't suppose you've any idea what's going on at Weatherall?'

'Where are you?' I said.

'On the way up there. And I'm not alone. Where are you?'

'You may be about to find out,' I said. I didn't have time to talk to her. I said I'd call her back later.

Quinn was the first to squeeze through. The hole was tight and muddy, and it was certainly a bit of a scrabble, but in moments there he was, back in Weatherall Fields.

'Want your shovel passed through?' Jack asked as Quinn on the inside rubbed the soil from his eyes. 'We might need something to defend ourselves.'

'Yes, drop it in the hole, I'll drag it through.' I insisted on going next, though if I'd been sensible, I'd have waited and let some of the larger members of our party make the whole bigger by their exertions. Halfway through I became stuck. I was well and truly wedged with only earth in front of my face and the ground feeling very tight around my middle. I tried to breathe in, but when I came to breathe out again the soil seemed to tighten around my chest. I wanted to shout for help, but I couldn't risk being heard, if one of the windows in reception happened to be open, or Vicki was emerging to collect some other dogs she wanted to feature in online show.

Quinn's hands grabbed onto mine and I found myself moving forward and up. Something lumpy in my jacket, probably the handle of Brownlow's extendable lead snagged on something, maybe a plant root, and I heard a tearing. It was at least my coat not me that was being ripped in two. Then, moments later, I was sitting on the grass on the other side.

'You okay?' Quinn leant back into the hole as my metal garden spade was passed through. Now I was armed and ready to rescue my dog. Quinn raised a hand to stop me.

'Let's wait for everyone shall we?' Alex was slim, fit and in her trendy dungarees perfectly attired for tunnelling. Whereas I'd emerged looking as rough as a badger's posterior, she, like a badger, came out looking as confident and poised as she went in. Even her asymmetric fringe was unruffled. Rouki made a bit of fuss and had to be told by both the guys on the outside and Quinn on the inside to hush. Even though – hopefully – there was no camera now watching for her to play to, she seemed to need to act out the jeopardy and drama with lots of 'Oh My God!' and 'I can't do this!'

Later, if we were successful, I could imagine her giving an interview about how the experience had 'put her in touch with her true self' and 'been an intense learning experience which had helped her grow as a person'. Now though, she was worrying about having earth in her mouth.

'Oh my God, there's not a worm on my tongue? Is there? Oh my God!' Jack and Carl joined us silently and with no drama, bringing the rest of the equipment. We had a shovel each. There were six of us. As far as I knew there were only two of them. We were ready to storm reception. Quinn though had disappeared in the direction of his shed.

'What do we do, Sophie?' asked Carl. 'Should we wait for him?' Before I could answer Quinn reappeared from the shed. He appeared to be holding a rifle. Rouki Bennett gasped.

'My God, is he going to shoot them?'

'Tranquilliser gun, not loaded,' Quinn grunted as he rejoined us, 'but they may not know that.'

I heard the faint wail of distant sirens. The police were surely coming. Quinn took the keys from his pocket as we shuffled in a line along the outside wall of the reception building, keeping close to the brickwork and taking little sidling steps. As I reached the window, which was open a crack, I could see in through the corner of the blind. Jonas was addressing the webcam with Brownlow sat in front of him, looking obediently towards the lens and somewhat disloyally grinning.

'No doubt, by now the police are on their way. But, if you've liked what we've had to say and have mobilised yourselves to join us in this day of action, then we know that for now at least we've nothing to fear.'

Jonas's eyes were shining with an almost religious righteousness.

'We know from all your posts, likes and words of support that you have, as asked, very kindly used your vehicles to block off every road for miles around. Now dear supporters – those of you who are willing to give a home to a former working dog – I ask that you leave your cars, your vans and your motorbikes. Make your way to our new, designated Former Working Dog Refuge and ring on the bell. We will be rehoming the dogs on a first come, first served basis, starting with our former pet detecting friend Brownlow here. Rescued from a cruel and negligent owner, all he is looking for is a home where he is treated as an equal and never made to earn his keep again.'

'But he is an equal! My equal. He loves his work and me. And I love him.' I said these words quietly, meaning only Quinn, who was beside me to hear. Inside the building, however Brownlow also heard me. 'A-woof!' Brownlow bounded to the window and stood up on his hind legs, placing his paws on the sill, tail wagging. 'Woof, woof, woof!' Horrified I'd given us away, I pressed back against the wall, hardly daring to breathe.

A helicopter suddenly zoomed in low overhead. It bore a black and yellow livery and the word 'police' written on its side. The noise was deafening. Someone, presumably Vicki, slammed the window of reception shut, no doubt so Jonas could continue to address his followers. Quinn raised his arm. 'Okay, everyone, we're going in. On a count of three.' Stealthily he stepped forward and unlocked the door to reception.

'One…' I gripped my shovel in both hands. 'Two. Three!'

Quinn flung the door back and with a mighty roar, rushed Jonas, aiming the tranquilliser gun right at his head. Rouki and Alex cornered Vicki, shovels raised, and Carl and Jack flung themselves at Jonas as he leapt across the sofa, evading Quinn and heading for the door. If Jack had been willing to clobber him with the shovel they might've stopped him, but when it came to actually committing an act of violence he hesitated. Jonas sprinted out the door.

'Stop or I'll shoot!' hollered Quinn, but Jonas took no notice, clearly not believing the threat.

'Get him, Brownlow!' I yelled. 'Get him!' Now Brownlow is no attack dog. He doesn't have the slightest bit of aggression in him, and he hasn't been trained to stop fugitives. He willingly bounded off in pursuit, in the direction as pointed, but I knew he was unlikely to bring down the fleeing man. Quinn though was sprinting after him, tranquilliser gun discarded to give him speed. I rushed outside to see Jonas race out through the gate of Weatherall, the police helicopter hovering above. Behind Jonas and gaining were Quinn and Brownlow. No doubt Jonas would head for a car or motorbike of one of his sympathisers and demand to be taken out of there. The first cars were in sight, parked in a queue up the lane.

Brownlow was gaining on Jonas. From just behind, Quinn shouted to him, 'Get him! Get him!' Thinking it a game, Brownlow jumped up at the man's back, toppling him into the long grass. Jonas was only down for a few seconds, dodging the dog and up again running. It had though given Quinn the few seconds he needed. With a flying rugby tackle Quinn took Jonas back down, the pair of them disappearing into the long grass.

I ran across the field, ready to use my shovel or my martial arts training. As I reached Quinn and Brownlow though, I found man and dog sitting side by side on top of Jonas. 'Good boy, Brownlow,' said Quinn. 'Have you got your dog lead, Sophie?' I handed over the lead, and Quinn wrenched Jonas's hands behind his back to tie them. Hearing a shout from the clinic building, I turned and raced back, shovel raised, intent on doing battle with Vicki. In the reception I could see the red-haired woman struggling with Rouki Bennett and Alex. She appeared to be as strong as an ox and was clearly getting the better of them both. I abandoned the shovel as a bit too drastic in the circumstances, now Brownlow was safe. There was no sign of Carl and Jack.

'Stand back, Rouki.' I span in with two quick taekwondo kicks and a punch. Vicki didn't even see it coming.

Carl and Jack reappeared in the doorway as I finished tying Vicki's hands. Carl was removing a blindfold from Clemency's face. 'Are you okay?'

'Um gosh yes, but gotta get the nestlings and fledgies fed.'

'Need a hand?' said Alex, 'my granddad had an aviary, and I think I can cope.'

My phone rang. It was PC Gemma Carmichael.

'Where are you, girl?' I said with some satisfaction, 'you've just missed out on all the action.'

'Get back inside Weatherall,' she barked. 'All of you – quickly! And lock the gates. Our chopper reports a large group of people making their way across the fields towards you – intentions unknown. Get inside. Lock yourselves in. Let us deal with it.'

'They're coming,' smiled Jonas looking over his shoulder, as Quinn hauled him into Weatherall's reception, Brownlow trotting at their heels. 'They're coming here in their thousands to liberate the dogs from their servitude, so they may live as our equals.' A group of people was reaching the main gates. Quinn pushed Jonas away from himself and pressed the button to close and lock the gates.

'Jonas thinks they're his followers, but who knows?' I said. 'Who knows what the rabble he's raised actually want or whose side they're on. Carmichael's right. We need to leave it to the police now. Things look like they might get ugly out there.'

Rouki was hugging her Cocker Spaniels. Alex had gone to help Clemency with the urgent feeds, and Carl and Jack were keeping an eye on our prisoners, who sat side by side on the reception sofa, tied up with dog leads. Quinn and I watched the mob advance via the CCTV. From a distance it was hard to see how many there were and with Carmichael's warning ringing in my ears, I was kind of expecting a 'Wicker Man' style lynch mob, or even a full zombie apocalypse of Let Dogs Be Dogs supporters. At school, bullies had so often outnumbered me, and I knew from painful experience what a large gang were capable of. I remembered Quinn saying the fence could be breached using power tools. I sincerely hoped there were no chainsaws out there, about to be used on the gates.

As the people came nearer, I was able to count them. Surprisingly, it didn't take that long. There were forty-one of them, including a baby in arms and an elderly woman walking with a frame. I recognised a man who had served me in the health food shop in the nearest village. I'd bought a box of walnut and mushroom pies and a carton of almond milk off him only the previous week, I thought, outraged at the notion he could now be trying to attack me. There were younger people too, filming their advance, and a man with grey floppy hair and sandals holding a quickly scrawled cardboard placard saying, 'Free All Dogs!' The thing was though, none of them looked particularly angry or scary. Again, like the march, most probably thought they were doing the right thing, getting behind a cause because it sounded worthwhile, or a friend had persuaded them to turn up. Several had dogs with them. I could see a Dalmatian and a Border Collie. They were normal happy dogs with normal, reasonably happy people.

'Err they look, okay, Quinn.'

'Most of them probably are. When they've not been manipulated and fired up by a load of hot air and nonsense. But I won't be opening the gates. The alarm's on again now. They may, if they've time, eventually discover our way in round the back, but I've given Carl the keys and told him to go and lock all the aviaries, kennels and buildings.'

'But I heard Jonas say there were thousands of people coming here. They might still be on their way. Leaving their cars and walking across the fields.'

'They might be,' said Quinn, 'but I'm willing to bet there aren't. You can fool a few of the people some of the time, but I can't imagine thousands believing the way to stop canine suffering in the world is to simply stop all dogs from working.'

Quinn buzzed the police in to Weatherall and they arrested Jonas and Vicki. Like me, the cops were concerned we might imminently be besieged by a hostile flash mob. To be on the safe side they called for further backup rather than immediately take the suspects out to their vehicles. PC Carmichael acted aloof and as though she didn't know me as her colleagues took our statements. Naturally she didn't bother to thank any of our team for apprehending the thieves either. It soon became apparent to everyone that the crisis had passed. As Quinn had predicted there was no rampaging horde descending on us. The modest-sized group of people outside the gates was dispersing, allowing the police to safely remove Jonas and Vicki from the premises. I glanced down at Brownlow who was lying at my feet in reception. He looked as tired as I felt. It was time to go home and make him his well-earned dinner.

Medalsum rang before we'd even driven away from Weatherall Fields.

'Sophie - oh my days! You guys are seriously awesome!' He'd been on tenterhooks watching on his phone alongside Skyla and Jamal as the whole thing played out. Despite my protests, he insisted on paying us a sizable bonus for recovering Tasha unharmed. In addition, he'd be sending Quinn and myself VIP tickets to his forthcoming Hyde Park gig. Brownlow's delicate eardrums weren't designed for concert going but Medalsum assured me he'd shortly be receiving a 'mega-goodie bag' of canine treats.

Back home in our little kitchen, I listened to Brownlow gulping down his dinner. After all the noise of barking, the helicopter and the rest, I almost didn't trust the peace that had finally descended. Quinn was probably feeling the same thing over at Weatherall, where caring for the needs of the furred and feathered residents had to carry on as normal. I was glad that at least the police could now charge Jonas and Vicki with offences that carried far more serious penalties than dog theft. For kidnapping and holding Clemency hostage and making threats to kill, they were both likely to serve some serious time in prison. As for Clemency, thankfully she'd seemed little the worse for her ordeal. Refusing the offer of a hospital check-up, she'd got straight on with feeding the young birds and making up puppy and kitten formula milk for the other orphans.

Unfortunately for the Brownlow and Gorrage partnership, once the police get involved in a case, they do tend to completely take it over. They insisted on being the ones who reunited all the stolen dogs with their owners, even those people who'd hired us to do it. Carmichael was tasked with returning Bianca to Melissa and Gavin Randall and then driving Tasha up to London to be reunited with Medalsum. I confess I felt somewhat miffed to be excluded from the joyful reunions.

As I checked my phone again, I noticed a strongly worded statement had recently appeared on the Let Dogs Be Dogs website, co-authored by Cass and Nat. They were distancing themselves and the organisation from the 'irresponsible and criminal' actions of Jonas and Vicki and went on to say that LDBD was going to go dormant for a while for a period of reflection and reorganisation. They would take time to consider how best to responsibly raise awareness of the welfare issues affecting working dogs. Going forward, peaceful campaigning and charitable work would replace any form of direct action. This was certainly a satisfactory outcome as far as we were concerned. Perhaps several of the dog owners needed to think a little harder in the future, before expecting their companions to undertake certain actions or experience certain things. I was however convinced that they were all basically good people whose loyal canine companions would be delighted to be returned to their loving care.

An email message from Melissa and Gavin pinged in, promising more gourmet doggie delights for my canine partner. While I was typing a reply, the doorbell rang, and I answered, still slightly warily, to find a courier holding a wicker basket tied with a big bow on top. I could tell by the loud sneeze coming from the shaggy dog directly behind me that this thank you gift was from Rouki Bennett and exclusively for me. As I unpacked the scented candles, soaps and shower creams I wondered if along with expressing her gratitude, Rouki was also dropping a not-so-subtle hint that I reeked. Sniffing my t-shirt, I couldn't really blame her. All that adrenaline and muddy tunnelling had made me work up an impressive sweat. I'd need to re-gift the scented candles and perfume diffusers to friends who don't have dogs with superior olfactory powers, but now that Brownlow was about to take a well-earned nap, I could go and have a long, luxurious shower. As I made my way to the bathroom, clutching Rouki's gifts, my phone once again started to belt out the Baha Men's famous hit. I hesitated, tempted by the thought of warmth, soap and steam. Then my conscience got the better of me.

'Hello? Brownlow And Gorrage.'

'Err hi, I've just got home, the door of my hutch is swinging open and it's getting dark. Lewis and Lottie are two little Dwarf Lops, I can't think of them wandering about out there on their own…' From the kitchenette, Brownlow heard me go back into the hall and take down his lead from the coat peg where I hang it. Immediately moving to my side, he gave a big yawn, stretched and looked up at me. His tail started to wag.

'Come on, boy,' I said, clipping the lead to his collar. 'A couple of rabbits need rescuing. Ready to sniff them out, Brownlow?'

Also by the author

Out Of The Frying Pan

How many artists does it take to solve a kidnapping?

Brighton sculptor Vonnie Sharpe's laidback routine is shattered when her flatmate Gina is carjacked during a bank robbery.

Gina's car is found abandoned on the South Downs but there's no sign of the quiet young chip shop worker. A worried Vonnie enlists the help of her arty friends in the race to find her. With a singer, actor and busker on her team, she half-wonders if she could've got Arts Council funding for her search.

Vonnie tracks down the bank robber, who insists he left Gina unharmed in her car. From here the trail twists and turns through art classes, language schools and escape rooms, as she narrows down her list of suspects. A ransom note arrives and it's Vonnie who the kidnappers want to deliver the money. With the cash drop imminent and not knowing who she can trust, she needs to find answers - and quickly.

£8.99

ISBN: 978-1-914322-07-5

Available from all bookshops or online retailers

Printed in Great Britain
by Amazon

19647119R00154